DATE			

AN ANCIENT EVIL

AN ANCIENT EVIL

The Knight's tale of mystery and murder
as he goes on pilgrimage
from London to Canterbury

P. C. Doherty

St. Martin's Press
New York

Library of Congress Cataloging-in-Publication Data

Doherty, P. C.
An ancient evil : the knight's tale of mystery and murder as he goes on pilgrimage from London to Canterbury / P.C. Doherty.
p.   cm.
ISBN 0-312-11740-X
1. England—Social life and customs—Medieval period, 1066–1485—Fiction. 2. Serial murders—England—Oxfordshire—Fiction. 1. Title.
PR6054.O37A82   1995
823'.914—dc20   94-46267   CIP

First published in Great Britain by Headline Book Publishing

First U.S. Edition: April 1995
10 9 8 7 6 5 4 3 2 1

To my baby son Mark and his vivid imagination

AUTHOR'S NOTE

By the mid-14th century, Oxford University had developed basically along the same lines as today. The halls or colleges and the faculties for different subjects were in existence. There was a central university administration where the proctors, as now, were responsible for student discipline.

One final note; in medieval demonology the term 'Strigoi' could be used to describe either the living dead or a powerful, evil spirit who takes possession of a living soul.

P.C. Doherty

The Prologue

The warm April showers had done little to clean the dirty
cobbles and mud-packed runnels of Southwark. Nevertheless,
the heavy rain was sweet to those who tended apple orchards,
flower banks, herb gardens or just grass for grazing; the shower
had also kept travellers safe as it confined the night hawks to
mere grumbling in the taprooms of the shabby ale-houses that
stood at the mouth of every street and alleyway in Southwark.
The black, long-tailed rats, however, knew the rain had softened
the mounds of refuse piled high in the sewers and now, their red
eyes gleaming, were busily foraging for tender scraps. A cat
keeping in the shadows of an alley wall also hunted, though it
suddenly stopped, ears cocked, one leg raised, outside the
cobbled yard of the Tabard inn which lay across the street from
the Abbot of Hyde's manor. The cat stared across the deserted
stable yard, quickly noting that the doors were all locked and
barred; no chance there to catch the soft mice shuffling among
the straw or greedily filling their small bellies in the bins of
bran, oats and other feeds. Instead the cat looked amber-eyed at
the light and listened to the raised voices and laughter that
poured through the glass of the great mullioned bay window at
the front of the tavern. Above the cat, the Tabard's sign
creaked and groaned in the soft April breeze. Somewhere a

horse neighed; a sleepy-eyed ostler opened the small barn door to ensure all was well and so the cat slunk on.

Inside the cavernous taproom of the Tabard, mine host Harry sat at the top of the great, long table and studied his twenty-nine customers and fellow pilgrims, his hands itching at the thought of the profit he would make both tonight and on their return from Canterbury. Harry picked up his great blackjack of ale, its froth bubbling round his mouth and nose while his wide, popping eyes once more surveyed his companions. Early tomorrow morning, before even cock-crow, they would start their long journey down the Rochester road to pray before the blessed bones of St Thomas à Becket in Canterbury. By the cock, Harry thought, a motley crew. On his left was the knight, his steel-grey hair falling to his shoulders, his face marked by lines of severity, his dark hooded eyes half-closed as he loosened his belt after a meal of partridge, quail and golden plover turned on the spit until the flesh became succulent white. The knight had said little; he had drunk and eaten sparingly, as had his son who sat next to him – a curly blond-haired squire, with face and manners as pretty as any maid's. He had talked even less than his father but had hung on the knight's every word, now and again stretching across with his knife to carve and dice his father's meal. A dutiful squire as well as a son, mine host Harry thought, and one who knows full well the rules of courtesy at table.

The knight's other companion, the cropped-headed, sun-browned yeoman in his coat of green, was listening patiently to the merchant on his left – a large braggart of a man with a proud face and forked beard under a large Flemish beaver hat which he refused to doff even when eating. Across the table, on Harry's right, the crafty-eyed lawyer was describing to the wealthy franklin a meal served to him at the Inns of Court. This lover of good food, with his daisy-white beard, listened carefully, licking his lips at the lawyer's description of the baked meats, fattened peacock and tangy fish sauces. Harry grinned to himself. He was glad he was not sitting next to the tousle-haired cook, who boasted he could prepare the sweetest blancmange. As the cook had sat down, thrusting one leg over the bench, Harry had glimpsed the open sore on the man's bare ankle. 'He will prepare no blancmange for me,' Harry quietly vowed to his old friend the shipman.

The host was also keeping an eye on the summoner with his fiery red face, black scabby brows and scanty beard. The man was covered with pustules, white and red, and his nose was fiery as a coal from Hell. He had, since his arrival at the Tabard, downed as much strong drink as all the other pilgrims put together. The summoner did not care a whit but, like the god Bacchus, wore a garland on his head. Nevertheless, he was still a man to watch for; Harry had twice glimpsed him trying to lift the trinket bag of silk that dangled from the franklin's belt. The other pilgrims were just as mixed. The lean-visaged pardoner, with his pouches full of rubbish to sell as relics, was a veritable scarecrow with his long yellow hair falling lank as a piece of flax around his shoulders. Beside the pardoner sat a reeve, thin as the pole he carried, hot-eyed, red spots of anger ever present on his high-boned cheeks, The miller was next – built like a battering ram, he was bald as an egg though his beard was red and long as a tongued flame. Harry looked once more at the miller and closed his eyes. He only hoped the loud-mouthed bastard would not pick up his bagpipes and start playing again. This would surely scandalize Dame Eglantine the prioress, who talked only in nasal French as she sat fingering the love locket around her neck or feeding slops of milk to the lapdog she carried everywhere.

'You are quiet, Master Harry?'

The taverner looked down at the monk and friar, bald-headed, brown as berries, their faces glistening with good living; Harry would not trust either of them as far as he could spit.

'I was thinking,' the landlord replied.

'About what?' demanded Alice, the broad, red-faced wife of Bath. 'Come on, sir, what were you thinking about?' She turned and winked lasciviously at Dame Eglantine's soft-faced chaplain.

'I was thinking how pretty you were,' Harry laughed.

The wife of Bath clapped her hands and her face broke into a gap-toothed grin. 'I have danced with five husbands, I am always prepared to step out with a sixth!' She moved her bottom, broad as a buckler, on the bench and flirtatiously adjusted the embroidered cloth around her shoulders.

Harry just stared down the table.

'I was thinking,' he said, 'how we have agreed that each should tell at least two tales. One will be for the day, but what about the nights?'

'I can keep you busy enough there.' The wife of Bath simpered to the laughs and catcalls from the others.

'No! No!' Harry banged on the top of the table and unhitched a small bag of coins from his belt. 'There's good silver in here and, by the cock, if any man disputes it I'll break his head with a quarterstaff! So, when we move out tomorrow to St Thomas's watering hole, let us tell a merry tale to instruct or amuse. But, at night,' his voice fell, 'let it be different.' He stared around the now quiet company. 'Let us tell a tale of mystery that will chill the blood, halt the heart and curl the locks upon our heads.' He looked slyly at the miller. 'Or, if you wish, your beard. The winner, the best tale, will receive this purse!'

The assembled pilgrims murmured quietly, now fascinated by their host's change of mood.

'Yes! Yes!' The pardoner's shrill voice broke the silence. 'Let us tell a tale of murder and death and let it not be too fanciful but spring from the heart, the life-blood, of each one of us!'

The rest of the pilgrims, full of hot food and strong wine, heartily agreed, eager to experience a tale of mystery as they sat, well fed, before the roaring fire of this or any other tavern on their way to Canterbury.

'So,' Harry asked, getting to his feet, 'who shall begin?' He glanced to his left where, throughout the conversation, the knight had hardly stirred but only gazed heavy-lidded into the darkness. Harry hoped the knight would tell the first tale tomorrow morning as they took the road out of Southwark; perhaps etiquette dictated that he should also be the first to tell a night story.

'Sir knight!' Harry exclaimed. 'Do you agree?'

The knight looked up, stroking his iron-grey beard. He wiped away the crumbs from his jerkin, which was still stained from the armour he had worn. He glanced sideways at his blue-eyed, fresh-faced son.

'I agree,' he replied quietly. 'And I shall speak first!'

Harry waved him to his own chair at the top of the table.

'Then, sir, of your kindness, take my seat and I shall serve you this tavern's best, a deep-bowled cup of the richest claret from Bordeaux.'

The knight obliged, moving silently as a cat. He sat in Harry's great high-backed chair, his elbows resting on its arms.

'I will tell you,' he began, 'a tale of terror and of mystery.' His voice rose. 'Of evil greater than that which prowls in the mid-day heat. About an ancient evil, spawned by the Lord

Satan himself, which had its roots during a time of war when Saturn ruled the stars and loosed his son, red-armoured Mars, to stalk the green meadows of England. A time of terror when even Pluto himself, Lord of the Underworld, paled at the horrors that entered the affairs of men.' The knight leaned back in the chair. 'My tale begins hundreds of years ago, just after the great Conqueror came here. So, gentles all, your attention as I describe these horrors sprung from the very pit of Hell.' And he began.

The Knight's Tale
PART I

The cruel-beaked ravens were gorged with human flesh, their silken jet plumage tinged with scarlet as they soared and dipped above the bleak battlefield. The ravens' usual resting place, the great donjon that soared into the sky above the river, was now engulfed in flames which roared fiercely up to the sullen clouds. Around the blazing fortress the dead lay thick as weeds. The huge siege towers that had been rolled against the donjon wall had also caught fire, their stout beams blackening and cracking into fiery cinders. The corpses lying there turned to bubbling fat and filled the air with the stench of burning flesh. In the nearby woods, an old hag-faced witch leaned against a tree; her spindly legs shook with terror, wispy tendrils of hair brushed her face as she stared at the great black cloud of smoke above the trees.

'They're burning the damned!' she screeched. 'They're sending the demons back to their master!'

The birds in the trees on the edge of the clearing heard her cracked speech and cowered on the branches as if they sensed what was happening. The villagers for miles around also hid, terrified at this day of wrath, this awful day of reckoning. They cowered in their mean huts but, pulling back the ox-skin coverings, they saw how the shapeless bracken was turning red, how even the great oaks standing in their ploughed fields seemed to bend and twist under a wicked wind that blew the smoke and stench of battle towards them.

Sir Hugo Mortimer, Lord of Oxford, knelt helmetless with his commanders in a circle and intoned David's psalm of praise and triumph over God's enemies. The prayer finished, Mortimer stood, his hatchet warrior face surveying the battlefield, and felt his elation marred by black despair at the cost of his victory.

'The widows will mourn for months,' he whispered, 'but at least their children are safe.' He gazed at the great keep, now hidden by sheets of roaring flames. He turned to his squire. 'How many did we lose, Stephen?'

'On the siege tower, my lord, at least sixty. In the keep well over two hundred.' Stephen wiped the bloody sweat from his face. 'Outside, amongst the peasant levies, God knows! Perhaps three, four hundred!'

Beside Sir Hugo an old, grey-garbed Benedictine monk stood, watching transfixed a dark-hooded figure bound in chains under the outstretched branches of a great oak tree.

'We should burn him, Sir Hugo,' the monk murmured. 'He comes from the bowels of Hell. He should go back there!'

Sir Hugo studied the ascetic, saintly face of the exorcist.

'That would be too simple, Father. He deserves a slower death.'

'No!' the exorcist protested.

He looked at that dreadful, silent figure fettered in chains, surrounded by Sir Hugo's best mercenaries. The soldiers had their loaded crossbows pointed at the prisoner as if daring him to move.

'Satan walks here,' the exorcist murmured. 'Not with snaky hair, bloated torso, spewing mouth and glowing eyes, but in this Strigoi.' He pointed a bony finger at the prisoner. 'He is the living dead. He came here under false pretences with smiling eyes and honeyed mouth to drink the blood of humans and wreak his fury on God's innocent children!'

Sir Hugo half heard the exorcist while staring blankly at the prisoner. He had captured him at last. His men had stormed the tower and forced this Strigoi, this devil incarnate, to the top of his terrible tower and given him a choice: to surrender to Norman justice or be burnt alive. The Strigoi had fought on, displaying incredible strength, seemingly impervious to any weapon except the most holy relics the exorcist had brought, which now lay in their chest in the cart guarded by several household knights. The rest of the coven had died in the flames, but the leader had surrendered, to be covered in chains from neck to toe, his face hooded lest he use his power against his captors. Now Sir Hugh had to decide what had to be done. King William had been most explicit: this diabolical stranger and his coven were to be wiped out root and branch, his terrorization of the countryside halted, his fortress burnt and a monastery built as reparation and as thanksgiving for God's good justice. As a reward, William the Norman had given Sir Hugo the surrounding land with its woods, fields, pastures, rivers and hunting rights, a fertile domain among the forests north of London.

Hugo blinked as the wind blew acrid smoke towards him. He coughed and turned his back, still unaware that the exorcist waited for a response. The king had also wanted to know how this stranger had come to England and Hugo marvelled at what he'd learnt: apparently this devil incarnate had travelled from Wallachia in the Balkans pretending to be a man dedicated to the service of God. He had taken over the old keep and rebuilt it, posing as a servant of God dedicated to Christ's work. At first he and his followers had been respected, even loved, by the petty knights, small landowners and villagers in the surrounding hamlets and villages. Then the terrors had begun; cadavers drained of blood were found in lonely copses, on the banks of streams or even on the king's highway. Children who went out to play never returned. Lonely merchants, tinkers and pedlars who had tried to push their journey one mile further as the day died and darkness fell and the inhabitants of small farms or lonely homesteads would be found as corpses, their faces white as wax, throats slashed from ear to ear, and their flesh drained of every drop of blood. Petitions had been sent to the great council in London and the king's justices dispatched with warrants to investigate. These, together with their clerks, chaplains and retainers had also been massacred, only a few miles from where Sir Hugo now stood. The king, however, had persisted, even sending his own son, William Rufus, and the cause of the depredation had been discovered, the bloody trail leading back to this awesome keep. So, the king, uttering great oaths and swearing vengeance, had granted Hugo Mortimer this wide domain and sent him to wage bloody war against these demons in human flesh. The saintly Anselm, abbot of Bec, had advised the use of England's most holy exorcist as well as sacred relics from the king's new abbey at Westminster.

The Strigoi, or living dead, had been trapped and now awaited punishment.

'Sir Hugo, what are you going to do?'

Mortimer looked at the exorcist.

'I am going to dispense the king's justice,' he replied.

And, cradling his helmet under his arm, Mortimer walked over to where the prisoner stood. The Strigoi's very silence and immobility increased the aura of terror around him and even the hardened Brabantine mercenaries were nervous and cowed despite their huge crossbows.

'You have decided, Sir Hugo?' The voice of the hooded prisoner was both gentle and mocking. 'You are a knight, Sir Hugo, you gave your word I would not die by fire.'

'Burn him!' The shout came from the exorcist standing beside Mortimer. 'Burn him now!'

'You gave your word, Sir Hugo. To die by fire or surrender to Norman justice.'

One of Mortimer's squires ran up. 'The cart has arrived,' he gasped. 'The casket is ready.'

Hugo Mortimer smiled bleakly. He drew his sword and grasped it under the hilt as if it were a cross.

'I gave my word,' he announced loudly, 'and now I pronounce the king's judgement. I, Hugo Mortimer, baron and king's justice in the shire of Oxford, pronounce judgement on you, a rebel, devil-worshipper, murderer and traitor caught in arms against your sovereign lord. You are to remain chained and be buried alive in the tunnels beneath your blood-soaked keep. The tower will be razed and a monastery built on this spot, to make it holy and offer reparation to our good Seigneur the Lord Jesus.'

Even the Brabantine mercenaries who heard this awful judgement gave a gasp of horror. The chained figure moved restlessly, the links of his steel bonds grating, clinking in the silence. The exorcist fell to his knees, hands clasped.

'He must burn,' he murmured. 'For God's sake, Sir Hugo, he must die by fire!'

'He will die a suffocating death beneath his own tower,' Mortimer replied. 'His body will remain manacled and it will be placed in a lead-lined casket also chained. It will then be placed in one of the tunnels beneath that—' Mortimer pointed to the still-burning keep, 'and the tunnel bricked up. Let him die slowly. Let him remember his evil deeds and the innocent

11

blood he and his followers have spilt!'

'Sir Hugo!' The voice spoke up, lilting, almost happy. 'I do not acknowledge your king or he whom you described as Le Bon Seigneur. I shall return!'

Sir Hugh sheathed his sword and shook his head. 'When the fires have died,' he ordered, 'let the punishment begin!'

Words between the pilgrims

'By the cock!' Harry the landlord growled. 'This is a bloody tale, sir knight.'

'More of the devil than of human kind,' the poorly garbed village parson commented.

'Yet he speaks the truth,' the wife of Bath exclaimed. 'In my pilgrimage to Cologne, as we went through the great forest, we were warned against those demons who suffer from blood madness, told how they worship the Lord Satan and spend the daylight hours in Hell but prowl the night looking for prey.'

'Succubi,' the pardoner interrupted. 'They are succubi, devils in human flesh.'

'They are as old as time itself,' the clerk from Oxford explained, eager to show his learning. 'The Greeks spoke of beautiful women called the Lamiæ . . .' His voice trailed away and he peered at the knight. 'Yes, such beings could be amongst us now,' he murmured. 'I have heard a strange story . . .'

Harry the taverner looked at him curiously; the clerk, so bookish and withdrawn, now appeared frightened as if the knight had reminded him of something.

'No more, gentle sirs, please,' Harry quickly intervened. 'Sir knight, continue your tale and give us every detail of this great mystery!'

PART II

Chapter 1

The riders reined in their horses and peered through the pouring rain. Above them the sky was overcast, the clouds thick and heavy as palls of smoke from which the rain fell in cold, drenching sheets. A crash of thunder and jagged lightning, flashing brilliantly against the skyline like a falling angel, made their horses skitter and whinny. The riders pulled their hoods closer about their heads but the effort was futile for the drenching rain had soaked their clothes clear through to the skin. The taller of the two wiped the water from his face and turned to his companion.

'Oxford at last, eh, Alexander?'

The younger, smaller man grinned despite the rain. The smile made his olive-smooth face boyish.

'Dry, Sir Godfrey!' he exclaimed. 'Soon we'll be dry! Yet, for soldiers like you, such weather must be an accepted part of life.'

Now the knight grinned as he stared down at the red-tiled roofs and yellow sandstone buildings of Oxford. At first he had resented the presence of the clerk, with his smooth hands, boyish face and constant good humour, but on their journey up from London Sir Godfrey had, in a rare happening in his life, discovered he genuinely liked another man. Alexander was no ordinary clerk. The illegitimate son of a northern knight and some lovelorn lady he had met while campaigning in Scotland, Alexander looked upon the world with amused eyes. He was an excellent mimic and a teller of droll stories and, despite his education in the halls of Cambridge, he always deferred to Sir Godfrey, though the knight often caught a flicker of mockery in the clerk's dark green eyes.

'Have you been here before?' Sir Godfrey asked.

'On one or two occasions,' Alexander replied. He stretched out a hand, ignoring the water that ran down his sleeve. 'To the east,' he explained, 'lies the castle. You can see it through the rain.'

Sir Godfrey followed his companion's pointed finger and glimpsed the high turrets of the castle.

'And there,' Alexander continued, 'are St Frideswyde's and St Mary's churches and the spire of the Trinitarian friary.'

'It looks so peaceful,' Godfrey murmured.

'So it should be. A centre for learning, the home of clerks, scribes and scholars.' The clerk flinched at the driving rain. 'Oh, for God's sake, Sir Godfrey, are we to go down or sit here until we catch the ague?' The clerk pulled back his hood. 'Mind you, what's the use?' he muttered. 'I'm as wet as a fish already.'

Godfrey stared at him. The clerk's black hair was now a wet soggy mess and his eyes were red-rimmed, for they had ridden hard through the storm. The knight pulled back his hood and scratched close-cropped hair.

'You should keep your hair cut,' he advised. 'In a fight it gives little for your opponent to hang on to and, in the rain, too little to soak.'

Alexander leaned forward. 'Aye, Sir Godfrey, but in winter my head's warm!'

The knight laughed and spurred his horse forward. 'We should have taken that tavern keeper's advice and stayed another day,' he remarked.

'Never!' Alexander shouted, coming up behind him. 'Did you see the size of the fleas in that bed? Give me God's clean rain any time.'

The knight spurred his horse on, but the smile died on his lips and his leather-skinned face became harder. He did not wish to show it but he was frightened. Oh, he had seen battles, the storming of gates and the terrible hand-to-hand combat in the blood-drenched fields of Normandy. Nevertheless, what awaited them in Oxford was something totally different. On their journey up from London he had hardly spoken to Alexander about it but he knew the clerk had similar fear; the terrors that awaited them lay like some invisible sword between them. Sir Godfrey wiped the water from his eyes and rubbed his smooth-shaven chin. He was scarcely past his twenty-fifth year, yet he felt like an old man; recalling the sights he had seen and the blood he had spilt, he wished he could have at least some of his companion's innocence. Alexander McBain was only a few years younger but he was a scholar, a clerk, skilled in parchment, cipher and the courtly hand, so what did he know about the real darkness of the human heart? How men could kill, stab and hack without a second thought? Or of others, more steeped in wickedness, who called on the Lord Satan and used magical arts to achieve their evil ends?

Sir Godfrey could hardly believe what the king's chancellor had told him in London. At first he had laughed, but the chancellor's wizened face had remained impassive as he described the terrible murders occurring in the king's own city of Oxford. Yet worse was to follow. The chancellor, closeted in his secret chamber at Westminster, had whispered about the origin of these murders – about secret rites and ancient evils that had once again surfaced to play their part in the lives of men. Sir Godfrey's blood had turned cold and, at first, he had refused to believe but the chancellor had been persistent.

'I need you in Oxford, Sir Godfrey,' he had insisted. 'The abbess, the king's own kinswoman, has asked for your presence and the king himself has now demanded it. In this matter we trust no other. However, you will have a companion, my young clerk, the Scotsman Alexander McBain. He will be your eyes and ears. Alexander is skilled in dealing with the subtleties and stratagems with which our good scholars in Oxford might try and trap you. Trust him. Trust him completely!'

Sir Godfrey cursed and patted his horse's neck. After that the chancellor had refused to elaborate, simply giving him two purses of silver and a fistful of letters and warrants declaring how 'the King's trusted servant, Sir Godfrey Evesden, and Master Alexander McBain, clerk, had been commissioned by royal authority to investigate certain brutal and bloody murders perpetrated in the King's city of Oxford'.

'There will be further help in Oxford,' the chancellor murmured, flexing vein-streaked hands over a charcoal brazier. 'The lady abbess will tell you more; she can be trusted. And the exorcist Dame Edith Mohun will be there to assist you.'

'An exorcist!' Sir Godfrey had exclaimed. 'How can an exorcist help?'

The chancellor's rheumy eyes stared back at him. 'You'd best be gone, sir. You are to be in Oxford by tomorrow nightfall.'

Godfrey wiped the rain and sweat from his face and dismounted as they reached the trackway leading into the city. Alexander did likewise.

'What's the matter, knight?'

Godfrey shrugged and grinned. 'An old soldier's trick!' he shouted back through the rain. 'Never enter a city by the main gate, you never know who is waiting for you!'

They skirted the city walls and entered Oxford by a postern door, then went by St Budoc's church and on into Freren Street, which stretched into the heart of the city.

The houses on either side of the street were so densely packed that their gables met to block out the rain; the roofs of the great mansions were drenched with water, while the huts of the poor artisans, patched with reeds, straw or shingles, had turned to a soggy mess. Godfrey wrapped the reins of his horse round his wrist and stared about him; despite the heavy downpour, the market stalls against the outside of the houses were laid out, forcing him and others into the middle of the street past the sodden piles of refuse that blocked the central sewer. Behind him Alexander lifted one boot and groaned. The mud and dirt were ankle deep and the clerk looked pityingly at a group of young urchins who, despite the weather, were playing in mud which crept half-way up their legs. He would have roared his annoyance at the stolid knight trudging ahead of him, but the noise was deafening. Students, either ragged-arsed commoners or bachelors in their dark shabby gowns, thronged the streets, shouting raucously at each other over the cries of traders.

In the short distance he walked, Alexander realized that Oxford, like Cambridge, was no common town for he heard a variety of tongues – Welsh, German, Flemish, Spanish, Italian and even those of visitors from farther east. At last Sir Godfrey turned off the trackway and led his horse into the yard of the Silver Tabard tavern. Alexander joyously threw his reins to the surly ostler, who cursed quietly at being dragged out into the rain.

'Something to drink and something hot to eat,' Alexander murmured, 'would be heaven on earth.'

'Not now,' Sir Godfrey muttered and, ignoring his companion's protests and the warm cloying smell from the taproom, the knight wrapped his cloak about him and slouched back out of the yard.

'Why?' Alexander shouted, coming up beside him.

'I hate cities,' Godfrey replied. 'I feel fenced in like a horse in a stable.' He glared at the clerk. 'Soon others will know we are here. They'll mark our faces and perhaps plot our footsteps. You know what we are going to deal with here, Alexander? Skilful, bloody murderers who appear like will-o'-the-wisps at night. They know the lanes, the gateways, the alleyways and the traps. Well, now's our chance to learn. Who knows, our lives may depend on it.'

The knight, with Alexander trailing behind, trudged through Carfax and along Catte Street, passing the sellers of illuminated parchments, most of whom had given up trying to do a day's business and had removed their precious wares into the front rooms of their houses. Suddenly the rain began to ease. They paused for a while at the Saracen's Head. Godfrey ordered cups of wine for both of them but then stood at the door drinking quickly, urging the clerk to do likewise, until Alexander felt his usual good humour strained to the point of breaking.

They went back into the streets, past the low, timbered halls that served as hostelries for students – the Eagle, the Falcon, the Wyvern and the Sparrow. They continued up School Street past the university church of St Mary's and into the High Street, pushing their way through the Straw Market until they reached All Saints' church. Sir Godfrey felt pleased and ignored his companion's black looks. At first the knight had dismissed Oxford as just a ragged warren of lanes, a labyrinth of dark runnels. Now he realized that Oxford was a city made up of small villages. The villages were the halls or colleges; each, enclosed by its high curtain wall, contained a hall as well as a library, refectory, dorters, workshops, forges and stables. Godfrey wiped the rain from his face and stared up at the looming spire of All Saints' church. Very snug, very close, Godfrey thought, but a death trap for anyone fleeing from the law or being pursued by some red-handed murderer.

They both stood aside as the church door opened and scholars in shabby tabards, tied around the waist by cords and leather straps, came out from the noonday mass. The students jostled and pushed each other, shouting raucously, and some sang blasphemous parodies of the hymns they had previously chanted.

'Sir Godfrey,' Alexander appealed, 'must we die here of the cold?'

The knight clapped his hands. 'You have earned your meal.' Grasping the clerk by the arm, he pushed him into the dry warmth of the Swindlestock tavern, shouting at the landlord for onion soup, freshly baked bread and dry bacon. They sat squelching in their clothes, both men eating hungrily from the hard-baked platters before leaning back licking their fingers and sighing with relief.

'Where to next, knight?' Alexander teased, his good humour now fully restored.

'To she who awaits us, the abbess of St Anne's.' The knight drained his tankard. 'You know why we are here?'

'A little. There have been terrible murders.'

'Not just that,' Godfrey replied. 'Oh, yes, the deaths have happened, and more. Did the chancellor give you any details?'

Alexander shook his head.

'At first,' Godfrey said, leaning back, 'the occasional student disappeared and their anxious relatives made enquiries but, of

21

course, such cases were dismissed out of hand.' Godfrey grinned wryly. 'After all, it's not uncommon for students and clerks to go on pilgrimages or become involved in some mischief more attractive than their studies. Nevertheless,' he continued, 'these disappearances became more frequent and none of the students was ever found. Then, three months ago, the murders began. The first was dismissed as the work of house-breakers, but now there have been three incidents, all of the same pattern. A house is broken into late at night, though there are no signs of entry. The entire family is killed – father, mother, children and servants. Their throats are cut and the bodies hoisted up on to the beams by their ankles, as a butcher would hang slaughtered pigs, to allow their blood to drain.'

Alexander blanched and gripped his stomach, hoping it would not betray him.

'The sheriff and the university proctors have all tried to reason it out but have been unable to discover anything. What has perplexed them,' Godfrey looked squarely at the clerk, 'is that each of the corpses has been drained of blood but there's no sign of this in the house.'

'So, what was behind these murders?'

'Not profit or gain; it's believed the murders are connected to some ancient rite involving the drinking of the victim's blood.'

Alexander gagged and the knight leaned over and picked up his tankard.

'You'd best drink,' he said softly. 'It will calm your stomach.'

'And why the abbess of St Anne's?' Alexander gasped, pushing the tankard away.

'She's the king's kinswoman and both the sheriff and the university proctors appealed to her for assistance. Apparently,' Godfrey played with the ring on his finger, 'the lady abbess is a scholar and knows something of the history of these parts. She believes the murders are somehow linked to terrible crimes that occurred in and around Oxford hundreds of years ago. She not only asked His Grace the King for help but sent pleas to the Archbishop of Canterbury as well as to the chancellor. They put their heads together and have sent an exorcist to St Anne's convent, an anchorite named Dame Edith Mohun. Our task,' Sir Godfrey continued gruffly, 'is to search out the murderers and hang them. There are to be no trials or public outcry.'

'Is that why they sent you?'

Godfrey grinned. 'Now and again there are cases discovered by the justices in eyre or the king's commissioners that cannot be dealt with in open court. Yes, I carry out judgement against them.'

'But this is different?'

'Oh, yes, master clerk. This time we deal with murderers who do not kill for profit or revenge but because they believe in ancient rites. These are the lords of the gibbet, the black masters of the graveyard, who reject the cross of Christ and put their trust in the Prince of Darkness.'

The clerk's face paled.

'So,' the knight went on, 'this is no mundane task of the chancery, some bill drawn up for a court. Your task will be to collect and sift the evidence, be my eyes and ears in this city of subtle knowledge. But enough, I have told you what I know. We'd best continue our journey.'

Godfrey led Alexander out of the tavern, up Northgate, past St Peter's church and into Buddicot Lane, where the stinking town gaol stood. Godfrey stopped and studied this for a while, intrigued by the soldiers wearing the sodden but colourful livery of the city standing on guard. A little farther along, at the end of the gaol wall, loomed a stark set of gallows with a rotting, bird-pecked cadaver gibbeted in its cage of iron bars.

'I have seen enough,' Alexander moaned.

'This time I agree,' Godfrey replied and took him back to the Silver Tabard where they collected their horses. They rode along the city wall to the convent of St Anne. A porter let them in, grooms running up to take their horses while a wizened old lay sister, casting disapproving glances at their rain-drenched garments, led them through the dank cloisters past the chapel and up to the abbess's chamber.

The lay sister knocked, then pushed open the door, ushering the two men into a warm, sweet-smelling chamber before withdrawing.

'What is it?'

Despite her age, the woman behind the desk rose quickly. She was dressed in a brown habit, her dark-blue wimple edged with gold filigree. She moved from the high-backed chair near the fire where she had been conversing softly with two men whose faces were hidden in the shadows.

Her face was narrow; it would have been saintly had it not been for the piercing dark eyes and hooked nose. Her lips were thin and bloodless. 'I am Lady Constance, abbess of this convent,' she said imperiously, though the words were accompanied by a generous smile. 'Sir Godfrey Evesden, and you must be Alexander McBain.' She allowed first the knight then the clerk to raise her vein-streaked hand to their lips.

'My lady,' Godfrey muttered, 'we apologise for our appearance but that is due to an act of God.'

The abbess shook her head and stepped backwards.

'You are most welcome, sirs, and come highly recommended by the king and the chancellor.'

Lady Constance stared at the two young men. Alexander she summed up as no more than a youth, exuberant, ever-smiling, full of the joys of spring. The knight was different. She saw the furrows around his mouth and the pain in his eyes.

'Master McBain, the chancellor says you are the most resourceful of his clerks and, Sir Godfrey, your feats in battle as well as in the tournament are widely known. I am,' she stammered, 'I am sorry about the recent death of your wife.'

Godfrey shrugged and looked away.

'Master McBain, the chancellor says you are a rogue,' she quipped, trying to lighten the mood. 'Well, are you?'

'If that's the same as resourceful, my lady, then yes I am.'

The abbess threw her head back and laughed like a young girl, clapping her hands softly. 'Yes, yes, resourceful, that's how he described you.' Her face grew serious and she cocked her head sideways. 'You are going to need all your skill and resourcefulness,' she murmured. 'Dreadful things happen here in Oxford. Believe me, sirs, you have entered the Valley of Shadows and Satan and all his fallen angels are camped about us.'

The abbess stared at them sadly and Godfrey sensed that when, or if, they left Oxford, their lives would have been changed by what had happened here. Lady Constance looked over her shoulder at the two men sitting silently before the fire and her lips moved as if she was talking to herself. She turned back and forced a smile.

'Matters will wait, you look cold and damp. Where are your saddle bags?'

'With our horses.'

'Oh, that can't do!' Lady Constance murmured. 'That can't do!'

She went back to her desk and, picking up a small bell, rang it vigorously so that it echoed around the stone-flagged room.

'Our visitors will stay in the guest house,' she told the lay sister who came in response to the bell's summons. 'Have their bags brought round.' She went over to the fire, murmured something to the two men sitting there and then returned. 'Come, I will take you.'

The abbess, walking forcefully, head erect, her shoulders straight as a knight's, went down the steps and into the cloisters. Godfrey looked up and saw the clouds were dispersing and already the sun was struggling to break through. Some of the nuns had come out to sit on benches along the cloister wall, awaiting the warmth of the strengthening sun while watching a host of small birds plunder the soft turf of the cloister garth for grubs and worms. They were almost out of the cloister when Godfrey and Alexander glimpsed a young woman seated by herself bent over a piece of embroidery. She looked up as they approached and both the knight and the clerk stopped and stared.

'A veritable Venus!' Alexander murmured.

Godfrey could only nod in open-mouthed agreement. The girl must have been seventeen or eighteen summers old. Her hair was not fair but golden and fell in rich cascades down her back, bound in place only by a dark purple headband with a spray of diamonds in the centre. Her gown was dark green, fringed at the cuff and neck with silver filigree. Godfrey noted the swell of her breasts, her slim waist and her delicate hands but it was her face that made his heart lurch and thrill with pleasure. It was oval-shaped, the complexion a dusty gold, with eyes as blue as the summer's sky and lips soft, red and full. The abbess had also stopped and looked back in annoyance, then she followed the direction of their glance and smiled faintly.

'Lady Emily,' she called out softly. 'Do these gentlemen know you?'

The girl rose shyly, her cheeks tinted with a blush; her eyes had the look of a gentle fawn.

'Lady Constance,' she stammered, her voice soft yet musical, 'I have no knowledge of them.'

Alexander swaggered forward. 'Accept my apologies, my lady.' He bowed to the girl. 'We did not mean to stare, it's just that we did not expect in a convent . . .'

'To find someone so young and comely,' Lady Constance broke in tartly, 'amongst us old sticks!'

'My lady,' Alexander replied quietly, 'beauty is a passing thing and has many forms. In you it takes one shape, in my lady Emily another.'

Both ladies smiled at the smooth, swift compliment. Godfrey could only stand and stare hungrily, making Emily blush even more deeply. The abbess reasserted herself.

'Lady Emily de Vere, may I present the king's commissioners in Oxford, Sir Godfrey Evesden and the clerk Alexander McBain.'

Both men paid their courtesies. Alexander, chattering like a magpie, made the young girl laugh so much she blushed and hid her face behind her hand as the clerk's stream of subtle compliments hit their mark like well-aimed arrows.

'Enough!' Lady Constance cried and led both men away.

Alexander looked over his shoulder and winked slyly at Emily, which only made her blush grow pinker.

'A true rose,' Alexander murmured.

Godfrey glared at him to hide his own confusion; he was always the same, he could wield an axe or ride a horse but any beautiful woman would tie his tongue in knots. Alexander jostled him.

'Come, sir knight! Have you ever seen such beauty?'

'Lady Constance,' Godfrey called out, trying to hide his

embarrassment, 'is the young girl one of your novices?'

'Oh, no, she's one of the king's wards, the owner of three manors and lush fields within a day's ride from Oxford. Her marriage is in the king's hands.'

'Most fortunate,' Alexander whispered.

Godfrey just walked on as Lady Constance took them across the rain-soaked grass to a two-storied sandstone building.

'The guest house is empty,' she explained. 'You will be the only visitors staying in it.' She showed them round the small buttery and the refectory where they would eat and introduced them to a red-cheeked lay servant.

'Mathilda will look after you,' she said. 'Of course, you cannot join us in our refectory, but your food will be sent across.' She touched Godfrey's wet cloak. 'Your chambers are upstairs. You can change your clothing, then I will bring my other guests across.'

'Has the exorcist arrived?'

'Oh, yes, we have given her a small cell built into the wall of the church near the sanctuary. She said she is happy there.'

The Prioress took her leave and Mathilda, a hearty cheerful matron of indeterminate years, showed them up to their sparse but comfortable chambers.

The soldier was running for his life, his tunic torn by the cruel, sharp-edged branches that leaned down to block his passage and claw his skin. All around him the wind moaning through the trees mocked his actions. He stopped, frozen, hands on his knees as he fought for breath. Was he safe? He had to be safe. He stood up, gulping in the fresh forest air. He wished he hadn't left the castle. Perhaps he should go back, take the relic and inform the sheriff of what he knew. Yet, what could he say? He was a thief and now Satan was rising from his throne to drag him to the deep pit where scorpions would gnaw at his innards for all eternity. After all, he had violated his oath; he was a soldier of a Hospitaller order, yet he had forsaken his vows, stolen a relic and fled west. He had hoped to reach Lundy Island and seek passage abroad; the princes of the Rhine, the archbishops of Mainz and Cologne, would pay richly for the relic he had filched from the high altar of his church in London. Now all had changed. He had gone down to the village to deliver a message to the miller and was returning to Oxford, whistling a song recalling warmer, brighter days in the wine-rich province where he had been born. He had been half-way across the simple bridge, above the cold, swirling waters of the river, when he had looked over and glimpsed the terrible scene on the far bank. A dark creature knelt over the body of a young girl, some country wench, her skirts pushed up revealing naked, brown legs. Disturbed by his approach, the hooded figure half turned and snarled, revealing the young girl's body soaked in blood, an awful, gaping wound in her throat. The creature had risen even as the soldier turned to run back along the bridge, his heart skipping with terror as he heard the pitter-patter of footsteps behind him.

The soldier had fled like the wind, his heart pounding fit to burst, his breath coming in short burning gasps until he had to stop. Surely, he thought, his terrible pursuer must have given up the chase? The Hospitaller froze. He heard a twig snap and realized all the birdsong in the forest had died. He drew his dagger and staggered on. He heard a chilling laugh behind him. He stopped, turned and whimpered in terror as he glimpsed the black-garbed figure skipping over logs, racing like a greyhound towards him. The Hospitaller fled on, his heart beating furiously in these, his last moments of life. Would he get back to the castle? The Hospitaller looked round. No sign of any pursuer.

So he paused, gasped for breath and, still grasping his dagger in his sweat-soaked hands, hurried on, ignoring the branches that tore at his face and the harsh, coarse bracken that stung his legs and impeded his progress. He caught a blur out of the corners of his eyes. Was the creature racing alongside him? The man moaned in fear of death. A terrible notion occurred to him. The creature, whoever it was, seemed to be playing with him and the Hospitaller was now sure that he had been ambushed. Had this demon been waiting for him? Where could it have come from? The friary? Those priests so sly and secretive? What dreadful mysteries did they hide?

The soldier staggered into a glade; at the far end a small waterfall gushed beside a track snaking between two trees. He ran towards this, but a hooded figure moved out to block his path. The soldier turned, his sweat-beaded lips curling and snarling, but another creature was behind him. Blind with fear, the man ran into the small stream and waded towards the waterfall. He was nearly there. His mind, twisted by fear, seemed to be saying he would be safe amidst the falling water. He tripped and fell against a rock. He flailed, trying to rise, and saw the hooded figure above him – the smiling face, the lips parted as if to give the sweetest of kisses. Another joined it. He was hoisted out of the water, held up and shaken like a landed fish. He threw his head back and screamed as one of his pursuers bit deep into his soft, fleshy throat.

Chapter 2

The Trinitarian friary stood on the outskirts of Oxford, its sprawling buildings bounded by a grey ragstone curtain wall. Beyond this, the land fell away in a sheer slope down to foul swamps and marshes which the friars, despite all their labours, could not drain. The marshes, covered in a treacherous green slime and straggling bramble bushes, stretched to the edge of a dark forest where the trees clustered so densely together that any who wished to challenge the forest's sinister reputation would find it difficult to penetrate. Edmund, prior of the friary, stood by the window of his high-vaulted cell and stared sorrowfully down at this silent, green darkness. He gently fingered the knots on the tassel of the cord tied around his waist, three in all, standing for the vows of poverty, chastity and obedience. Edmund had never questioned these vows. He was a scholar, an ascetic, happier amid the vellum, parchment and leather of the library than running a religious house, especially with his knowledge of the dreadful secrets it held.

Edmund had been a friar for thirty years. As a young postulant, he had heard the stories and legends of this place. The novices used to scare each other by lying awake at night and whispering all sorts of ghostly and ghastly stories. Edmund had always ignored these. His responsibilities had grown to include the care of these novices, the running of the infirmary and, above all, the care of the scriptorium where the brothers painted, in breath-taking colours, beautiful books of hours or copied the writings of Chrysostom, Eusebius, Athananasius and the other great fathers of the church. The supervision of the friary, the administration of its estates, the discipline among the brethren and the spiritual welfare of the community had always been in the firm hands of the abbot. Now the brutal and sudden death of Abbot Samson had shattered all this.

Edmund had been harshly reminded that these legends and stories were now a very grim reality and he did not know how to cope. Naturally, he had done his best. He had brought in an old hag from the forest to wash Samson's body and dress it for burial and had informed the rest of the community that the abbot had died of a sudden seizure brought on by some morbid disease. The sooner the requiem mass was sung and the corpse buried before the high altar, he had suggested, the better. The brothers had accepted this, except for the ancient ones such as Lanfranc, who worked in the archives, and Matthew the librarian. They had their suspicions. During chapter meetings, their rheumy old eyes would challenge Edmund, as if daring him to announce that the ancient evil over which the friary had been built was free to exert its baleful influence again.

Edmund closed his eyes and whispered a short prayer. The old ones would keep their vows of silence, but for how long? No one really knew the secrets of the friary. These were only handed over to each new abbot, who swore a solemn oath never to divulge them. Edmund was supposed to have no knowledge of them. He did not want to act as abbot and yet it would be months before the mother house in France authorized the election of a successor to Samson. Edmund wiped his wet lips with the back of his hand. He had sent letters under secret seal across the Channel but all he had received was the strict instruction to keep silent. Edmund glared once more at the green marshes; time was running out. The litany of horrific deaths in the area was growing by the month. Men, women and children were being barbarously murdered and there seemed to be little anyone could do to stop it.

The prior wove his long fingers together nervously. Why, oh why, he wondered, had Abbot Samson broken his vow and unlocked the iron-bound door leading to the vaults? No abbot was supposed to do that but Samson, ever headstrong, had not only opened the vaults but disturbed the chain-bound coffer. And someone had been with him – a stranger who had slipped into the friary as silent and deadly as some bat. Abbot Samson had personally met the shadowy figure at the gate and taken him to his own quarters, where they had stayed until the rest of the community had retired. Prior Edmund had glimpsed these strange happenings but ignored them till he woke late at night soaked in sweat and shaking from horrible nightmares. Edmund had hurried down into the vaults to find the abbot dead, no mark upon his body but his face convulsed in a terrible grimace, mouth gaping, eyes open. There was no sign of the mysterious visitor. Edmund had stepped into that grey, evil-filled vault and looked at the coffer, now disturbed, the rusty padlock forced, the chains cast back, the lid slightly shifted to one side. Edmund had moved the lid back and brought down a new padlock, fastening it securely.

He had kept his eyes turned away, but even he had been shocked by what he had glimpsed: the uncorrupted body of a handsome youth, eyes closed as if in a deep, peaceful sleep. Edmund had stared around that vault. He was sure the coffer had been ransacked, but he could not tarry. He had removed the hammer and crowbar Samson had used and dragged the abbot's body out, re-locking and re-sealing the door to the vaults. He had pulled the corpse out of the tunnel and, under the cover of darkness, carried the heavy-boned body to the abbot's study, where a servitor found it the following morning. Why, Edmund moaned, had the Abbot opened the vault? What had happened to him? What had he seen? What had he done? Were those marshes at the foot of the hill responsible? Had Samson been looking for gold, new-found wealth to drain the marshes and turn them into fertile pasturelands? Who was his mysterious visitor? Edmund turned his back on the window and glared at the locked door of his cell. He must stop this; he kept hiding from the rest of the community and already they were beginning to sense something was wrong. He picked up his crucifix from the prie-dieu beside him and clutched it to his chest. The sheriff had said help was coming, but what would happen when it arrived? Abbot Samson's death and the horrific murders were terrifying, but so might be these royal commissioners with their power to question and threaten.

The prior leaned against the prie-dieu, half listening to the birds who rustled their wings in the eaves of the friary roof. Perhaps he should take matters into his own hands? Confront Lanfranc and Matthew and demand to see the secret chronicle? He tapped his fingers on the wood, remembering that secret doorway, the awesome, slimy, rat-filled passageway beyond and that lonely coffer. Prior Edmund was a good but weak man; he shivered and, bowing his head, begged God for help against the powers of darkness.

The friar's anxieties and fears would have turned to heart-throbbing terror if he had known of the meeting being held in the depths of the forest just beyond the friary. The sombre, cowled figures had entered it by secret paths, not stopping till they had reached a glade surrounded and darkened by great oak trees. In the centre of the clearing were oblong stone plinths ravaged by age and covered with moss. Once these had formed a great altar used by the Druids, who had slaughtered their victims there before hanging them from the branches of a nearby oak as an offering to the gods they worshipped. The group of black-cowled figures now used the stones as benches, sitting there in silence, merging with the darkness. In the faint daylight seeping through the trees they looked like monks coming together to worship in some ancient cathedral. Indeed, they regarded this place as a church, calling it their field of blood, for it was protected by ancient evils and reeked of terrible sins. They were safe here, wrapped in the darkness, away from prying eyes and straining ears. They sat silent as the weak sun, dipping in the west, was hidden by clouds. Their leader sighed – the only noise to break the silence, for no animal ever went near the glade. Its green, sinister silence was never broken by the chant of birdsong. The leader sighed again.

'We have come,' he intoned. 'We are assembled here in order to draw strength and plot our course. I have news. The king's men will be here soon. We cannot stop their journey any more than we can resist the power of the so-called sacred relic.'

'We should have destroyed that!' One of his companions spoke up.

'We cannot. It's too powerful and, if displayed in our midst, might unveil our true natures.'

'Then what shall we do?'

'First, we leave the relic. Second, we pretend. Let the king's men chase their moonbeams and will-o'-the-wisps. They will soon tire and their master will grow weary. They will be recalled; this kingdom is at war with France and the king needs every man. Yet, while they're here we must be careful.' He paused and took a deep breath. 'The spirit of our Master is now free,' he continued, 'and the rumour of his return has gone out. Our existence is known in Paris, in the great cities along the Rhine and in the villages beyond the Danube. Soon, those from where our Master came will hear of us.' The leader looked round the ancient circle. 'We shall re-open the sacred groves and take strength from our enemies, for their blood is our food.' The leader stopped and waited until the thin rays of daylight died among the trees. 'Light the torches!' he ordered. 'The Dark Lord awaits us!'

A tinder was struck and each lit the flambeau he carried. They all stood and moved in procession to stand in a circle around the great oak tree, whose branches thrust up like dark fingers towards the sky. The tree had always been twisted and, in the natural hollow of its branches, the Druids had once placed the wicker baskets containing their human sacrifices. Now it bore its own grisly burden: the corpse of the Hospitaller.

At the convent, Godfrey had unpacked his bags, stripped, washed and made himself as comfortable as possible on the small cot bed. He stared around the cell, stark and austere, and was wondering how long it would be his home when he drifted into sleep. He was roughly woken by a grinning Alexander.

'Come on, soldier,' the clerk jibed. 'Food is served.'

Godfrey sat up, sniffed the savoury odours and went downstairs to find a bustling Mathilda had laid out cups of wine, some cheese, pure flour bread and two bowls of steaming hot broth. Both men wolfed the food down and had hardly finished when Dame Constance returned with the two strangers Godfrey had glimpsed in her chamber. One was short, with the rosy red cheeks of a maid, tufts of blond hair pressed down over his thinning scalp. He waddled rather than walked and, with his protuberant belly and stuck-out chest, Sir Oswald Beauchamp, sheriff of Oxford, reminded Alexander of a very fat pigeon he had once owned as a pet. Nevertheless, despite his bland features, the sheriff was a shrewd, calculating man with restless eyes and a mouth as thin as a miser's purse. He had the irritating habit of scratching the point of his nose until the skin had begun to peel off. His companion, Nicholas Ormiston, proctor of the university, was an oldish-young man; although of no more than thirty summers, his thin face was already lined, his hair fast receding and his shoulders stooped after years of study. Nevertheless, his quick, dark eyes were friendly and welcoming.

Dame Constance finished the introductions and shooed Mathilda back to the convent kitchen, closing the door firmly behind her.

'You have eaten and drunk well?' she asked, coming back to sit at the head of the small table. 'Good! Good!' she continued, not waiting for an answer, and carefully folded back the sleeves of her gown. 'What you are about to learn, as king's commissioners, is both bloody and sinister. Terrible murders have been perpetrated in Oxford and we think more will occur. Sir Oswald?'

'Yes, yes,' the small man muttered officiously and, plucking a small piece of parchment from his wallet, tossed it on to the table.

Alexander picked it up and studied the six names on it.

'Who are these?'

'The names of students from Stapleton Hall in the Turl who have disappeared over the last few months.'

'Disappeared?' Alexander clicked his fingers. 'Like a mist? No trace?'

'None whatsoever.' The proctor intervened in a deep mellow voice. 'They took their belongings, what few they had. One or two of them were glimpsed walking along the High Street before they vanished. They came from different parts of the kingdom except for one, Guido, who was a Fleming. Their families are anxious for they too have neither seen nor heard of them.'

'But there's more isn't there,' Godfrey interrupted, 'than the disappearance of these six young men?'

'Yes, yes, there is. In the city, over the last few months, houses have been broken into,' the sheriff replied. 'Though I use that term wrongly, there was no sign of violence against doors or windows. Different households,' he murmured as if talking to himself, 'each time with the same result. Every man, woman and child in that house is killed, their throats cut and the bodies drained of blood. Yet the assassins disappear as quietly and mysteriously as they came.'

'There is no connection,' Godfrey asked, 'between any of the families killed?'

'None whatsoever.'

'And are the houses plundered?'

'Coins are taken, gold, silver but nothing else.'

'And is there any sign of resistance?'

Beauchamp shook his head. 'That's what's terrifying. The rooms are awash with blood but there's no mark of violence, no sign of a fight, never once are the neighbours aroused. It's as if—' The sheriff nervously rubbed the end of his nose. 'It's as if some demon can move through walls and doors, quietly kill, drink the blood and disappear.'

'Are the victims old?' Godfrey asked. 'Surely a young man would put up some form of resistance?'

'One family had two young sons,' the proctor replied, 'one

fifteen summers old, the other seventeen. They died like the rest.'

'And the streets are patrolled at night?' Godfrey asked.

'We have beadles, officials from the university and some soldiers from the castle,' Beauchamp snapped. 'They are now too terrified to venture out at night and what is the use, Sir Godfrey? Not even a beggar or the occasional whore has glimpsed anything amiss.'

'Some witches' coven is responsible,' Dame Constance intervened. 'A group of Satan worshippers who have studied the legends.'

The sheriff shook his head in exasperation. 'Lady, lady, we have heard these stories before, nothing but legends.'

Alexander moved his wine cup aside and rested his elbows on the table. 'I collect legends,' he smiled, 'my own people's stories of Oengus and his war dog.'

'These are different,' the abbess responded curtly. She drew in her breath. 'Many years ago,' she began, 'shortly after the Conqueror subjugated this country, a young man arrived in what was then the small village of Oxford. He came from the east. No, not a Saracen or a Turk, but from the countries north of Greece hemmed in by wild mountains and dark forests. He was apparently a kindly man much given to the service of God and the rendering of good works. He drew others to himself. They took over a derelict keep and, digging stones from the local quarry, rebuilt and refurbished it.' Dame Constance sighed. 'England was in turmoil at the time and many such strangers arrived. At first, the local people welcomed this stranger and his companions who prayed so much and did such good work among the poor, especially tending to travellers on the road going up to the northern shires or to those who took barges along the river. They even built a bridge across the Cherwell.

However, within a year of the stranger's arrival, strange deaths began to occur; men, women and children were found with their throats cut, their bodies drained of blood.' Dame Constance smoothed the top of the table with her fingers. 'To cut a long but brutal story short, after months of such horrible crimes the blame was squarely laid at the feet of the stranger and the mysterious order he had founded at the keep in which they dwelt.' She licked her lips. 'Appeals were made to London. The king sent soldiers north and, after a vicious and bloody battle, they burnt the keep and either killed or hanged whoever lived there.' She fell silent and stared down.

'And the stranger?' Alexander asked.

'According to the legend, Sir Hugo Mortimer, the Norman commander whose descendants still own land hereabouts, burnt the keep to the ground. Underneath it Mortimer found secret tunnels and passageways, so he had this wicked stranger placed in a lead-lined coffin, bound with chains and buried alive.'

The abbess paused. Godfrey realized how quiet the guest house had become, the only sound being the water dripping from the eaves outside. Alexander sat fascinated, the other two men looked subdued.

'What are you saying, Lady?' Godfrey asked.

'I haven't finished. According to the legends, a monastery, later taken over by the Trinitarian friars, was built on that site. The centuries passed and the old sins, reeking of an ancient evil, were laid to rest by masses and prayers.'

'But now you say the curse has returned?' Alexander queried.

'Yes.' She smiled faintly. 'I study the stars and their different constellations. Oh, I know the church condemns astrology, but the planets have moved into some deadly configuration and the spirit of that accursed stranger has come back amongst us.'

'What proof do you have of that?' Godfrey asked.

40

'Nothing, except the series of bloody deaths which evokes an evil past and, God knows how, perhaps the death of Abbot Samson at the Trinitarian friary.' She licked her dry lips. 'Although a healthy man, Samson died suddenly and, rather mysteriously, his body was coffined immediately and laid to rest before the high altar.' She shrugged. 'Both I and the sheriff attended the funeral mass. There is something sinister at that friary.'

'And these disappearances?' McBain spoke up. 'Surely the Master and fellows of Stapleton Hall have investigated?'

'Yes, they have and, no, they know nothing,' Ormiston replied.

'Sir Oswald,' Godfrey said, 'as we came into the city we noticed the town gaol heavily guarded. Why is that?'

'Last night,' the sheriff replied, 'another household was attacked – a spinster and her two sisters, seamstresses from the parish of St Thomas à Becket.'

'What happened?'

'Nearby was found a student, Eudo Lascalle, a Brabanter by birth. He was found deep in his cups lying in an alleyway, unarmed, unscathed, but covered from head to toe in someone else's blood. He has been lodged in the town gaol because, ostensibly, he is another riotous clerk.'

'And has he confessed?'

'To nothing but drinking too deeply of new ale in the Cock and Hoop tavern.'

'And the house?'

'Boarded up and guarded. You see,' the sheriff continued, 'so far there are rumours, whispers in the city, but nothing else. If this story came out it would fester old grievances, particularly between the townspeople and the university.' He shrugged. 'There would be riots and neither the city nor the university authorities want that.' Sir Oswald heaved himself up from the table. 'We have done everything.' His voice quavered. 'Guards, officials, street patrols but, as I have said, they too are frightened out of their wits.'

'And how did our lady abbess get involved?' Alexander smiled dazzlingly at Dame Constance.

The abbess flushed slightly, like some young maid accepting a compliment.

'I am a lonely woman and Sir Oswald and Master Nicholas often do me the honour of dining with me. At first, I thought the deaths were part of the bloody business of living but, as they continued, I remembered the legends and the university kindly allowed me to consult certain manuscripts kept in St Mary's church. Only then did I suspect.' She swallowed hard. 'I wrote to the king and the archbishop.' She spread her fingers. 'The rest you know.'

'This house, have the corpses been removed?' Godfrey asked.

'No,' Sir Oswald replied. 'The corpses were discovered by a journeyman trying to sell trinkets. Until tomorrow he, too, is cooling his heels in the town gaol. As usual, we will wait until nightfall to have the corpses removed.'

Godfrey rose to his feet. 'In which case, let us see them now.'

The proctor shook his head. 'I cannot go with you,' he whispered. 'So much blood, so many deaths.'

'I'll go,' Sir Oswald said. He looked warningly at them. 'I hope you have the stomach for it.'

They said their farewells to the abbess and went to collect their horses from the convent stables and rode back into the city. The murdered women had lived in an alleyway just behind a row of houses near Carfax. Two soldiers wearing the livery of the city stood on guard outside the door. They looked nervous and pale, but were pleased to see the sheriff and his companions. They immediately broke off their whispered conversation with the dark, gowned priest standing in the shadows.

'Must we stay?' one of the guards whined as the other gathered the reins of the horses.

Sir Oswald kicked aside the dirt and refuse of the alleyway.

'For God's sake!' the sheriff snapped. 'The dead can't hurt you!'

'No,' the fellow retorted, 'but those who hunt in the darkness can.'

'Guard the horses!' Sir Godfrey ordered curtly.

'Father Andrew!' Sir Oswald exclaimed. 'You have heard the news?'

The priest stepped out of the shadows. He was of medium height, pleasant-faced, youngish, though his black hair was prematurely grey. Godfrey noticed his tired eyes but also the laughter lines around the firm mouth and chin.

'Yes, yes, I have,' the priest replied. He stared at Godfrey and Alexander and his eyes became watchful.

Sir Oswald introduced them.

'You are most welcome,' Father Andrew murmured. He sketched a blessing in the air. 'As St Peter says "Be on your guard: Satan has come into this city and leaves his mark all around".'

Sir Oswald grunted and, pushing by, drew his dagger and cut the wrapped seals on the lintel. He then took a key from his pouch, unlocked the door and pushed it open.

Godfrey and Alexander, Father Andrew following, entered the musty darkness. Alexander felt the hair on the nape of his neck curl and sensed a dreadful presence even before Sir

Oswald struck a tinder, making an oil lamp splutter against the gloom. A pitch torch in its iron bracket also flared into life. Alexander looked round and nearly fainted. The room was simple – an earthen floor, a table, some shelves built against lime-washed walls, a small hearth, a cooking pot over the white ashes and a wire basket of bread which had been hauled up into the rafters away from foraging mice. Some jars, a clay dish, a pewter pot, knives and skewers hung above the hearth. All these simple things only enhanced Alexander's terror, for the walls were splattered with blood, the table glistened with gore and on the floor the corpses of the women lay like hunks of meat, their heads thrown back, gaping wounds like second mouths in their throats and the bodices of their simple dresses caked with blood. One look at the bluish-white faces and Alexander could stand no more; catching his mouth in his hand, he followed the priest, equally shocked, back into the gloomy alleyway. In the room of death the sheriff turned to stare at Sir Godfrey. He, too, was pale and, although he had seen such horrors before, his lean face glistened with sweat and fear had enlarged his eyes. He leaned against the wall, not caring about it being blood-stained, and closed his eyes.

'*Kyrie eleison, Christe eleison, Kyrie eleison.*' He breathed the words of the mass, 'Lord have mercy, Christ have mercy, Lord have mercy.'

At last he opened his eyes and stared up at the rafters and the three pieces of hacked rope which still hung there. Then he looked at the victims' feet, noticing how the ankles were still bound with cord. He grasped Sir Oswald by the shoulder.

'Is that how you found them?' he asked.

'Yes, strung up like pullets. The rest is as you see.'

'Nothing else?'

'Nothing, nothing taken, nothing disturbed. The upstairs

chamber is like a thousand others.' The sheriff jerked his head. 'Only this abomination.'

'And the neighbours heard nothing?'

'Before God, Sir Godfrey, nothing at all!'

'And the student Lascalle?'

'He was found at the mouth of the alleyway sodden with drink.'

Sir Godfrey turned and went back outside, breathing in the evening air as if trying to cleanse his mind as well as his lungs of the sights he had seen. The sheriff came out, locking the door behind him.

'You have seen enough?'

Alexander still leaned against the wall retching, Father Andrew gently patting him on the back.

'Oh, Christ Jesus,' the Scotsman breathed. 'I pray never to see the like again. Sir Godfrey?'

The knight closed his eyes. 'I have seen cities taken by storm,' he said, 'towns put to the torch after pillage and rape, but, before God, there is something evil in that room. So orderly, so neat, except for those three bodies and the blood-spattered walls.'

'Did you examine the corpses, Sir Oswald?'

'My physician, Gilbert Tanner, inspected them. There were no marks or bruises on their bodies, though their mouths were gagged before they died.'

'God have mercy on us,' Father Andrew whispered. 'Sirs, I must return. Master Sheriff, if there is anything I can do . . .'

The priest walked back up the alleyway. The knight watched him go. 'A good man, Sir Oswald?'

'Yes, he is parish priest of St Peter's, a church very near the castle. He has been here for five years and tends the poor. He, too, believes this is the work of darker forces.'

They walked up to where the soldiers had taken their horses, far enough away that it seemed as if they wanted to put as much distance as they could between themselves and that blood-soaked, two-storied house. They remounted. Sir Oswald curtly reminded the soldiers of their duties, and they returned in gloomy silence to the convent. At the main gates the sheriff gathered the reins of his horse and warmly clasped first Sir Godfrey and then Alexander by the hand.

'Tomorrow, sirs, I shall return. But enough has been done. I believe you are to meet the exorcist tonight. God keep you.'

Godfrey and Alexander shouted their farewells and rode into the darkened courtyard of the convent.

'Something to eat?' the knight queried as the groom led their horses away.

Alexander stopped, his ears straining into the darkness.

'Can you hear it, Sir Godfrey?' he asked, ignoring the question. 'The nuns are at vespers.' He smiled weakly. 'Perhaps we can gain a glimpse of the fair Emily.' He pulled his face straight. 'I want to go to church tonight. If what we saw at that house is what we face then we need God's protection.'

Sir Godfrey shrugged and followed him along the winding, cobbled path towards the convent church where a lay sister let them in. The nave was dark except for one torch spluttering feebly against the darkness. The lay sister led them past the shadowy columns to a bench before the rood screen. In the sanctuary beyond, the high altar was ablaze with lighted candles, the nuns in their choir stalls on either side sweetly chanting David's psalms. Alexander searched the pews, his eyes hungry for a sight of Emily, and he smiled as he glimpsed her sitting beside the abbess, the sheen of her blonde hair covered with a light blue wimple. The girl looked up quickly, caught his glance and smiled, making Alexander's heart leap with joy. Then he looked at the other dark cowled figures and his fear returned. He glanced sideways and saw Sir Godfrey's eyes were closed and his lips moving. As he caught a verse chanted by the nuns, Alexander, too, closed his eyes.

'From the evil one,' he whispered, 'and from the terror which stalks at mid-day, Lord deliver us!'

In the anchorite cell built into the wall of the convent church, the exorcist Dame Edith Mohun was also reflecting upon her arrival in Oxford. It had been strange, she thought, to leave her little, stone-walled cell, the sanctity of her London church and the daily routine of prayer, meagre meals, meditation and sleep. Edith knelt upon the beaten earth floor and confessed her own pride and cowardice. She had been safe there; she was always protected against those terrible visions, those horrific nightmares in which demons appeared to her with great heads, long necks, lean visages, sallow skin, savage eyes and flame-vomiting gullets. Now she would hear their voices again, dark and dreadful, as she once more looked upon the wickedness of man. Edith sensed the evil of the coming confrontation. Something hideously vile was awaiting her in the dark, fetid streets of Oxford, something she had met before – but this time it could be more real, more threatening. This would not be some poor boy or girl possessed by demons but a more terrifying reality, that dreadful alliance between man's free will and the power of evil. What the abbess had told her had evoked Edith's memories of the dark forests and lonely, haunted valleys of Wallachia and Moldavia, places unused to the cross or the real power of Christ. She had experienced real evil there and it had pursued her. But how could this evil be destroyed? By just three people – a knight, a clerk and a recluse who had lost her sight, her very eyelids being sewn together to block out the sun?

47

Edith crouched on the cold floor. What form would this evil take? Where did it hide? Edith had in her youth seen the popular carvings, the pictures in which Satan was depicted as some monstrous beast with hooked nose and curling serpent hair. But she knew differently. Satan was a beautiful young man with a silver tongue who would always appear to be most pleasing. She must not forget that; appearances were deceptive. Satan himself could quote the Scriptures and she would have to be on her guard. She touched the wooden cross at her throat and muttered her disbelief at what Dame Constance had told her. She knew all about the Strigoi, the living dead, but she could hardly believe that they were here in England, a country sanctified, covered in churches, where the cross had replaced the sacred oak, the Druids' magic and the sacrificial ring of stones. Perhaps, she concluded, evil never disappeared but just sank beneath the surface, biding its time. Then she looked up as she heard the insistent knocking on the wooden door to her cell.

'So it begins!' she whispered. 'So it begins!'

Chapter 3

Sir Godfrey and Alexander were finishing their evening meal of beef broth, cheese and bread when there was a knock on the door and the abbess swept in. Alexander and Godfrey rose to their feet.

'I have a visitor,' the abbess said. 'Dame Edith Mohun!'

The grey-garbed woman came out of the darkness and moved quietly into the room. Alexander could only gape. The blind exorcist was of medium height. She was dressed in a simple grey robe, her snow-white hair hung free to her shoulders. A dark blue bandage covering her eyes emphasized her skin, creamy soft and smooth as a maid's.

'Must you stand and gape at me like yokels?' the blind woman asked, smilingly. She turned. 'Especially you, Sir Godfrey Evesden, the king's champion and most intimate counsellor. I have heard of your bravery.'

The knight wiped his mouth with the back of his hand as he stammered his own greeting back. Dame Edith walked closer as the abbess left the guest house, closing the door softly behind her. Dame Edith grasped the knight's hand.

'I was only teasing. I did not mean to embarrass you, sir.' She turned towards Alexander. 'Master McBain, Scotsman and king's clerk, student from the halls of Cambridge, if I had a coin for every time you have been in love—' Her smile widened. 'I could feed the poor of London.' She walked towards the clerk and extended her hands. Alexander knelt and kissed the soft, warm skin. The exorcist gently stroked his face. 'You are brave,' she whispered, 'and you'll need all your courage, both of you, in the dreadful evil we face here. But come, let me share your meal.'

She walked to the top of the table. Alexander hastily brought her a stool, watching her curiously; despite her lack of sight, the exorcist was unerring in her movements.

'What are you staring at, Scotsman?' she asked.

'My lady,' Alexander stammered. 'You can see?'

The exorcist smiled. 'In a way, yes, I can. If you picture something in your mind and refuse to accept the darkness, it's wonderful what you can do.' She gripped the goblet of wine Alexander pushed towards her. 'Except read, read, read!' she whispered. 'I miss the world of books. When this is all over, will you read to me, Alexander?'

'From what, my lady?'

'Oh, the manuscripts you collect. The stories about your great heroes, Macbeth, Malcolm Canmore?'

'Of course,' Alexander replied. 'I will read to you.'

Dame Edith nodded. 'And do you know what we face here?' she asked abruptly.

'I do,' Sir Godfrey answered hastily, 'but the clerk knows little. Well, not as yet.'

Dame Edith turned back to Alexander. 'The sheriff and proctor know but, although they are here and listen, they do not accept the evil that is in this city. They are like us all, they have faith only in what they can see, hear, touch, taste and smell. Many years ago,' she continued softly, 'as the lady abbess has told you, before this place of learning with its halls, schools, castles and proctors was built, a great evil crossed the seas and took up residence here. It was vanquished but not destroyed, driven away but not burnt out. Now an evil that is not destroyed is like smoke; it may be trapped but, when it discovers a crevice or crack, it will pour through.' She paused. 'Are you frightened, Alexander McBain, of what you can't see?'

'Lady, I never think of it.'

'And what *do* you see?' she insisted.

'Perhaps only half of what I should,' Alexander jokingly replied.

'No, be serious,' Dame Edith breathed. 'What happens if there is more to our reality than what we see. We are like a fly, Alexander, which lands on a piece of bread and thinks that only what it can see and taste exists. We are like that, Alexander. We are small creatures in God's cosmos and we reach the arrogant conclusion that only what we see actually exists.' The exorcist's voice rose. 'Now as Christians we know different. We believe our reality is only part of a greater one and that beyond the veil exist spiritual beings who, like us, are in a state of conflict. The Apostle himself says that we do not fight against flesh and blood but against all the forces of Hell.'

'The Church also teaches,' Alexander interrupted, 'that Christ is always with us and that his strength will suffice.'

'Oh, in the end it always will, but we must draw a distinction between the battle and the inevitable victory. Now we tend to think of all evil as man-made – the robber, the adulterer, the ravisher and the murderer – but there is another dimension and within that the evil we see forms a pact with the evil we can't.' Dame Edith patted Alexander's hand gently. 'I do not mean to preach, but what you saw in Oxford tonight gave you a glimpse of what I witnessed.' Edith paused, her sightless eyes staring into the night, summoning up the shadows from her own past.

'Once upon a time,' she began, 'I was young and comely.'

'Domina, you still are!'

Edith smiled. 'Flattery is the sweetest wine, Scotsman. I was a young girl,' she continued, 'the only child of a doting father, a widower. He was a humble knight who owned some lands that stretched down to the shoreline in Northumberland. I was caressed and I was spoilt, I was given a fine education at the local convent. One day, when I was fifteen, my father visited me. Stephen Mohun came with him.' She laughed sweetly. 'I would have taken him on the spot, for I loved him dearly and I would not be brooked.' She turned her blind face towards Sir Godfrey. 'Within a year I was out of the convent and Stephen Mohun's wife. He was the youngest son of a great family. We lived with my father, who named Stephen his heir. Now, my Uncle Simon was a Hospitaller in a local commanderie.' Dame Edith shook her head. 'Golden days. We fed ourselves on meals of glory, the great feats of Charlemagne's paladins and, when Pope John and others began to preach a crusade, we answered. My father raised loans on his land and we joined a Hospitaller expedition to aid the Franks in Greece.' She shook her head. 'The foolishness of youth. We became mercenaries, fighting alongside our small Hospitaller troop as it made its way into Wallachia to protect the Christian communities there. Do you know the country?'

Alexander shook his head.

'Always dark, mountains black as night, slashed with precipitous gorges, covered in sombre forests and watered by treacherous, rushing rivers.' The exorcist stopped speaking, lifting her head as if straining to hear something. 'Even now,' she murmured, 'I dream I am back there. A terrible demon-filled place.' Her mouth fell slack, open. 'I can't describe what happened, but the convoy I was with was ambushed, massacred almost to a man. I and one other escaped, but he soon died of terrible wounds to his neck.'

She paused. Alexander and Sir Godfrey sensed, from her quick breathing, how she did not want to describe the terrors of losing her family. The exorcist shook herself free from her reverie.

'For a while I wandered like some beast in the forest. At first I thought the only dangers were the Turks, the wild bears and savage wolves but they were mere childish fantasies against the real terrors that existed.' She stopped and laughed. 'I was arrogant. In my earlier studies, I had learnt the Greek myths and the story of the Lamiæ, ghastly women who lured handsome youths to drink their blood and eat their flesh. In those dark forests of Wallachia, I learnt such dreams were part of our reality. One day I was in a village begging for food and drink. I was invited to attend the funeral of a young man who had fallen from a tree; his body was laid out and I was asked to join the funeral banquet prepared around the corpse. I ate and drank everything I could. The body was buried in a small graveyard next to the church. I went back to the forest and thought nothing of it. I kept clear of the village because a troop of Turkish Spahis—' Dame Edith gazed blindly at Sir Godfrey, 'Turkish cavalry entered the area. One night I was sitting by myself before a small fire when a dark figure appeared between the trees, walking towards me. I could not see the glint of any weapon and the man's hands were outstretched in a gesture of peace. I invited him closer, telling him to warm himself by the fire.' Dame Edith paused. 'The figure moved soundlessly towards me. His features were shadowed but, when he sat down, the fire flared and I went cold with terror. His face was white, the eyes red-rimmed and dark-shadowed; it was the same man whose funeral I had attended the previous week. He just sat watching me and I could do nothing. I was frozen with terror. He grinned, baring his teeth like a wolf, rose and slipped silently back into the forest.'

Alexander stirred uneasily, for the woman's story awakened fresh memories of his own nightmarish experiences in the city.

'At first,' Dame Edith continued as if talking to herself, 'I dismissed it as a phantasm, but the next morning I noticed that the area at the other side of the fire still bore the imprint of where he had sat. I went back to the village headman, thinking perhaps that the young man had not really died but had been buried by mistake.' The exorcist chewed her lip. 'Sometimes that happens – the victim falls into a deep swoon, with no trace of a heart beat, and is declared dead. He is buried in a shallow grave, revives and digs himself out.' Dame Edith paused, listening to the night sounds. Alexander, sitting beside her, struggled to control his own fears.

'Continue, domina,' he whispered.

'The village elder listened carefully to what I described and his terror was apparent. He immediately ordered the men back from the fields and imposed a curfew at night. He told me that the young man, who had been excommunicated by the local priest, had become a Strigoi, one of the living dead.' Dame Edith wetted her now dry lips, her voice dropping to a whisper. 'Of course, I dismissed it as peasant superstition, so the headman told me to wait. He sent for others from the village council and, with the priest's permission, the young man's grave was re-opened. I'll never forget the sight. The corpse was still warm, flesh-coloured with no greenish tinge of corruption. The limbs were pliable, not stiff, the head turned to one side rather than facing the sky. The elder pronounced himself satisfied, a stake was brought and driven straight into the young man's heart.'

The exorcist's mouth opened and closed. 'I will never forget his scream. It was horrible, soul-chilling.' Dame Edith sighed. 'The corpse was later burnt. I never discovered whether the man I had seen was a ghost or a demon. A few days later the Turks captured me.' Her voice hardened. 'They discovered I was a woman and tried to abuse me. I fought back savagely, so they thrust a red-hot iron bar against my eyes, turning them to water and blinding me for life.' Edith abruptly paused. 'Do you hear them?' she asked softly.

Alexander and Sir Godfrey, absorbed by her story, looked up.

'No, what is it, domina?' the knight asked.

Edith raised a finger to her lips. 'Listen!'

They strained their ears and heard a faint squeaking from the darkness outside.

'Bats,' Sir Godfrey said. 'They probably nest under the eaves.'

'I wonder?' the exorcist replied. 'In Wallachia the peasants claimed that bats were the emissaries and heralds of the Strigoi, the blood-drinking night stalkers.'

Alexander shook his head. 'Domina, the next thing you will be saying is that those bats were also sent.'

'They could have been.'

'Then by whom? Are you saying these Strigoi, these night stalkers, are lurking near here? If so, we'll hunt them down and kill them as your village elder did in Wallachia.'

'I have only told you half my story, McBain!' Dame Edith snapped. 'There's worse to come. I was captured, blinded, my eyelids sewn up. I became a slave in the fields, to all intents and purposes a peasant in Wallachia. Believe me, Alexander, there's none lower under Heaven than these peasants. At first I dismissed them as ignorant, crude and unlettered, but they taught me more than I had learnt in any school or in the libraries of our monasteries.

'Four years into my captivity, the village I lived in was attacked by greater demons. Three cruel, evil men, real sons of Satan, had been executed. The village priest, a holy man, urged that the corpses of all three malefactors be burnt. The Turkish commander just laughed and the bodies were left to hang.' Edith paused and shook her head. 'The first attack came within a week. A young girl was found, her throat ripped from ear to ear, her body drained of blood. Attack followed attack, each more gruesome than the last. The Turks moved soldiers in to the area, Spahis and even a crack troop of janissaries. They scoured the countryside but could find no trace of these mysterious attackers.' Dame Edith grasped Alexander's hand. 'Listen!' she hissed. 'One day I was in the wood picking berries – I did such things to train my mind and overcome my blindness. A young lad from the village had led me there. Suddenly he tugged at my cloak and begged me to crouch behind a bush. I did so and the boy whispered that he had seen a Spahi coming towards us but that there were attackers waiting for him in the trees. I heard the sound of commotion, the neighing of a horse followed by the most heart-rending scream. The boy beside me eventually fainted away in a dead swoon.' The exorcist pressed Alexander's hand as a child would his father's. 'I stayed by that boy for over an hour, lost in a blind hell and listening to the most dreadful sounds.' Dame Edith stopped talking and stared at her companions.

'What is it?' Alexander asked.

'The young boy revived. I half carried him back to the village. For two days he cowered in his hut, unable to speak. Then he told us what he had seen. The Spahi had been attacked by a family of woodcutters, a husband and wife and their son, a young man of no more than seventeen summers. They looked, the boy said, no different from other humans, but the speed and strength of their attack was unbelievable. They sprang at the Spahi bringing both horse and rider to the ground. The son ripped the soldier's throat with one awful bite, like a fox with a chicken or a weasel with a rabbit. They then strung the poor man up and drained the corpse of blood. Before he fainted, the boy saw them begin to drink the blood.'

Alexander stared at the exorcist, then at Sir Godfrey. He would have dismissed the tale as fanciful, if it hadn't been for the stark terror on the woman's face and the beads of perspiration that ran down to soak the bandage across her eyes. Sir Godfrey had seen fear affect many, but he could remember nothing to equal the sheer terror that now gripped this usually serene woman.

'At first no one believed the boy, but a watch was set upon the woodcutter's hut. The woodcutter, his wife and son acted as normal. They looked no different, their attacks were not governed by any change in season, by the sun or the moon. Only one thing was noticed. The local priest declared that, although the woodcutter and his family came to church, they had stopped taking the sacrament and always seemed to position themselves so they did not have to look directly at the altar whilst mass was being celebrated.' Dame Edith's grip on Alexander's hand tightened. 'Remember that, and you, Sir Godfrey. Forget the old wives' tales about crosses or spells or any talismans such as garlic or plants.'

'What happened?' Alexander insisted. The chill from the woman's hands seemed to spread into his own body.

'A new Turkish commander was appointed. A wise, old man. He ordered the corpses of the three malefactors to be burnt and the immediate destruction of the woodcutter and his family. They were to be taken at dawn, killed, their bodies destroyed, their house razed to the ground.'

'And the order was carried out?' Sir Godfrey asked.

'Yes, the attack was launched but the woodcutter and his family fought like demons. They seemed to possess superhuman strength, speed and agility. The village elder who witnessed it reported that before the young man was killed eight janissaries lay dead.' The exorcist let out a sigh. 'And that's when the real terror began. You're a soldier, Sir Godfrey, when your enemy falls you forget him.'

'And these revived?'

'Oh, no, worse than that! One of the janissary officers suddenly turned on his own men and began to kill them. The Turks realized they were not fighting flesh and blood but spirits that moved from one body to another, like someone moving out of a destroyed house to a more fitting abode.'

Sir Godfrey shook his head. 'Domina, that's impossible!'

'Is it? Read the gospels. Do you remember when Christ exorcized the man, the demon inside begged for a place to be sent to? I have conducted many an exorcism, the procedure is always the same. You ask the demon to name itself and then you begin the solemn ritual. The demon will usually shriek for a place to go and the exorcist's answer is always the same: "To Hell's dark abyss". But what I witnessed in Wallachia was different. These spirits were lords of Hell, having the power to move from a corpse to a living body. That is why the peasants call them Strigoi; they are spirit walkers, the living dead.'

'But why the blood-letting?'

Edith thumbed the crucifix at her throat. 'The Strigoi demon inhabits a man's body and turns him into a killer, the blood-letting is what they want. They draw strength from it.'

'What happened in that village?' Sir Godfrey asked.

'The Turkish commander did a brave thing. He broke off the attack and asked the priest to bring down the ciborium bearing a consecrated host. The priest did this, holding the ciborium aloft as the soldiers launched a second attack. Only this time, when they eventually killed the woodcutter and his wife, they used Greek fire and the bodies were burnt immediately. Apparently, if this is done quickly, the exorcism is complete and the demons must return to their dark pit.'

The exorcist's voice faded away and Alexander stared into the blackness of the night.

'Is that what we face here, domina?'

'Yes, Alexander. We do not fight flesh and blood but the very lords of Hell.'

'And there is no way of detecting these possessed creatures?'

'No, there is not. They will speak, they will sing, they will cry, they will eat and they will drink. They act as normal people, be they villeins or lords. But one thing I know is that they cannot take the sacrament during mass. If they are exposed, and that is difficult, they will soon show their true natures.'

'How many could there be?' Alexander asked.

'I don't know. There could be one, there could be six, ten, twenty, thirty or forty.'

'Can the number grow?'

'No, apparently not, but unless the body inhabited by a Strigoi is killed and burnt the demon passes to someone new. It's like some terrible plague that kills and passes on.'

Alexander closed his eyes and muttered a prayer for strength.

He shivered as he remembered the ghastly scenes in that house. 'Surely not,' he murmured. 'Perhaps it could be something else? How do you know the creatures responsible for the deaths we've heard about are Strigoi?'

'For two reasons. First, the university has great archives and libraries. In one there is a chronicle written by a monk of Osney. Now, it's full of strange stories – of apparitions, miraculous cures and dreadful events. The monk wrote about fifty years after the Conquest and in this chronicle, which the abbess read out to me, there is a reference to a strange order which landed on the coast of Kent, then moved to Oxfordshire. They took over and repaired an old, disused keep in the wilds of the countryside. This group posed as religious men and women, pilgrims carrying out some solemn vow – until the grisly killings began.'

'These were Strigoi?' Alexander interrupted.

'Yes, they came from Wallachia or a place close to it, Moldavia, one of the Balkan principalities. William, the first Norman king, destroyed the entire tower . . .'

'And the Strigoi?'

'God knows, but I suspect that not all their bodies were destroyed.'

'Why do you say that, domina?'

'I suspect that the leader of these Strigoi, the ones whom William the Norman destroyed, was imprisoned in some vault. That resting place may have been disturbed and the Strigoi's spirit is now free to roam where it wishes.'

'So,' Sir Godfrey intervened, 'there might only be one?'

'Yes, but he's a prince amongst them and has summoned his vassals to his aid.'

'Why cannot we destroy his resting place?' Alexander asked.

Dame Edith smiled. 'But where is it? And the real damage has already been done: the spirit is free. Perhaps even the body.'

'How do the Strigoi select those they'll possess?'

The exorcist smiled. 'People think that only the evil can attract such demons. Sometimes they do, but the spiritually weak, those not prepared, those who do not take the sacrament regularly are all vulnerable to attack.'

Sir Godfrey leaned over. 'Your story isn't finished, is it, domina?'

Alexander felt the exorcist's body tremble with fright.

'Because I had been instrumental in tracking down the killers, the Turkish commander allowed me to be ransomed by the Hospitallers and returned to England. Now, before I left, this man, a good Muslim, told me something very strange.' Dame Edith eased the bandage round her eyes.

'Which is?'

'He told me that just before the last Strigoi was destroyed in the bloody carnage around the woodcutter's house, he shrieked out a terrible prophecy.' The exorcist crossed her arms and bent over as if in pain.

'Domina, you must tell me!'

'The Strigoi shrieked, "Tell the blind one we shall all meet again. She will be older and be in the company of a king's son!"'

Alexander gasped in terror.

'Oh, don't you see,' Edith whispered, 'the terrible deaths in Oxford and your name, McBain, which means "son of a king". When the news of the murders reached London and the chancellor asked who should go with me, I learnt about you and knew for certain what demons awaited me in Oxford.'

Alexander stirred restlessly to hide his own panic.

'So, the Strigoi knew me before I was born?'

'No, but they prophesied that one day you would be their enemy.'

'But there's a flaw. How can these Strigoi from Wallachia be the same as those prowling the streets of Oxford?'

'I shall tell you, McBain. You asked if the Strigoi could

61

possibly multiply themselves. They cannot. But regard them as an enemy force that crosses a great river and establishes a bridgehead to allow others to follow.' The exorcist pushed her face close up to Alexander's. 'If we do not destroy the Strigoi here, they will extend their power and others will come.' She gripped the clerk's wrist. 'Alexander, believe me! Days of terror are upon us!'

Dame Edith rose and slipped out into the darkness, leaving Alexander and Sir Godfrey numb and more frightened than they had ever been in their lives. Alexander drew a deep breath, rose, went to the window and gazed up at the stars.

'In God I put my trust,' he muttered and began to chant the great prayer of St Patrick: 'Christ be beside me, Christ be before me, Christ be within me.'

Sir Godfrey joined in, then the knight stood up, genuflected to the east, crossed himself and quietly went up to his chamber. For a while Alexander just sat by the fire and watched the sparks jump like miniature imps in their own small Hell.

'Alexander, my boy,' he whispered, 'you have seen the days!' He smiled to himself. 'You will be a hero, Alexander. Say your prayers, boy, and keep your sword arm strong!'

For a while Alexander hummed to himself but, just as he began to feel drowsy, he recalled the words of a great Gaelic epic: 'Those who fight monsters must be careful not to become monsters and remember, when you stare into the Pit of Hell, the Pit of Hell glares back!'

Chapter 4

The next morning Sir Godfrey and Alexander broke their fast in the small refectory. The merry-faced Mathilda served them manchet loaves, jugs of ale and cheese made from ewe's milk which tasted tart and spicy. Sir Godfrey had already said his prayers, kneeling beside his bed, dedicating all his actions to the five wounds of Christ and asking for the Blessed Virgin's protection. Alexander, more practical, had prayed as he dressed. Now both men sat chewing the bread and cheese and reflecting on what the exorcist had told them the previous evening. Alexander picked up one of the small, white loaves and broke the silence.

'I eat only this,' he said. 'A Jewish physician from Salerno told me that rye bread not only turns your bowels to water but gives you strange dreams.'

'We don't need strange dreams,' Sir Godfrey growled. 'We are living in a nightmare. Those corpses, that silent, dreadful house and Dame Edith. What do you think of her, Alexander?'

'I studied in the halls of Cambridge, Sir Godfrey. I was lectured in logic and the subjects of the quadrivium and trivium. I move in a world which depends on touch and taste but,' the young clerk scratched his tousled head, 'St Paul says we not only fight flesh and blood but legions of infernal beings, those lords of the air who wander through God's creation, ever ready to destroy the work of Le Bon Seigneur.'

Sir Godfrey grumbled to himself.

'Did you say something?' Alexander leaned across.

'I fight flesh and blood,' the knight replied. "Last night we saw the work of flesh and blood.'

Alexander shook his head. '*Sic et non*, as the great Abelard would say. Yes and no, Sir Godfrey. What happens if the people who perpetrated those horrible murders either are possessed by demons or really believe they are something else?'

'What do you mean?' the knight asked brusquely.

'Well, in Cambridge there was a man whom people dismissed as an idiot. He lived in the cellars of a tavern on the road out of Trumpington. He really believed he was the Angel Gabriel and nothing anyone could say would persuade him differently.'

'And?'

Alexander grinned. 'What happens if he really was?'

Sir Godfrey just popped a piece of cheese into his mouth and ignored Alexander's wink. The young clerk drained his jug of ale.

'Sir Godfrey, whoever the killers are, we are about to enter the Valley of Death but,' Alexander couldn't resist gentle banter, 'we have your sword, my brains and the prayers of Dame Edith.'

'I think we might need more than that.'

The knight and clerk looked round in surprise at the exorcist standing in the doorway. Both men rose in embarrassment. Alexander noted that Dame Edith was dressed as a lady; she had changed her grey gown for one of dark blue trimmed with silver piping and a veil and wimple of the same colour covered her head. Once more Alexander was struck by how, despite the blindfold across her eyes and the snow-white hair peeping from

underneath the wimple, Dame Edith's face was soft and comely
as a young girl's, her lips full and red.
'God does not intend us to be miserable!' she exclaimed,
walking forward. Alexander bit his lip and blushed, for the exorcist seemed to
read his mind. He was also fascinated at how she could walk
with such a firm step and stately poise. She sat down at the
head of the table with as much grace as one of the queen's
ladies-in-waiting. Her hand went out.
'You have eaten well?' She took a small loaf and broke it in
her hand.
'The freshest bread and cheese, domina,' Sir Godfrey replied.
'And ale, richly brewed; what more could a man ask?'
The exorcist laughed merrily. 'Aye, what more, Sir Godfrey?
You should fortify yourselves. The devil can use an empty
stomach and a weak spirit to his best advantage. You have said
your prayers?' she asked quietly.
'Yes, domina.'
'And you have planned what to do?'
Both men looked at each other in concern.
'If you are to enter a maze,' the exorcist said, 'it's best if you
feel for the wall. What do you know already?'
Alexander pushed his trencher away. 'You want some ale,
domina?'
'A little, a small cup.'
Alexander rose and went into the buttery. He came back,
filled the cup to the brim and put it gently into the exorcist's
slender fingers.
'Your hands are warm.' The exorcist smiled. 'The blood
runs hot in your veins, Alexander McBain, and that's good. But
my question?'
'What we know is very little,' Sir Godfrey replied, watching

65

the exorcist intently. He could almost swear she could see every movement they made.

'And yet?' she asked sharply.

'And yet, domina, there are a few loose threads. First, those students who disappeared from Stapleton Hall in the Turl. We should go there. Secondly, this strange business at the Trinitarian friary, that too should be visited.'

The exorcist nodded.

'After all,' Sir Godfrey continued, 'the friary is built on the site where the Strigoi's tower once stood and there is the matter of the sudden and mysterious death of Abbot Samson. We should also visit the Mortimer family.' Sir Godfrey looked at Alexander. 'Where is their manor?'

'Between here and Woodstock.'

'And, finally,' Sir Godfrey concluded, 'we should interrogate that student imprisoned in the town gaol. He may have something useful to tell us.'

'Then,' Domina Edith said, wiping her fingers on the napkin, 'we should begin immediately.'

The men looked at each other in surprise.

'I am coming with you,' the exorcist added defiantly. 'I may be blind—' She chuckled merrily. 'But it will be good to be out in the world again and listen to the affairs of men.' Her face grew solemn. 'I may be of some assistance.' She stood and gently touched Alexander's ears. 'You can listen with them and you can listen with the soul.' She held up her hand in mock imitation of a vow. 'You have my word, if I am a hindrance I will stay here, but I would love to come.'

Alexander glanced at Sir Godfrey, who just shrugged and spread his hands.

'Of course, domina,' the knight replied as Alexander pulled a face at him. 'But you must put yourself in no danger.'

'Danger?' The exorcist put her head back and laughed. 'Sir knight, I have lived in danger all my life!

The conversation ceased at a loud knocking on the door. The abbess entered, leading a rather dishevelled soldier; his boots were caked in mud and there were flecks of dirt on his shabby tabard. The fellow bowed at all three of them, but Alexander could see he was fascinated by the exorcist. The abbess, standing behind him, scowled, her face showing her disdain for the man, who smelt of horse sweat and kept wiping a runny nose on the back of his hand.

'He's from the sheriff,' she announced.

'Well, man?'

'Sir Oswald,' the messenger closed his eyes, 'Sir Oswald sends his, sends his . . .'

'Compliments,' Sir Godfrey suggested testily.

'No, sir, his greetings. He desires your presence in the castle immediately.'

'Why?' Alexander asked.

The fellow opened his eyes. 'God knows, master, but they did bring a body in this morning. All blood and gore seeping through a sheet. It was still dripping when Sir Oswald ordered it to be taken down to one of the cellars.'

'Another death,' the exorcist murmured. 'Perhaps we should start at the castle.'

The messenger was dismissed and Godfrey and Alexander collected their sword belts and cloaks. The exorcist remained to exchange pleasantries with the abbess, who was anxious to learn what Dame Edith might require.

'Only a horse,' the exorcist said, as both men came back down the stairs. 'Something gentle but strong. A sweet-natured palfrey.'

The abbess agreed and led them to the stables. As they

67

passed the rain-soaked gardens they heard a young girl singing. Alexander stopped.

'That's a French song, isn't it? *"La Belle Dame sans Merci"*, "The Lady without Pity".'

And, without being invited, Alexander walked through a gap in the privet hedge that shielded the singer. His face softened as he glimpsed the Lady Emily standing next to a small fountain, a brilliantly white dove resting on her gloved hand. She was stroking its breast gently, singing to it, completely absorbed in what she was doing.

Sir Godfrey joined him. Both men stood in speechless admiration, for the early morning sun caught the young woman's unbraided hair and created a golden aureole around it. In her long dress of murrey, bound at the waist by a silver cord, she reminded Alexander of a fairy princess he had glimpsed in a Book of Legends in a wooden-panelled library at Cambridge.

'A vision!' he murmured.

The girl kept singing. Godfrey could only stare, wondering why his heart skipped a beat, his pulse and blood raced and his stomach tingled with excitement.

By the rood! he thought, I have only met her twice and I stand like some lovelorn squire!

The two women also joined them. The dove fluttered. Emily stopped singing as she realized she had an audience. She placed the bird gently on the ground and coyly looked at them from under her eyelashes.

'Good morning, sirs,' she murmured.

Alexander took a step forward, his boots crunching on the gravel path. The dove fluttered its wings and rose, soaring into the air to circle above the girl. Alexander sketched the most courteous of bows.

'Mistress, I apologize, but that song, I have never heard it sung so beautifully.'

'My mother taught it to me.'

Alexander looked up at the circling bird. 'Is that a pet?'

'Of sorts.'

Alexander watched the bird circle, a flurry of white against the early morning sky.

'Then, mistress, it is the most fortunate of doves!'

'Why, sir?' Lady Emily's eyelashes fluttered as she glanced straight at him.

Godfrey felt a pang of envy, for the girl was struggling to hide her laughter.

'Mistress, to be held by you!'

Now the girl blushed. Dame Constance noisily cleared her throat but the exorcist laughed, as if echoing the young girl's merriment.

'You have met Dame Edith?' Sir Godfrey found his voice, louder than he intended.

Dame Constance bustled in and made the introductions. Emily swept forward to exchange the kiss of peace, her red lips gently brushing the cheeks of the exorcist.

'You are beautiful,' Dame Edith whispered, stepping away. 'And a fine singer.' She looked in Alexander's direction. 'Do you really know that song?' she queried.

Alexander, eager to seize every second, thrust one leg forward, head back, arms on his hips, taking up the pose of a professional jongleur.

'If the lady Emily will accompany me. How does the first verse go?

'La nuit devient trop tard.'

Alexander's rich tenor voice broke into song, Emily joining him on the third line. They sang a duet as sweet as any Sir

Godfrey had heard. By the time they had finished, even Dame Constance's severe face was lit by a smile. The exorcist clapped her hands, but Sir Godfrey could only stare, torn between envy at Alexander's easy gallantry and the sheer vivacity of the girl. 'This will not do! This will not do!' Dame Constance declared in mock severity. 'Master McBain, the sheriff awaits you.'

Alexander caught Emily's hand, raised it to his lips and pressed his mouth against her long, cool fingers. Revelling in their smooth silkiness, he allowed his lips to linger while he glanced cheekily at the girl from under his eyebrows. For her part Emily acted the perfect coquette, reluctantly withdrawing her hand when etiquette and Dame Constance's grim look demanded it.

'Mistress,' Alexander murmured, 'you should sing again.'

'A perfect accompaniment,' Emily softly replied.

Alexander stepped back and once again bowed but, instead of turning, walked backwards as if he found it impossible to tear his eyes away. Emily collapsed in giggles. Dame Constance strode on, while the exorcist gripped Alexander's hand.

'Come, sir,' she whispered. 'You have the abbess's tolerance, even acceptance. Do not push matters further.'

Sir Godfrey, however, did not move and waited until his companions had gone back beyond the privet hedge that cordoned off this small pleasance. He then walked forward. He tried to smile but found it false so kept his face straight. Emily looked at him strangely; she saw the passion in his face and fire in his eyes and realized this man did not believe in dalliance. She folded her hands across her stomach.

'Sir Godfrey, you tarry?'

The knight put his hand out and Emily placed her fingers gently within his. The knight then brought her hand up to his lips, brushed it gently and let it fall away.

'Lady, in all things I am your servant.'

Emily blushed, but this time not from coyness but at the passion in Sir Godfrey's face. She opened her mouth to speak but Sir Godfrey turned on his heel and strode away to join the rest at the stables. The servants had led out a small grey palfrey and Alexander was gently assisting the exorcist into the saddle. She turned her face towards Sir Godfrey.

'I know what you are thinking, Sir Godfrey,' she called out briskly. 'I may be blind, but I am not helpless. I can ride a horse as well as a babe suckles its mother's tits.' She tapped the wooden hilt of the long dagger she usually carried under her cloak, which was now lashed in its sheath to the saddle horn. 'And, if it comes to battle, I can deal as good a blow as I get.'

The exorcist grinned. 'But make sure you don't come too close. Sometimes it's hard to tell friend from foe.'

Alexander bellowed with laughter at her short speech as he and the knight mounted.

'Sir Godfrey!' the abbess called, 'the clerk tells me you wish to seek out the Mortimer family?'

'Yes. I believe they have a manor between the city and Woodstock?'

The abbess shook her head. 'No Mortimers live there now. I am sorry, I should have told you before; their only descendant is Sir Oswald Beauchamp, the sheriff. I thought you knew that?'

Sir Godfrey shook his head. 'No, I didn't,' he muttered, 'but I won't forget it.'

They rode together out of the convent buildings, Alexander leading the exorcist's horse by the bridle. They had to pull aside as the town bailiffs trundled by with a cart carrying the body of a suicide to Eastgate to be buried in the city ditch. Then they made their way up the High Street towards the castle. After the yesterday's rain, the thoroughfare was muddy and the rain had swollen the sewer in the centre of the street to overflowing. Nevertheless, the prospect of a better day, as well as the chimes of the bells of different churches and the cries of the apprentices, had brought the crowds out. Benedictine monks in their black habits, Carmelites in white, friars in black and grey and throngs of students – some in gaudy attire, others ragged, yellow-faced, with bitter faces and hands constantly resting on their daggers – shouldered their way through the streets. Servants trotted by, carrying books to the schools. A priest, preceded by a silver cross, mumbled prayers for the repose of the soul of the corpse bobbing up and down in a cart behind him. Now and again Alexander spied the different professors: the doctors in their mantles of crimson cloth, the fur-lined hoods of the theologians and the brilliant white caps of the Masters of Arts.

There was a purposeful air in most of the crowd as they hurried in and out of the many halls that lined the High Street or pushed into the cookshops to break their fast, attracted by the savoury beef and onion smells that hung heavy in the morning air. Peasants in their wooden clogs and brown and green hoods jostled wealthy burgesses in wool-lined cloaks. Busy serving girls hurried along the stalls with their baskets, quietly mouthing the things they had to buy. Alexander watched them all, noting particularly the hostility when town and gown met. Here a group of students forced a trader out of their path, almost pushing him into the stinking sewer. A burgess half drew his sword as he heard salacious whispers directed at his young daughter, whose pretty face peeped out from a damask-covered hood. All the time students talked in loud raucous voices as they prepared for a day's learning in the schools and Alexander caught snatches of their songs. City beadles and university officials kept an eye on the busy throng. All were armed with staves but, as one moved, Alexander glimpsed the pommel of a sword beneath his cloak. Sir Godfrey, too, had noticed this; he leaned back in his saddle.

'There's a tension here,' he declared. 'It reminds me of a barnyard full of fighting cocks.'

'There's always tension,' Alexander sourly observed. 'The students hate the citizens, the citizens hate the students. It was the same in Cambridge.'

No, Sir Godfrey thought, looking around, this is different. He wondered if the mysterious murders had intensified the curdling dislike between the university and the town. They cleared the High Street and went past St Martin's and on to St Peter's church. Here they stopped and stared curiously: the church, set in its own grounds a few paces from the High Street, was now boarded up, its windows shuttered, the main entrance door firmly padlocked, though the small hall beside the church was busy enough. Sir Godfrey looked at the ragged men and women who thronged outside its doorway chattering to the priest they had met the previous evening. He had set up a small stall at the entrance to the hall and was serving the poor or, indeed, any caller, bowls of hot pottage and small loaves of bread. Father Andrew saw them and grinned. He handed the ladle to a tousle-haired young man and came forward to greet them.

'Good morrow, sirs.' The priest stared around Alexander at the exorcist, sitting absorbed in her own thoughts.

'Father Andrew.' Alexander clasped the man's hands and stared at his saintly face. 'May I present Dame Edith Mohun.'

'The exorcist?'

'Yes,' Alexander replied. 'You have heard of her?'

The priest approached, took the exorcist's hand and kissed it gently.

'I was born in Whitby in the north but served as a curate at St Dunstan's-in-the-Fields. Your reputation was known even then.'

'Reputation for what?' Dame Edith tartly asked. 'Hiding away from everyone?'

Father Andrew laughed and stepped back. 'For your prayers and good works.'

Sir Godfrey pointed to the table, the steaming cauldron and the poor people thronging about it. 'Like yourself, Father Andrew.'

'It's the least we can do,' the priest replied. 'So many people come to Oxford. The price of a bed or a loaf of bread would tax even the wealthy. It's good to use the revenues of the Church for such matters.'

Sir Godfrey nodded. He had seen such sights before, wandering labourers, poor students, even entire families. He recalled the debates at the great council held by the king last Easter; how the roads were being thronged as the lords used their fields and arable pastures to grow sheep and grow fat on the profits of wool while the poor were turned out of their homes. The exorcist, who had smelt the savoury odours from the cooking pot, pushed her palfrey forward.

'You do good for the body, sir priest. But I hear no bell for mass or the creak of anyone going through your door.'

Father Andrew laughed.

'Domina, you can see as well as any person with keen eyesight. The church is barred because the roof inside has grown weak, the beams are cracking.' Father Andrew laughed again. 'I know the Church is supposed to be the gate of heaven but we should not take that too literally.'

They laughed at the priest's sally, made their farewells and continued along the streets, across the drawbridge and up into the castle. Servants took their horses and a busy-eyed steward led them up to a comfortable solar on the second floor where Sir Oswald Beauchamp and the lanky, dark-faced proctor, Nicholas Ormiston, were waiting for them. Introductions were made and pleasantries exchanged as a servant took round a tray of goblets of sweet white wine and a plate of figs dried and sugared. As they all sat around the small table in the far corner of the solar, Alexander seized the initiative.

'Sir Oswald, you are a descendant of the Mortimers, of the lord who first challenged and destroyed the Strigoi?'

Sir Oswald shuffled his feet and stared down to hide his embarrassment.

'It's something I don't like to mention,' he muttered. 'My mother was the last of the Mortimers and she was only too pleased to take my father's name.'

'Don't be too hard on Sir Oswald,' the proctor intervened. 'Were you also told, master clerk, that I, too, am a relative of the Mortimers?' He grinned sideways at the sheriff. 'Albeit the link is a weak one.'

Dame Edith just sat listening attentively, her head slightly cocked to one side. Alexander glanced at her in puzzlement. She was old and yet young, distant even holy. She could talk like a trooper but had a sharp practical mind. Father Andrew was right, she could see better than even the most sharp-eyed. The exorcist turned to Alexander and smiled. The clerk noticed how white and even her teeth were.

'I am listening, master clerk, and I am fascinated. Tell me, Sir Oswald, did your family have any legends about the Strigoi?'

Beauchamp shrugged. 'Nothing was written down,' he replied slowly. 'Just legends and folklore passed by mouth from one generation to the next. Sir Hugo was seen as a great champion of both Crown and Church.'

'Where is he buried?' Dame Edith asked.

'He was of Norman blood and owned lands on both sides of the Channel. He lies buried under the high altar at Caen in Normandy.'

Dame Edith whispered something under her breath. Alexander was sure it was 'Then at least he's safe'.

'What other legends were passed down?' Dame Edith abruptly asked.

Sir Oswald leaned his elbows on the chair and stared up at the heavy-beamed roof, his embarrassment apparent to all.

'There wasn't much,' he replied haltingly. 'More like a nightmare you can only faintly remember. Oh, we knew about the legends of the Strigoi and Hugo's destruction of his tower. Sometimes the stories were just rejected as legends but at other times there was a feeling of unease that the Strigoi curse might return to take its vengeance.'

'There is one story.' The proctor spoke up, looking quizzically at his distant kinsman. 'You remember, Sir Oswald?'

'Oh, yes!' The sheriff closed his eyes, chewing his lip as he tried to remember. 'An old saying in the Mortimer family,' he murmured. 'Ah, I remember now, that's how it goes.' He opened his eyes. 'Mortimer, beware when the devil from the old keep comes to the rock near the new keep!' He shrugged. 'That's it!'

'What does it mean?' Alexander asked.

The sheriff shrugged. 'God knows, I'd tell you if I did.'

The exorcist had now turned in the direction of the proctor as if studying him intently.

'You, sir, you are a Doctor of Theology?'

'Yes, domina.'

'Skilled in philosophy and logic?'

Ormiston laughed like a young boy. 'Well, so they say. I

76

have those who praise me and others who criticize me. There is a great deal of learning at Oxford but very little charity. Why do you ask?'

Now the exorcist smiled. 'You must find it hard to believe in devils and Strigoi, people who shift their shape and feast on human blood.'

Ormiston shook his head. 'When I was younger, yes,' he replied slowly. 'But I believe in the powers of darkness. Go out into the countryside, domina, you'll find those going to church on Sunday who, the night before, have danced in moonlit glades offering sacrifice to Cernunnos, the horned god.' Ormiston shifted on his seat. 'Three years ago, in this very city, I presided at the trial of a student who had fashioned an image of a rival from the fat of a hanged man then scored it with pins.'

'Such things are common,' Alexander jibed.

Ormiston looked bleakly at the clerk.

'Oh, no, he wasn't tried for that. What the court wanted to know was why the image's legs were broken on the very morning, master clerk, when his rival's legs were crushed by a cart in Carfax.'

The proctor leaned forward. He pushed his face towards the exorcist as if he believed she could really see from behind her blindfold.

'Oh, I believe in evil, Dame Edith. Satan can walk the alleys of Oxford as he can any moonlit glade.'

Dame Edith now looked straight at Beauchamp.

'Do you have doubts, Sir Oswald?'

The sheriff squirmed in embarrassment. 'Dame Edith, I am an officer of the crown. I hunt down outlaws. I trap felons and hang murderers. I don't know what you mean by Strigoi, devil-worshippers.' His hands flailed out. 'To me they are just filthy murderers.'

Alexander stared obliquely at the exorcist. He, too, had the same doubts as the sheriff and was intrigued that the knight, his more practical companion, had not questioned what the exorcist had told them the previous evening.

'All I can say,' Dame Edith replied, 'is that we do deal with murderers but, whether you believe it or not, they act on the authority of higher, darker powers. They believe that human sacrifice and the drinking of human blood strengthens their cause. These are the Strigoi, shape-shifters, what others would call vampires.'

Sir Oswald got to his feet.

'Well, whatever they are,' he muttered, 'they have killed again. You'd best come and see.'

And, taking two of the sconce torches from the wall, he gave one to Sir Godfrey and, with Dame Edith resting on Alexander's arm, he led them out of the solar down a narrow, spiral staircase and into the cellars of the castle.

Chapter 5

The sheriff dismissed the two soldiers on guard outside the rusting dungeon door. He inserted a key and led them into the high-ceilinged, fetid cell. The place had been swept clean; two oblong boxes lay next to each other on the flag-stoned floor. Dame Edith whimpered and stayed near the door; Alexander caught her sense of dread. The sheriff, turning his face away, pulled back the lids of the two makeshift coffins. The human remains in each were disgusting. Ormiston immediately left the cell. Alexander closed his eyes, trying hard to control his stomach. Sir Godfrey pushed forward and stared down. The girl's throat looked as if it had been bitten out, her body drained of every drop of blood. She looked grey and ghastly in the flickering torch-light. The man had been mutilated beyond belief; his throat, too, had been slit but his body bore strange marks, crude carvings in the flesh, as if someone had tried to sculpt the antlers of a deer on his chest and arms.

'We've seen enough,' Sir Oswald muttered. 'For God's sake, man!'

Sir Godfrey simply stared. He'd seen worse in the ditches and battlefields of Normandy but this was different. He had no difficulty in accepting what Dame Edith had said. He'd met evil before, in all its forms, but this was something new – a purposeful, deliberate malice, murder carried out in the name of some ancient rite.

'Close them up!' Sir Godfrey ordered. He stared at Alexander's white face. 'Not here,' he said. 'We can't talk here.'

Sir Oswald had the dungeon locked and took them back to the solar, where he testily ordered a servant to fill their goblets. Ormiston and Alexander looked as if they wished to retch. Sir Oswald's hand shook as he handed out the wine cups. Dame Edith sat as if carved out of stone, her lips, thin and bloodless, pressed tightly together.

'What makes you think the two we have just seen were murdered like the rest?' Alexander asked. 'I take it they were not found in the city?'

'No,' the sheriff replied, 'in the woods to the north. The girl was found near a ford. The same party of hunters discovered the soldier's body placed like an animal's carcass in the branches of an oak tree.'

'Is there anything special about the places where they were found?' Sir Godfrey asked.

'The ford is used by many people, but the glade? Well, there are legends that it was once used by pagan priests, long before the Romans came.'

'So, how did the hunters find it?'

'They didn't, their dogs did. They caught the smell of blood and led them straight to it.'

'You say he was a soldier,' Alexander commented. 'The man was as naked as the day he was born. Did you know him, Sir Oswald?'

'Yes, I did,' the sheriff replied, leaning back in his chair, 'or, at least, I think I did. He came to the castle here and gave his name as Reginald Bouilang. He was wandering the countryside, offering his sword to the highest bidder. He claimed to have served in the retinue of some great lord in France. I offered him a bed and the normal wage of a serjeant and he accepted.' Beauchamp shrugged and looked at the knight. 'You know the sort, Sir Godfrey? The roads and lanes are full of them. They go from castle to castle offering their services. He seemed able enough, quiet and industrious. He mingled with the rest of the garrison as if he had been born here and they never gave him a second thought. Yesterday he was sent to one of the millers in the local village to find the price of corn and flour.'

'You said you *thought* you knew him?' Sir Godfrey intervened.

'Yes, yes, I did.' The sheriff plucked a small scroll of parchment from his wallet. 'At about the same time as his corpse was brought back here with that of the girl, I received this proclamation from the sheriff of London about an outlaw, Jean Mabille.' He waved the parchment. 'According to this Mabille was a serjeant in the Hospitaller order based at Clerkenwell just outside London. He apparently absconded from there with a purse of gold and, more importantly, a precious reliquary containing a piece of the true cross. The description of Mabille fits that of the dead Bouilang.'

Sir Godfrey sighed and slumped back in his chair.

'I suppose you've searched the man's possessions?' Alexander asked.

'Yes, yes, I have and it didn't take long. A battered saddle bag full of bric-à-brac, a change of clothing, two stilettos and an empty purse – but no gold or reliquary.'

'Could he have hidden them anywhere?'

Sir Oswald shook his head. 'I have thought of that. No one saw the dead man act suspiciously and I have searched the castle myself. I know every brick of this place. He could have buried them anywhere: in a field or beneath some tree in the forest.' The sheriff threw the piece of parchment on the table. 'I'll write back and tell them that Mabille's dead and the gold and reliquary have disappeared.'

'Wait! Wait!' Dame Edith raised one white hand. She leaned forward. 'We have two deaths here. The girl was taken near a ford. Has that ever happened before, Sir Oswald?'

'No, never. All the deaths have occurred within the city.'

'But the soldier,' Dame Edith continued, 'was not only murdered outside the city but used as a victim in some sort of sacrifice.' She paused, lacing her fingers together.

'What are you implying, Dame Edith?' Alexander asked.

'Oh, clerk, use your logic. First, none of these murders has occurred beyond the city walls and, yet, now we have two. Secondly, a soldier who has stolen a precious relic – and I suspect the relic is genuine, not one of those traded by pardoners up and down the kingdom – is killed in the same wood as the girl. Thirdly, he was a fighting man, he would not have given up his life cheaply. Ergo, I believe the soldier was ambushed; these Strigoi, these murderers, were waiting for him. The poor girl was just unfortunate. She wandered into the wrong place at the wrong time.'

'Do you think the soldier was killed for the reliquary?'

Dame Edith laughed sourly and shook her head.

'These Strigoi would be frightened of such a relic, as they are of the sacrament. Oh no, if the soldier had had it on his person he would have been safe. They would never have approached him. I think that, somehow or other, this soldier, and the reliquary he carried, caused grave inconvenience and distress to these murderers and they punished him with death.' She shook her head. 'I don't know why, how or when. But we should find out where the poor man hid the reliquary and that might lead us to his murderers. Sir Oswald, do you have any clue?'

'One thing,' the sheriff replied. 'Mabille slept in the guard house with a number of others. As I said, his possessions were few and I have been through them. But, above his pallet bed, he had scrawled some words on the wall as if to remind himself. "*Le chevalier outre mer*", the knight from across the sea.' Sir Oswald shrugged. 'But, what it means is a mystery. Now . . .'

He rose, went to the door and whispered to the captain of the guard and then came back.

'I have one final thing to show you,' he declared, 'the imprisoned clerk, a Brabanter called Lascalle. He was the student found near the house when those women were massacred. He was covered in blood but protests that all he is guilty of was drinking too much ale in the Sparrow's Heart tavern.'

'And what do you think, Sir Oswald?' the knight asked.

'I have been to Lascalle's hall,' the proctor interrupted. 'He is not the most industrious scholar in Oxford. He is a toper, a roaring boy who neglects his studies and is more often drunk than he is sober. He hails from Dordrecht and enjoys the patronage of one of the queen's knights, but he lives a conventional life, nothing remarkable.'

'He should hang!' Sir Oswald snapped. 'He cannot remember anything. He was found near the house, his dagger was missing and he was covered in blood.'

'Sir Oswald, as sheriff you have no authority over him,' the proctor insisted. 'He should either be tried by the university or by the Church. He is a clerk in minor orders.'

The sheriff made a rude noise with his mouth but Alexander could see he was not prepared to push matters further. In any case, the conversation ended when the door was flung open and two guards pushed the hapless Lascalle, his ankles and wrists loaded down with chains, into the room.

He was not a pretty sight. His florid, wart-covered face was unshaven and dirty, his eyes were red-rimmed through lack of sleep and his hair, smeared with mud, was dishevelled and spiky. His tattered gown still carried blood-stains mingled with his own vomit and the dirt of much of the dungeon he had lain in. He stared speechlessly at the sheriff's grim face and fell to his knees, arms clasped, as he whimpered for mercy in a patois Alexander found difficult to understand.

'You can speak English!' Ormiston insisted. 'Master Lascalle, you stand accused of the most horrible murders.'

'Innocent I am!' the clerk wailed. 'Innocent I am! I will take any oath! I will purge my innocence!'

Alexander got up, stood over the prisoner and grasped him by the elbow.

'Courage!' he whispered. 'For God's sake, man, get on your feet and answer the questions.'

'This is my court!' the sheriff snapped.

'No, it is not,' Sir Godfrey quietly intervened. 'We hold the king's commission in this matter.'

When Lascalle heard this he began to shake and would have fallen on his knees again if Alexander, wrinkling his nose at the foul stench of the man's body, hadn't held him firmly by the arm. Sir Godfrey got to his feet and poked Lascalle in the chest.

'I will listen to you,' he said softly. 'You will tell me the truth and, at the end, if I believe you are innocent, you might walk from this castle a free man. If you lie? Well, I couldn't care if you were related to all the cardinals in Rome, you'll hang from the castle walls.' He seized the man's unshaven chin between his fingers and squeezed it gently. 'Now, the truth!'

Lascalle drew in a deep breath. 'Two nights ago, I went to the Sparrow's Heart tavern. There's a servant wench there,

Roseanna, who likes young students.' Lascalle licked his lips. 'Free with her favours she is. But that night she would have nothing to do with me – one of your young lords was passing through Oxford. So I sat by myself and began to drink. I was joined by another student, very well dressed he was, with a purse full of silver, and one pot of ale followed another. I remember going outside, vomiting in the cesspit and coming back for more.' His voice faltered.

'And then what?'

'The next minute I was being kicked in my ribs by the watch, dragged to my feet, my hands bound. I was slung into the Bocardo and accused of some murder. God knows why! My dagger's gone.' Lascalle blinked and stared round. 'I never killed anyone,' he whimpered. 'As God is my witness, I don't know where this blood came from!'

'Who was this student, your drinking partner?' the exorcist gently asked.

Lascalle stared at her. If that hawk-faced knight frightened him, this woman with her bound eyes, quiet face and snow-white hair terrified him out of his wits.

'What is all this?' he wailed. He stared beseechingly at the proctor. 'Who are these people? Why should I be questioned by the king's commissioners?'

Sir Godfrey tapped him gently on the cheek.

'Just answer the questions,' he persisted.

'I don't know the student. He was short, russet-haired, clean-shaven.'

'Which could be said of a thousand other students,' Alexander remarked dryly.

'Well,' Sir Oswald barked, 'shall we hang him?'

'Wait!' Dame Edith got up and, without any help, went and stood in front of the prisoner and touched his face. 'Sir Oswald,' she said, 'you have a chapel here?'

'Of course!'

'And the blessed sacrament is kept there?'

'Of course!'

'Tell your chaplain to bring a host.'

Sir Oswald was about to protest, but Sir Godfrey nodded, so he hurried off.

The group in the solar remained silent. Lascalle, moving now and again, looked everywhere except at this strange, blindfolded woman. She stood like a statue, not even flinching as Lascalle moved his arms and legs in gusts of stale sweat. At last Sir Oswald returned, followed by a priest, a cope across his shoulders, in his hands a small pyx.

'Now, Lascalle,' Dame Edith said, 'are you prepared to take the sacrament and swear on it that you are innocent?'

The young clerk nodded. The priest approached, opened the pyx and held up the small, white wafer.

'*Ecce Corpus Christi*,' he intoned. 'Behold the body of Christ.'

Lascalle closed his eyes, head back, and opened his mouth. The priest had almost laid the wafer on his tongue.

'Stop!' Dame Edith seized the priest's wrist. 'I am sorry, Father, I meant no blasphemy. But Lascalle here is not perhaps in a proper state to receive the sacrament.'

The priest put the host back in the pyx, covered it with the end of his cope and stood back. Sir Oswald whispered that he could go.

'Why did you do all that?' Sir Godfrey asked.

Dame Edith tapped the manacles around Lascalle's wrists.

'He's no Strigoi,' she murmured, 'nor a murderer. Sir Oswald, let him bathe and change, give him a hot meal for charity's sake and let him go.'

Sir Godfrey concurred with this and Lascalle, gabbling his thanks and vowing he would light a thousand candles for Dame Edith, was hustled out of the chamber.

'If he was one of those we are hunting,' Dame Edith explained before anyone could question her further, 'he could not have taken that sacrament. Believe me, sirs, you would have seen a man in a frenzy such as you've never witnessed before. Anything holy, really powerful, weakens their strength.'

'I don't believe it,' Ormiston murmured.

Dame Edith laughed. 'Don't you? Tell me, if you had committed some terrible crime could you take the oath and the sacrament and still say you were innocent?' She shook her head and walked back to the chair. 'Or have you seen Christians bait Jews with a piece of pork? Or Christians being forced to renounce the cross of Christ? No, no,' she whispered, tapping the side of her head, 'in here, according to your state, angels or demons work.'

'What are we to do?' the sheriff snapped. 'Order everyone in Oxford to take the sacrament publicly?'

The exorcist gazed in his direction. 'It may well come to that, Sir Oswald. Believe me, when you consider what we face, it may well come to that.'

A short while later Sir Godfrey and Alexander, with Dame Edith comfortably ensconced in the saddle of her palfrey, left Oxford castle. They went through the Great Bailey and then into Newington Hall Street. Outside Trillok's inn, where the street widened, Sir Godfrey stopped.

'We could talk about what we've just seen,' he murmured. He waved a hand at the students, scholars and tradespeople pushing by him. 'But God knows who could be listening. So where to now, eh?'

Alexander felt tired and rubbed the side of his face. He

would like to go back to the convent of St Anne's, not just for some food, refreshment and rest, but to see the lady Emily. As Sir Godfrey solicitously asked the exorcist if there was anything she needed, Alexander stared at the half-timbered walls of St Mary's College farther down the street. The building brought back memories of his own hall at Cambridge and his exuberant, happy days there.

I do not like this business, he thought to himself, God be my witness, I don't! He wistfully recalled his days in the royal chancery, riding around London, meeting friends at a riverside tavern, being party to important decisions, enjoying the power of being so close to the high and mighty in the kingdom. He felt homesick for his tidy chambers above a shop near St Paul's, his books, his manuscripts, the easy pace and routine of his life – mass in the morning, breakfast in one of the cookshops, a hard but rewarding day drafting letters or sealing documents. In the evening he would visit friends, perhaps take a barge down river to one of the palaces where they could use their status as clerks to dine and feast at their own leisure. Or, if the mood took him, join the choir at St Paul's in their polished wooden stalls as they sang Salve Regina. A beggar whining for alms caught his attention. The man's face was covered in rotting sores, he limped along the side of the houses, using a crude staff as an awkward replacement for his leg, which had been sheered off just under the knee. The beggar's face was raw with pain, he whimpered for alms, one skeletal hand thrust forward. Alexander walked over and tossed a penny at the man.

'Is that all?' the beggar asked spitefully.

Alexander gave him another coin and the man hopped off without a thank-you or a backward glance.

It's all dirt, Alexander thought, horrible murders, devil-worshippers, the world's gone mad.

'Alexander!'

The clerk started and gazed around. Sir Godfrey, holding the reins of their horses, was staring at him strangely.

'Alexander, are you well?'

Don't you care? Alexander thought, gazing at the knight's handsome but hard face. *Aren't you frightened? Don't you have a home, loved ones?*

The knight stared grimly back. 'Alexander McBain, have you lost your wits? We have to move on. Dame Edith says we should visit Stapleton Hall. The students who disappeared from there . . .' The knight angrily waved Alexander over. 'Come on!' he rasped. 'You are daydreaming like some milkmaid!'

The clerk bit back his angry reply. The exorcist leaned down from her palfrey and gently tousled his hair, a soft warm caress like a mother's.

'Don't be angry, Alexander,' Dame Edith murmured. 'We are all tired. We are all frightened and the sooner this business is done the sooner we can go home!'

Alexander nodded and grasped the reins of her palfrey. With Sir Godfrey leading, they entered Cheyne Lane, turned left at Peter Hall and went down towards Stapleton. They entered the hall by a side entrance. A porter called grooms to stable their horses, then took them across the grassy quadrangle, round by the chapel and library, to the provost's chambers in Palmer's Tower. No one was there. A servant told them the provost was in the library, so they were taken farther up the narrow, wooden stairs. The day had become overcast, the clouds threatening rain, so the long library chamber had been lit by candles placed on the rim of a wheel and hoisted up by pulleys. A table, with benches on either side, ran down the centre of the chamber. The walls were lined with cupboards, their doors open to show books, bound in leather and dark-coloured vellum, securely held in place by stout chains. The servant left them there, closing the door behind them. Dame Edith sat on a stool, Sir Godfrey standing beside her, as Alexander walked down the dusty, eerie chamber.

'You like our library?'

Alexander's heart skipped a beat as a dark, hooded figure shuffled out from the shadows. A claw-like hand pulled back the hood, revealing iron-grey hair swept back from a high, domed forehead, the muddy skin of a face enlivened by green eyes and with a sharp, bird-like nose above thin, bloodless lips. The man stretched out his hand.

'Thomas Wakeham,' he announced, 'provost and treasurer of Stapleton Hall.'

Alexander forced a smile and introduced himself and his companions. The provost stared curiously at Dame Edith. He dismissed Sir Godfrey with a flicker of contempt, as if any man who bore arms was beneath his notice, and turned his back on the knight, a sour smile on his face.

'Master McBain, we expected you. Proctor Ormiston explained why you were coming. You,' he flickered a glance over his shoulder, 'and your companions.'

Sir Godfrey patted Dame Edith's hand. 'Stay quiet,' he murmured.

'I need no second bidding,' she whispered back.

Sir Godfrey strode across the library floor and gently pushed Wakeham round.

'Yes, you should have been expecting us. I bear the king's commission.'

Wakeham stepped back, some of the arrogance draining from his face.

'And our questions are simple,' Sir Godfrey continued. 'A

number of scholars who have lived and studied at this hall have disappeared without explanation or trace. Why?'

'I don't know,' Wakeham replied petulantly. 'We have conducted our own searches. We sought the advice of both the sheriff and the proctor.' He wriggled his bony shoulders. 'They have gone.'

Sir Godfrey was sure the man was about to turn his back on him again.

'Master Wakeham!' he exclaimed, 'I appreciate you are busy, but so am I. We take our authority from the king, so you will stand and answer our questions!'

Wakeham looked slyly at Alexander, licked his lips and decided discretion was the better part of valour. He pushed his bottom up against a table and folded his arms.

'Yes, sir, scholars from this hall have disappeared. We have found no trace of them but there was a connection between them. They belonged to a secret society who called themselves the Luminosi – the Enlightened Ones,' he translated patronizingly. He waved bony fingers at Alexander. 'As Master McBain knows, Oxford and Cambridge are riddled with such societies. Young men in pursuit of secret knowledge: the philosopher's stone, the mysterious alchemy, the cabbalistic writings of men like Roger Bacon. I could name at least thirty such societies in both universities at the present time.' He pushed his bottom farther on the table. 'I am correct am I not, Master McBain?'

'Aye, you are,' Alexander grinned. 'When I was at Cambridge I belonged to a group called the Scelerati, or the Sinners. We were in pursuit of a different type of knowledge.'

'Surely,' Sir Godfrey persisted, 'members of this group, friends of the missing students, still study here.'

'I wish you were correct,' Wakeham replied. 'But, no, they

91

were a small, self-contained group, quite isolated. They attended lectures in the schools, disputations here in the hall. They did not roister or get drunk, so they were left alone.'

'And their belongings?' Alexander asked.

'Nothing much,' Wakeham replied, 'quills, the occasional book, clothing, rosary beads. And all these have now been sent back to their families.'

'Did you find anything remarkable?'

'Yes, I did. Each had letters, small strips of vellum issued by the sheriff and by Proctor Ormiston. The one from the sheriff allowed them passes out of the city gates after curfew.'

'And the one from Proctor Ormiston?'

'Licence to study at the university library in the church of St Mary.'

Sir Godfrey glanced at Alexander.

'Strange.' Dame Edith spoke up abruptly. 'Neither the sheriff nor the proctor told us this.'

'Well,' Wakeham clutched the voluminous sleeves of his gown. 'I can tell you no more, sirs.' He stood, lips pursed.

Sir Godfrey and Alexander thanked him as courteously as they could, helped Dame Edith to her feet, walked out of the library and across the wet grass towards the main gate. The sky had grown darker, the day was drawing on. A cold biting wind stung their faces and chilled their fingers as they stamped their feet, waiting for the porter to bring out their horses.

'Are all scholars so welcoming?' Sir Godfrey grumbled. 'By the rood, Alexander, you'd think we were the Inquisition!'

'To men like Wakeham you are,' Dame Edith replied tartly. 'This is Oxford, sir knight, where they do not take kindly to outside interference.'

Grooms brought their horses and they went out through the gateway into the street. They were about to move off when the tousle-haired porter who had taken them to Palmer's Tower suddenly slipped through the gate and caught the hem of Alexander's coat.

'Please!' he hissed, his red-rimmed eyes large and tearful. 'Those scholars who disappeared. I was their servant. I know nothing except this . . .'

'Except what?' Alexander asked, stepping closer.

'Go to the Mitre tavern. Ask for a servant girl there, Laetitia. She knew the Brabanter. She may know more.'

And, before Alexander could question him further, the man turned and fled back into the hall.

'Strange upon strange,' Sir Godfrey commented, leading them off down the darkened Turl. 'The Mitre is in Carfax, isn't it?' He looked over his shoulder at Alexander.

The clerk nodded.

'Well, we'll go there. And let's hope it doesn't rain.'

They forced their way up the street, unaware of the cowled figure staring down at them from the top casement of one of the overhanging houses. The man pushed open the rickety, wooden window, covered with thin greased parchment. He strained his neck to glimpse the two men, Dame Edith riding behind them, making their way through the evening crowd towards the High Street. The man's eyes, dark as bat's wings, were cold and hard. He watched, as a hunting snake would eye its quarry, his lips pressed close together, humming the tune of a jig he had heard in one of the taverns.

'They are moving on,' he murmured to a second cowled figure seated on a stool in the far corner of the empty, musty room. 'They have talked to Wakeham, but he's so ignorant and arrogant he'll have told them nothing. But the servant, he may have been useful. Shall we kill him?'

'No,' the other replied gently. 'Why pursue minnows when

we have such fat pike in the pond?'

'Are they dangerous?' the figure at the window asked.

'Yes, they are. The knight is a killer, one of the king's best swordsmen. He is ruthless, with a sense of duty found in few others.'

'And McBain?'

'A court fop, a dandy. Or so he pretends. But his brain is razor-sharp. He's like the knight but, perhaps, lacks his courage.'

The man closed the window and stared across at his black-masked master. 'It's the woman, isn't it?'

The seated man nodded.

'A canting, dangerous bitch!' he spat out. 'Sooner or later, and it will be sooner rather than later, she'll smell something wrong – the relic, the soldier's death. She'll marry them together.'

'What shall we do?'

The master sucked in his breath through the slits of his mask.

'Our leader will soon join us. So, for a while, let's avoid them. If they keep coming on, we'll kill them all!'

Chapter 6

The taproom of the Mitre was thronged with students and tradesmen. The rushes underfoot had turned to a muddy mess as sweating scullions and serving girls brought platters of red meat from the kitchens and hot pies from a nearby cookshop. Potboys rushed around serving jugs, blackjacks and flagons of frothing ale or deep-bowled cups of wine. In one corner five scholars practised a carol. Alexander smiled when he listened to the words for, though the song was in Latin, the scholars were really singing a salacious ditty about the mayor of Oxford's daughter with wide generalizations about the morals of Oxford women. Thankfully, the traders seated around didn't realize the insults the grinning scholars were bellowing out; they were intent on filling their bellies and discussing the day's trade. Beggars hopped around – Alexander glimpsed the one he had seen earlier in the day. Two tired-looking whores touted for business, but their faces were so raddled with paint and their fixed grins showed such blackened teeth that they would find little custom that night. Alexander smiled at them and tossed each a coin. They grasped the coins without a word of thanks and fought their way to the great tuns of beer where the landlord stood taking orders for the strips of beef roasting behind him in the kitchen. Jostled on every side, Dame Edith between them, Alexander could see Sir Godfrey was fast losing his temper – his hand was already on his sword. The clerk grabbed one of the serving wenches.

'Laetitia?' he bawled in her face.

The girl shook her head.

'Not here yet!' she yelled back. 'Not till the bell sounds for vespers. She has other things to do.'

'Oh, for the love of God!' Godfrey shouted at Alexander above the hubbub. 'Hire a chamber.'

Alexander did and the sweaty, greasy-aproned landlord led them up some rather shaky wooden stairs to a small, white-washed chamber above the taproom. It was a bare, gaunt room, and none too clean, but at least they were quiet and the raucous noise of the taproom merely a constant hum. They ordered ale, bread and some dried, cooked meat with a dish of onions. Dame Edith picked at her food, but Sir Godfrey and Alexander ate with gusto.

'There's nothing like tramping the streets of Oxford,' Sir Godfrey said sourly, 'to give a man an appetite.'

'But was it worth it?' Alexander asked. 'Dame Edith, are you tired?'

'Confused,' she smiled, 'very confused. So, let's see, master clerk, what we do know. First, there are legends that hundreds of years ago a Strigoi leader built a keep and terrorized the countryside. He and his coven were destroyed by Sir Hugo Mortimer, an ancestor of our good sheriff Sir Oswald Beauchamp. Moreover, if we believe what we heard this morning, Proctor Ormiston has some Mortimer blood in him as well. Secondly, the Strigoi leader seems to have reappeared, formed a coven and perpetrated terrible murders here in the city. What else?'

'There are the students,' Sir Godfrey remarked, taking

the tankard away from his lips.

'Ah, yes, thirdly, a group of students from Stapleton Hall, who call themselves the Luminosi, disappear without trace. No one ever discovers any sign of them. What's even stranger,' Dame Edith continued, 'is that this group vanished one by one but none of their group lodged any objection or complaint with the authorities.'

'We are not too sure of that,' Sir Godfrey intervened. 'Provost Wakeham was hardly helpful and Ormiston and Beauchamp could have been more forthcoming. Surely they thought it was strange that all the students who disappeared applied for licences to avoid the curfew and visit the university library? I intend to question them on that.' He grinned his apology. 'But, Dame Edith, you were saying?'

'Fourthly,' the exorcist continued, 'these killers strike at night. They can massacre an entire household without rousing the neighbourhood or being detected by the watch and, according to appearances, it looks as if they were invited. Master McBain, who would you invite into your lodgings at the dead of night?'

'A nun!'

Dame Edith laughed. 'But what would she or her ilk be doing in the narrow lanes of Oxford after the curfew?'

'An official,' Sir Godfrey suggested. 'A person with a warrant. Someone who had every right to enter a house.'

'Perhaps,' Dame Edith replied. 'But what else do we know?'

'Well, fifthly,' Alexander said, 'we have the strange business at the Trinitarian friary. We have yet to visit there.'

'Yes, we should,' Dame Edith murmured. 'There is the matter of abbot Samson's sudden mysterious death and we must not forget that the friary is built over the site of the Strigoi's keep.'

'Sixthly,' Sir Godfrey added, 'we have the strange case of

the Hospitaller fugitive. Why was he killed? Deliberately ambushed in those woods outside the city? Where did he hide his famous relic? And what do the words *"Le chevalier outre mere"* mean?'

'Hush!' Dame Edith sat up straight. She felt her heart skip a beat, a tingle of fear shivered the nape of her neck.

'Dame Edith, what's the matter?'

The woman trembled and put her arms across her chest. She felt her throat constrict and her mouth went dry.

'I heard a sound.' She grasped Alexander's wrist. 'Master McBain, indulge an old woman, look outside!'

Alexander stared at the wooden shutters, straining his ears for any noise above the rumble from the taproom below.

'There's nothing,' he whispered. 'The wind's picking up, that's all.'

Sir Godfrey got up and strode to the window. He opened the shutters and stared down at the dirty, cobbled street in front of the tavern. He glimpsed the light peeping from the half-open door and the huge, cracked sign creaking gently on its chains. He glanced to the left and right. The cold breeze caught his face, ruffling his hair.

'Nothing there.' he announced, but he, too, was apprehensive. He felt the same flutter of excitement in his stomach, the same tension in his neck and shoulders, that he had experienced in France when he had gone out at night to spy out the position of the French and knew their scouts were hunting him in the darkness. He looked down again. Two students rounded the corner, drunkenly singing a song. They stopped and waved up at him. Sir Godfrey sighed and closed the shutters. In the street below the two scholars quickly sobered up and slipped into the darkness, while above, on the sloping tavern roof, the black-cowled figure smiled at his narrow escape. He padded softly along the ledge and, skilfully as any cat, jumped the gap on to the roof of the adjoining house.

Inside the chamber Dame Edith relaxed.

'Whatever it was,' she whispered, 'it's gone.'

'Tell me, domina,' Alexander said, 'you are a woman of considerable spiritual power. You see with your soul?'

'No, Alexander,' she replied, 'that's only what people say. I am just a hair on God's hand. What I do, I do for him.'

Alexander grimaced. 'What I am asking,' he continued haltingly, 'is that you claim these Strigoi are flesh and blood?'

The exorcist nodded.

'But they can be weakened by powerful relics, killed by the sword and destroyed by fire?'

'Yes, it must be fire,' she said. 'Remember, Alexander, what I have told you. If you kill them, their spirits simply enter their companions' bodies and make them stronger. They must be plucked up like dead twigs and thrust into the heart of a fire. But, I'm sorry, you have another question?'

'Yes, and I'll put it bluntly. Could you sense one of these Strigoi? Could you, moving amongst a crowd, stop and recognize one?'

'No, they are well disguised but, once they are discovered, perhaps I could. I remember once,' she continued, 'being in a town in France, I forget its name. A convicted murderer was being led across the town square to be executed at the same time as I passed. I experienced a deep terror, so violent I swooned.'

'Are you saying,' Sir Godfrey asked curiously, 'that these Strigoi wander throughout Europe?'

'Oh, yes, Sir Godfrey, there are different types of diabolical possession and this is the worst. I am sure the malefactor who died in that square was a Strigoi. Sometimes they exist by themselves, although they are more powerful if they group into a coven under a master. You see, one by himself can be discovered, but a group, cunningly led, masquerading under some pleasant guise, protecting each other, can live undetected for years.' Dame Edith sighed and rubbed her hands together. 'Yes, sometimes I can sense the malevolence of the Strigoi, but first they must reveal themselves.' She smiled. 'I have no secret power. Any man of goodwill would become uneasy in their presence.' She paused at a loud knock on the door and the red-faced taverner waddled in, clutching a thin-faced girl by the wrist.

'This is Laetitia,' he announced. 'But she can't stay up here talking for long.' He winked at Sir Godfrey. 'My, it's a bit cold, who has had the shutters open?'

Sir Godfrey pointed to the big, thick, tallow candle. 'I did. That creates a rather nasty stench.'

'What's the matter with it?' the taverner asked. 'It's good pig fat.' He gestured towards the casement window at the far end of the room, unshuttered but sheeted in small squares of glass. 'There's not many taverns can boast glass windows. You didn't try to open that one, did you?'

Sir Godfrey wearily shook his head.

'Good!' the taverner grumbled, 'because it might fall out.'

Alexander took a coin from his purse and, smiling, pressed it into the taverner's hand. 'Thank you, my host,' he said. 'Leave Laetitia here.' His smile widened as he looked at Laetitia's thin, anxious face. 'Don't worry,' he told her gently. He pulled a stool across.

The taverner clumped out of the room, slamming the door behind him. Laetitia sat and stared; the clerk looked friendly but she was frightened of the grim-faced knight and the strange old woman with her white hair and the bandage around her eyes.

'What do you want?' Laetitia blinked furiously to hide her fear.

Alexander touched her hand gently. 'Just a few questions.'

'I've done nothing wrong,' she protested. 'I'm a good girl. I work hard.'

'What about the Brabanter?' Alexander asked.

'Oh, he's gone.'

'We know that,' Alexander persisted gently, 'but he was sweet on you.'

The girl pulled at a loose thread on her thin smock then gently patted her greasy brown hair.

'He bought me trinkets,' she said shyly. She looked up under her eyelashes. 'Do you want to know where he's gone?' She shook her head. 'I don't know.'

'No. We want to know about his companions. They called themselves the Luminosi. Wasn't Eudo upset when they disappeared?'

'Oh, no. He said that they had been sent to different parts of the country on some mysterious secret errand. He claimed he might have to go too.'

'Who was sending them?'

'Oh, someone they called the Gar . . .'

'The guard?'

'No, something like that, Gardia?'

'Guardian?' Dame Edith suggested softly.

'Yes, that's it!' The girl clapped her hands as if she had solved a word game. 'The Guardian was sending them.'

'And who was the Guardian?'

Laetitia licked her lips and rammed her hands in her lap. 'I am a poor girl,' she added archly.

Alexander pressed a coin into her fingers. The girl looked up. She glimpsed the white face pressed against the casement window behind her three interrogators. She didn't blink, she just stared; the face was white, the eyes large dark pools of murderous malice. A finger came up to the face's lips as a sign for silence. Laetitia's jaw dropped. She blinked and, when she looked again, the face had disappeared. Dame Edith felt a thudding in her head. She stared in the direction of the window.

'What is it?' she exclaimed, grasping Alexander's wrist.

She felt a pang of terror as Laetitia jumped up, sending the stool behind her crashing to the floor.

'I've got to go!' the girl gabbled. 'I have to go down now!'

Alexander, caught between Dame Edith's reaction and the girl's sudden outburst, stared at Sir Godfrey, who simply shrugged.

'Girl, come back!'

Laetitia had reached the door, her hand on the latch.

'No!' No!'' she hissed. 'Touch me and I'll scream! I'll scream and say you tried to do things to me!'

'Hush!' Alexander said, getting to his feet.

The girl opened her mouth.

'No, no,' Alexander exclaimed hurriedly. 'You can go, but what's frightened you?'

Laetitia shook her head. Alexander stared over her shoulder at the window, but saw only the darkness outside. He looked back at the girl.

'Listen,' he offered, 'go now, but if you wish to see me again come to the convent of St Anne's and ask for Alexander the clerk. I'll give you a gold coin.'

The girl nodded and fled out of the room.

'What got into her?' Sir Godfrey asked.

Alexander pulled a face.

'She was frightened,' Dame Edith replied, crossing her arms. 'As I am. Sir Godfrey, Master McBain, I swear we are being watched. The Strigoi know you are in Oxford. At first they will use fear to weaken our defences but be on your guard, for they'll strike as swiftly and deadly as vipers!'

With the exorcist's sombre warning blighting their moods, Sir Godfrey led his companions out of the tavern and through the darkening streets, ill lit by the occasional lamp over a door post. They crossed the city and did not relax until they reached the ivy-covered walls of St Anne's convent, where a cheery, garrulous porter let them through the postern gate.

'The abbess is waiting for you,' the fellow said. 'She has been waiting all day.'

He would have launched into a longer speech but Sir Godfrey told him to be quiet and tossed the reins of their horses at him. Dame Edith said she was tired and wished to rest. A lay sister led her away to the church while another took Sir Godfrey and Alexander up to the abbess's parlour. Dame Constance was busy sealing a number of letters and lecturing a whey-faced novice on how to melt the wax and fold the parchment so it didn't crack. As soon as Sir Godfrey and Alexander were announced the abbess dismissed the girl, who fled with a look of relief. The abbess pushed her chair up to the pine-log fire. She served them mulled wine, using a cloth to take the hot jug out of the inglenook and fill their goblets to the brim. She then sat down between them, stretching her thin, long fingers out towards the blaze.

'You had a fruitful day?' she asked.

Sir Godfrey gave her a brief description of the day's events. The abbess nodded.

'Lady,' Alexander said, seizing upon a silence in the conversation, 'your porter said you had been waiting for us all day.'

'Yes, I wanted to see you,' Dame Constance replied. 'Not

about the matters in hand but about Lady Emily de Vere. I will choose my words most carefully. Lady Emily is not what she appears to be.' Dame Constance watched a log snap in a splutter of red sparks. 'She is an orphan, the king's own ward, a wealthy heiress, but she is not as naive and helpless as she may appear. Behind that pretty face is a brain that would be the envy of any chancery clerk as well as a determined will. She can be not only stubborn but wilfully obstinate, as I have found to my cost. She chose this convent because it is near her estates. She insists on regular visits and accounts from her stewards. She even has the king himself wrapped around her little finger – though, I concede, that would not be hard. Our noble Edward, God bless him, can resist anything but a pretty face.' Dame Constance paused and sipped from her goblet. 'For a young woman of such tender years, Lady Emily has won herself powerful concessions. She will not only acquire her estates when she comes of age but she has the king's own vow that she will be allowed to marry for love and not made to enter into any arranged contract.' Dame Constance coughed. 'She is shy, but that is her buckler or shield against the world. You see, her mother died young and she watched her father being killed at a bloody tournament near Osney. He was dragged from his horse and, by the time the physicians got to him, he was a living wound from head to toe. He died in the most terrible agonies, which Lady Emily witnessed. I believe this, too, has saddened her soul.'

'Thank you for telling us this,' Sir Godfrey said. 'But,' he grinned sheepishly at Alexander, 'how does it concern us?'

'Because, sir knight,' Dame Constance snapped, 'I may be a virgin consecrated to God, innocent when it comes to the cravings of the flesh and the lures of the world, but, sometimes, I do enjoy the cunning of the serpent.' She laughed. 'Let us not beat about the bush, or play cat's-cradle with each other. Lady Emily is a lovely young woman. You are both smitten by her, are you not?'

Both men stared, embarrassed into the fire.

'Lord save us, you men!' she breathed. 'So valiant in war, little doves in love.'

'You are most forthright!' Sir Godfrey growled. 'Any man would be taken by Lady Emily.'

'Ah!' Dame Constance moved the sleeves of her gown. 'But let's bite into the core of the apple. You see, Lady Emily is smitten by both of you. That marks a radical difference in her affairs!'

'Has she said as much?' Sir Godfrey silently cursed himself, aware that he sounded like some lovelorn squire.

The abbess smiled primly. 'Not directly. However, from the little I have seen and the few words she's said, you don't have to be a wise woman to detect the signs.'

Alexander squirmed in pleasure, smiling to himself as he looked into the fire. He hated this business in Oxford but, if and when it was finished, how could he keep the attention of Lady Emily? His face darkened as he recalled the abbess's words. He stared across the fire at Sir Godfrey and was shocked to see the hard, calculating look in the knight's eyes. We are rivals, Alexander thought. God knows how this will end.

Sir Godfrey was thinking much the same thoughts. He regretted that his friendship with this dry-humoured, sardonic clerk might end in a bitter feud but he was equally determined. He, who thought all love had died in him, loved the Lady Emily passionately.

'I can read your thoughts,' the abbess murmured. She took the silver chain from around her neck and held it out towards the two men. 'Swear!' she urged, 'swear by this cross you will not feud over Lady Emily. At least,' she added, 'not until this business is finished!'

Both men stared at her. Dame Constance's face became severe. She felt like threatening to send the young woman away, but what was the use of an oath sworn under duress? Her face softened.

'Please,' she said. 'For the love of Christ! For my sake! For the sake of those killed by these terrible murderers! On your loyalty to the king and to the Church, I beg you swear!'

Both men's hands went out to touch the crucifix.

'You have my oath,' Sir Godfrey declared.

'And mine,' Alexander added.

Then Dame Constance put the chain back around her neck.

'Good, then tonight you will be my guests at high table. You, Dame Edith, and, of course, the lady Emily.'

In her cell in the convent church Dame Edith carefully washed the dust from her face and hands. She rebound the silken blindfold around her eyes and knelt before the crucifix.

'I have met them again,' she whispered. 'They were there, Lord, tonight. Somewhere near that tavern.' She shivered and stared sightlessly at the tortured face of her Saviour. 'But there was something else? What was it, Lord?' She leaned back on her heels and let her mind float like a feather on the breeze. She allowed the distractions to flood in – the noise and stench of the city, the sweet smell of parchment at Stapleton Hall library, the sense of terror in the small chamber at the tavern, the premonition . . . Her heart skipped a beat. She clambered to her feet, biting her lower lip in anxiety.

'Oh, Lord!' she prayed. 'Oh, no!' She had recalled the premonition, lasting only a few seconds, she had had when Laetitia had refused to talk any further.

'I put my hand down—' Dame Edith spoke to the gaunt, whitewashed walls. 'I put my hand down. I touched McBain's. His hands are usually warm, soft and supple but, for those few seconds—' She raised her finger to her lips. 'For those few seconds,' she whispered, 'McBain's hand was as cold and as hard as ice.'

In the abbess's parlour Dame Constance was insisting on refilling her guests' cups to celebrate the oath they had sworn when suddenly a lay sister, veil flying, bustled into the room without knocking.

'Oh, mother abbess! Mother abbess! You must come now! You must come now!'

Dame Constance rose to her feet.

'For God's sake, woman!' she snapped. 'What is the matter? Have the French landed? Has the king arrived? Dame Veronica! Why aren't you working in the infirmary?'

'I was,' the white-faced nun gasped. 'And then I visited the cemetery to lay flowers on Dame Richolda's grave.' She paused, mouth gaping. 'I can't say,' she spluttered. 'You must come! Mother, you must come – and your guests, please!'

Dame Constance collected her cloak and coolly lit two tapers. She gave one to the infirmarian and, followed by the knight and clerk, walked out of the convent, through the cold darkness, around the church and into the cemetery. The graveyard was bleak. A night breeze rustled the yew trees and sent the dry leaves of autumn fluttering across the wet grass, while the wooden grave crosses creaked and moved in their beds of earth.

Alexander looked around and shivered. He cursed as an owl flew down, almost skimming their heads as it pursued some small night animal into the corner of the graveyard. He saw the ghostly wings flutter a little, the bird swooped, there was a thin scream and the bird of night rose and disappeared into the dark branches of a tree. Dame Veronica hurried before him and stopped in the middle of the cemetery, which was dominated by a great wooden cross carved in the Celtic fashion. A small stone altar lay beneath it and, in front of the altar, Alexander glimpsed three upturned crosses. Dame Veronica pointed, then turned away. Sir Godfrey took one of the tapers and squatted down, Alexander standing behind him. They stared, hearts chilling at the sights that greeted them, trying to ignore the gasps and cries of the abbess.

'Who could have done that?' Dame Constance hissed. 'Some macabre joke!'

'Three crosses,' Sir Godfrey said thoughtfully.

He pulled one out of the ground and placed it flat on the earth. He drew his dagger and prised loose the dead bat that had been pinned to the centre of the crosspiece. He gouged the cross where his name had been crudely scrawled.

'Three crosses,' he murmured. 'Each with a bat nailed through it and our names carved beneath: Sir Godfrey Evesden, Alexander McBain and Dame Edith Mohun.'

He got to his feet and kicked down the other two crosses, then, trying to control his fury, he stacked the three crosses on top of each other.

'Dame Constance?'

'Yes, Sir Godfrey?'

'Have oil poured over these and burn them immediately.'

The abbess nodded at the infirmarian. 'Do it!' she ordered quietly. 'And do it now! Get a scullion from the kitchen to help you!'

Dame Constance then led her guests back to the warm cosiness of her parlour.

'Who did that?' she asked, slamming the door behind her. 'Is it some scholar's joke?'

'No.' Sir Godfrey leaned against the fireplace, sipping from his wine as he stared into the fire. He looked over his shoulder at the white-faced clerk. 'It's beginning,' he said. 'We have learnt the tune, we have memorized the steps and now the dance of death is about to begin. Dame Edith is right: the Strigoi know we are in Oxford and they have sent us our first warning.'

Both men returned to their rooms, promising themselves and Dame Constance that they would not mention this matter to anyone. They washed and changed, each taking great care with his toilet, until a lay servant came to invite them down to the abbess's comfortable refectory – a small hall with a raised platform under a blue and gold canopy. Dame Constance sat in the centre, with Dame Edith on her right and Lady Emily on her left. The two men sat opposite. At first the conversation was stilted and Alexander became convinced that the exorcist knew something was wrong. However, both men had eyes only for Emily, who looked ravishing in a white veil bound by a gold circlet and a blue and silver gown lined with costly sable fur. Her every movement was delicate and both men caught her exquisite perfume, a deep musk mingled with some sweet herbs. She looked at them coyly and Dame Edith found it difficult to conceal her smile. She is a minx, she thought, pure steel hidden in the softest velvet; she has a deep fondness for both of these men and intends playing them like a fish. Dame Edith half listened to the courtly conversation. She hoped this beautiful maiden would not provoke any jealousy between the two men whom Dame Edith also had a secret fondness for. They are good men, she thought, they have their passions and their weaknesses but they are pure at heart, good-willed, strong and courageous.

Alexander noticed how the exorcist was hardly eating but simply playing with the small, white loaf she had broken up on the silver salver before her. He reluctantly tore his eyes away from Emily.

'Dame Edith,' he said, 'you are very quiet.'

'Master clerk, my apologies, but I was thinking.'

'About what?' Alexander teased, revelling in Emily's sweet smile. 'Your visit to Oxford or perhaps your journeys elsewhere? You have travelled more than any person here.'

Dame Edith caught the hint and launched into a vigorous comparison of the University of Oxford with those at Padua and Genoa in northern Italy. Dame Constance, who had now overcome her shock at the blasphemy she had seen in the graveyard, breathed a sigh of relief and raised her hand as a sign for the steward to serve the splendid meal she had ordered. She made sure both the knight's and the clerk's wine cups were regularly filled and watched the wine, the good food, the presence of a beautiful woman and the marvellous anecdotes of the exorcist work their magic and ease the terrors of the day. The meal was a sumptuous one: swan cooked in chaudron, beef steaks roasted in a sauce of brown sugar, black pepper, ginger and cinnamon; salads garnished with pot herbs, green porrey made out of a mixture of vegetables; small, white loaves, lamb cooked in garlic and rosemary; peas and onions with civets and, to follow, honey toasted over pine nuts.

Dame Constance looked around at her guests, pleased that the meal was a success and, at an opportune time, declared she would retire. She left her guests chattering away. Even Dame Edith was laughing at McBain's descriptions of trying to write in invisible ink. Dame Constance thanked her cook and kitchen retainers and went back to her own chamber. A servant had built up the fire and refilled the jug of wine warming in the inglenook. Dame Constance knelt at her prie-dieu, lit the two great candles fixed in iron spigots on either end and began her prayers. She softly chanted the psalm and thought she was dreaming when she heard her name called.

'Constance! Constance! Oh, Constance, open the window!'

The abbess stood, one hand going to her mouth. It had been so many years since anyone had called her simply by that name, not since she had been a girl in her father's manor and other children had come to invite her out to play.

'Constance! Constance!'

The abbess hastened to the window, pulled back the shutters and looked out into the darkness. A cresset torch flickered near the entrance way, shedding some light, but not enough for the abbess to catch a glimpse of the caller.

'Constance!'

The voice was much closer. She felt the ivy shift and move around her. She looked first to the right, then, immediately beneath her, she saw the figures, dressed completely in black, with dark-rimmed eyes and grinning mouths in pallid faces. It was a nightmare, she thought, and averted her eyes. But when she looked again they were still there – four, five figures clinging like black bats to the ivy, all grinning up at her. Dame Constance closed the shutters with a bang and ran screaming for the door.

Words between the pilgrims

'By the cock!' Harry the taverner declared, staring at the expectant faces of the pilgrims grouped around the great table of the taproom of the Tabard tavern. 'By the cock!' he repeated, 'a nightmare story, sir knight. Please go on.'

The knight shook his head and pointed to the candle.

'The hour's growing late. Enough for one night. There is always tomorrow. Perhaps, after supper tomorrow, I can continue.'

'But who are these killers?' the fiery-faced summoner demanded. 'Oh, come, sir knight, do not play such tricks or devices.'

'No,' Harry the taverner intervened. 'The rules are set, the principles firmly laid down; each pilgrim is to tell his tale without carping interruptions.'

'But do such creatures exist?' the pardoner asked, flicking his lank, yellow hair back from his thin, cadaverous face. 'Strigoi, night-walkers, creatures from Hell? Sir knight, this is nonsense!'

A chorus of agreement greeted his words.

'I am not too sure,' the clerk of Oxford interrupted. 'Sir knight, your story has woken memories – anecdotes, tales I have heard. Your description of the university is correct in all

113

its forms. I do know there was a provost at Exeter Hall called Wakeham and, in the rolls of the city, Sir Oswald Beauchamp was the king's sheriff.' The Oxford clerk paused. 'But was he not killed in a fire? And Proctor Ormiston? A strange fellow, whose disappearance from the university was cloaked in mystery.'

The clerk caught the knight's unspoken plea for silence.

'Why?' the portly friar interrupted. 'Are you saying this tale is true?'

'I, too, recognize names,' the poor parson declared, crouching next to this dirt-stained brother, the ploughman. He leaned forward, clutching the cord of the purse slung round his neck.

'Whom do you know, Father?' the knight asked.

'Why the priest at St Peter's, Father Andrew. In my younger years, when he served as a curate at a church in London. A holy man much given to works of charity.'

'Ah, yes,' the irrepressible Oxford clerk declared, one bony finger pointing to the ceiling. 'St Peter's has now been renovated. Father Andrew is dead – I have seen his tomb before the high altar. He was much revered for his good works.'

'So, this story's true?' the franklin asked, scratching his snow-white beard.

'I haven't said that,' the knight replied, glancing quickly at his son, who sat looking at him strangely.

'But do such things exist?' the hard-faced lawyer persisted.

'I have told you,' the wife of Bath trumpeted, 'when I was on pilgrimage to the tomb of the Blessed Virgin at Cologne . . .'

'More like looking for another husband,' the monk snickered.

'Well, even if I was, I certainly wouldn't choose someone like you!' the wife of Bath replied tartly. 'I have heard about the Strigoi, the living dead.' She adjusted her wimple, her podgy white hands flickering in the air. 'No, no, listen, all of you. According to what I know, Strigoi are men and women possessed by evil spirits and these spirits make them live on human blood, which strengthens their bodies as well as the demons within.'

The wife of Bath drained her cup.

'Whilst at a village just outside Cologne, I heard such a story about a young man called Ulrich, a tiller of the soil. Though physically strong and rarely ill, Ulrich began to have difficulty in breathing.' The wife of Bath leaned her elbows on the table and beamed at her fellow pilgrims, pleased that she was now the centre of attention. 'This began after a quarrel with his brother over a piece of land. Ulrich became weak and began to spit blood. He died and his body was buried in the local graveyard. Sixteen years later he reappeared in the village, claiming he had not died at all but had been dug out of his grave and revitalized by one of these Strigoi masters.'

'What happened to him?' the prioress asked, her large eyes rounded in fear.

'Oh, he was burnt as a witch. But the important thing is that it confirms the knight's story: these Strigoi are controlled by a hierarchy of masters and they never die unless destroyed by fire. What is more,' the wife of Bath added warningly, 'these Strigoi masters can appear as angels of light, lawyers, summoners, even pardoners.'

'Who knows—?' The nun's priest spoke up in a thin, reedy voice. 'Who knows, one of us could be a Strigoi.'

'Is that possible?' The cook, still chewing on a piece of dried meat, bawled down the table at the knight. 'Sirrah, is that possible?'

The knight's eyes never left the monk's face. 'Oh, yes,' he replied quietly. 'As my story says, such beings only reveal themselves either when they choose to do so or if, unwittingly, the sacrament or some great, holy relic is brought into their presence. Even then they will try to escape, gabble some excuse but, if they cannot—' The knight paused and leaned back in his chair.

The pilgrims shivered as the great tavern creaked and groaned around them.

'Go on!' the shipman urged.

'If they cannot,' the knight continued, 'they will reveal their true natures and it is the most terrible sight.'

The monk, now digging his berry-brown face into the largest tankard of ale Harry the taverner could provide, coughed, spluttering with laughter, and slammed the tankard down on to the table.

'Nonsense!' he declared in his rich, sonorous voice. 'Tiddle-piddle stories to frighten children!'

'Why do you say that?' the knight gently asked.

'Well, I have been with the Trinitarian friars in Oxford,' the monk replied. 'I have stayed in their guest house. I never heard of any legends about the Strigoi, tunnels or empty tombs. I am sure the good brothers would have informed me of them. Indeed, I studied a history of the house and I read no such legend there. So, it's all fiddlesticks!'

The knight shrugged and smiled. 'I never said it was true,' he pointed out. 'Mine host asked me to tell a tale. Whether you believe it or not . . .' He spread his hands and pushed the chair back. 'But now, good sirs, ladies, I must retire. I bid you good night.'

'You'll finish the tale tomorrow?' the cook shouted.

'Oh, yes,' the knight promised. 'Tomorrow my tale will be told!'

His son dutifully followed him out of the room and up to the chamber they had rented above the taproom. The squire lit the candles on the table and helped his father divest himself of his leather jerkin, taking from the saddle bag a clean nightshirt and fresh woollen leggings for the morrow. As he had on countless occasions, the squire watched his father stand beside the lavarium and wash his naked body. He felt the usual care tinged with fear at the horrible scars and wounds that marked the knight's body from neck to toe. He had long stopped asking his father where such wounds were inflicted for, when he did, the same reply was given: 'In the service of God and for the glory of the Church.'

'Father?'

'Yes,' the knight answered wearily, towelling his body roughly and slipping the nightshirt over his head.

'Father, is your story true?'

'What do you think?'

The squire stared back and the knight grinned.

'Then get some sleep, son. Tomorrow is another day and I have a different tale to tell.'

The squire undressed and lay on the pallet bed as the knight began the ceremony he performed every night. He pulled his great sword from its sheath, pressing its tip to the floor, and knelt before it, his hands on the crosspiece. He blessed himself and began to pray. The rite never changed: one paternoster, three aves and a special prayer the knight had memorized asking Christ to deliver him from all evils. After that the knight re-sheathed his sword, took a small leather bottle of holy water and blessed both their beds, making the sign of the cross above them. He then kissed the precious reliquary at his throat and climbed into bed.

The squire watched his father close his eyes.

'Father?'

'Yes, my son?'

'What was Mother like?'

'Beautiful as the night,' the knight replied. 'Dark raven hair, skin like silk, lustrous blue eyes and a smile you'd never forget.'

'And she died giving birth to me?' The squire always asked the same question.

The knight looked over, his eyes crinkled in a smile.

'Don't tax yourself. She caught a fever, weakened and died. I mourned her passing, but her soul is with God and her spirit comes back to watch over both of us.'

'Is that why you left England?'

'I am on my own crusade. I am searching for something and, when I find it, you will know.'

'What do you think of our companions?' the squire asked abruptly, propping himself up on an elbow. 'The other pilgrims?'

'A mixed crowd,' his father replied. 'The good, the bad and the indifferent. But a word of warning – keep well away from that monk!'

'Why, Father? He likes hunting and I noticed he flirts with the prioress, but what harm can he do?'

'Keep well away,' the knight repeated. 'Now, go to sleep. The hour is late and tomorrow our journey begins.'

'One final question, Father?'

'Ask it.'

'Why are we going to Canterbury? I mean, to give thanks to the Blessed Martyr?'

'To give thanks,' the knight replied, 'and to ask for his blessing.'

'Will you make your confession there?' the squire persisted. 'And ask to be shriven?'

The knight laughed and propped himself up. 'What do you know about my sins?'

'Nothing.' The squire quietly cursed himself. 'It is just that before we left Minster Lovell, you killed a man down on the banks of the Windrush.'

'He drew his sword and challenged me,' his father replied. 'I had no choice. I reported his death to the sheriff and my yeoman took an oath that I killed in self-defence. Now,' he pulled the blanket up over his face, 'go to sleep!'

The squire lay there, eyes staring into the darkness. Yes, he had heard about his father slaying the man near the river, as he had about other men his father had killed. But why? the squire sleepily wondered. Why did his father on certain occasions always ensure that the corpses of the men he killed be burned immediately?

They woke early the next morning, the taverner's trumpeting voice rousing them from their slumbers. They joined the rest of the heavy-eyed pilgrims in the taproom to break their fast on bread, cheese, cold bacon and watered ale. After that, they collected their baggage and stood in the great cobbled yard as grooms and ostlers brought out their horses. There was a great deal of confusion, shouts, the neighing of horses and the jingle of harness. At last they were all mounted and Harry the taverner led them out on to the High Street of Southwark, past St George's church and on to the old Roman road of Watling Street which would lead them south-east to Canterbury.

The day proved a fine one. At first there was unease as they entered the open countryside; they had heard about the outlaws and wolfsheads who plagued such deserted areas and preyed upon hapless pilgrims. Harry the taverner, however, soon mollified them, pointing out that the knight was armed and there was a goodly number of robust fellows in their company who would frighten off any outlaw.

119

They rode through the bright spring sunshine past great open fields where the green, rain-drenched shoots were beginning to appear. The knight began his tale for the day. It was about the Theban knights Arcite and Palamon and their rivalry for the hand of the beautiful sister of the queen of the Amazons. He had finished the story by the time they reached St Thomas's watering hole. Here they had to pause for a while. The miller was as deep in his cups as the night before and had continued to sup from a wineskin ever since they had left the Tabard. Harry the taverner tried to reason with him.

'No, by God's soul!' the miller cried. 'I will not keep quiet. I insist on telling my tale now and, if I am drunk, blame it on Southwark ale. However, hearing our knight talk about Oxford, I'll tell you a tale of a different ilk! About a stingy carpenter who lived in that city and his weasel-slim wife Alison, who was as hot for bed sports as any woman could be.'

The reeve, a carpenter by trade, heard this and immediately a great quarrel broke out between the two which lasted until they'd finished their journey for the day. No one really paid much attention to the miller. He had been drunk since the day he joined them and, by the time they had finished supper, he was snoring in a corner, one arm around his bagpipes. They waited until the servants had withdrawn from the room they had hired then begged the knight to continue his tale.

He was standing by the window staring out into the darkness, watching the shadows in the trees across the road from where the tavern stood.

'Come on, sir knight,' Harry called cheerfully. 'For pity's sake, sir, you began a tale last night which terrified us all. We won't rest secure in our beds until you have finished it once and for all!'

The knight stared into the darkness. He was sure he was

being closely studied, either by someone trailing the pilgrims along the Watling Way or by one of his travelling companions. He did not know, but kept a watchful eye upon the monk. He sensed the man's cheery bonhomie hid deeper, darker waters. Harry the taverner repeated his request, the knight smiled and came back to the head of the table.

'I shall finish my tale,' he declared. 'Now listen well!'

PART III

Chapter 1

Dame Constance's screams at what she had seen roused the convent and brought Sir Godfrey and Alexander running from the refectory. They gathered in the abbess's parlour and, for a while, Dame Constance could hardly speak but sat quivering with fear. Only when Alexander carefully forced a cup of wine between her lips did she relax and describe, in halting phrases, the nightmarish scene she had glimpsed from her window.

Sir Godfrey immediately ordered all doors and windows to be locked. He hurried across to the guest house, Alexander accompanying him. He donned his hauberk and great sword belt and strode out into the darkness, sword in one hand, dirk in the other. Alexander, similarly armed, followed him around the convent buildings yet they could discover nothing amiss. Only the nightbirds chattering in the trees, the occasional howl of a dog and faint noises from the light-filled windows of the convent broke the silence. They searched the grounds until Sir Godfrey became concerned that the men Dame Constance had glimpsed might have entered the building by some postern door or open window.

'You go back there, Alexander,' he ordered. 'I'll finish searching here.'

Sir Godfrey walked to the far side of the convent away from

the church and into the large orchard that stretched down to the boundary walls. He caught the sweet-sour smell of rotting apples underfoot but, as he entered the trees, he sensed there was something awry and cursed the wine that had fuddled his wits. Holding his knife and sword before him, he strode through the orchard into a small glade and realized what was wrong. A deathly stillness had fallen; not even the chattering of a nightjar, the hoot of an owl or the rustling of night animals in the overgrown grass disturbed the silence. The knight walked into the centre of the glade. The clouds had broken and the trees were bathed in the silvery light of a hunter's moon. Sir Godfrey paused. He listened to the sound of his own heavy breathing, then gave a strangled cry as five figures detached themselves from the trees and walked towards him. Dressed completely in black, they blended into the darkness. Their faces were hidden by masks, so that Sir Godfrey could glimpse only the glint of an eye, the faint patch of skin above a mouth. He adopted a fighting stance, resisting the urge to flee back to the convent.

'We mean you no harm, Sir Godfrey Evesden,' the central figure declared. His words, though, were followed by a snigger that turned a solemn reassurance into a menacing threat. 'Well, we mean you no harm for the present. What happens in the future is a matter for you to decide.'

Sir Godfrey stepped back; the figures stayed still.

'Who are you?' the knight challenged. 'Why are you here? What do you want with me? Why frighten a poor old abbess in the dead of night?'

'Come, come, Sir Godfrey,' the voice replied. 'We know why you are here and the commission you carry. Go back to your masters in London and take the snooping clerk and that blind-eyed bitch with you. Tell the king this is no matter for you, no conspiracy against the crown, silent treason or the corruption of officials. And lower your sword. If we wanted your life we could have taken it.'

'So, what do you want?' Sir Godfrey snapped.

'To finish our work here.'

'Which is?'

'None of your business, knight!'

'Then how will you finish it?' Sir Godfrey persisted. 'By murder? By shedding the blood of innocents? By terrible crimes perpetrated in the dead of night? By slitting the throats of innocents and drinking their blood?'

'No different from what you do, Sir Godfrey,' the voice replied. 'Have you not fought on the battlefields of France where the dead are piled waist-high or taken a barge along the river Thames and seen the corpses bobbing like bits of refuse? Human life is cheap, Sir Godfrey. So easily,' the voice chuckled, 'and so pleasurably replaced.'

'You are devil-possessed assassins!' the knight retorted.

'We all have our different lords, Sir Godfrey, but enough is enough. We have frightened that old bitch the abbess. She should not have brought you here and we have delivered our warning to you. Be out of Oxford within three days!'

'And if not?'

'Then we shall meet again.'

The figure stepped back, retreating within the trees, and disappeared. Sir Godfrey sheathed his sword and dagger and leaned against the cold bark of a tree. He waited until the tremors racking his body ceased and then walked back to the convent building.

Alexander was waiting for him just within the entrance. He took one look at Sir Godfrey's face.

'You've seen a ghost, sir knight?'

'Worse, clerk, I've seen the devil himself!'

And Sir Godfrey gave Alexander a curt description of the meeting in the orchard. The knight sat on a bench and leaned his head against the lime-washed wall, staring up at a gaunt, black crucifix.

'They came to frighten,' he murmured, 'and to warn.' He glanced at the clerk. 'If they knew what little progress we are making, they would not have bothered.'

'Everything hinges,' McBain replied, 'upon one fact.'

'Which is?'

'How, in sweet God's name, do they get into these houses without any hue or cry or disturbing the neighbours?'

Alexander went back into the refectory and brought back two goblets of wine. He handed one to the knight and grinned.

'Dame Constance has retired. Dame Edith is praying in the church and I have given my personal assurance—' His grin widened. 'My personal assurance that Lady Emily is safe.' He paused. 'We could do one thing, Sir Godfrey.'

The knight looked at him quizzically.

'We know the Strigoi are in Oxford this evening. Perhaps they plan to make another visit elsewhere. Let us walk the city – see what does happen at the dead of night in the alleys and streets of Oxford, who does prowl around.'

Sir Godfrey felt tired, still slightly fuddled after the meal of rich food and heavy drink. However, he accepted the wisdom of the clerk's words and, within the hour, booted, cloaked and wearing their weapons, they left the convent and began their journey around the sleeping city of Oxford.

They went along the streets, covering their noses at the stench of the refuse piled in the ditch near Holywell, past Smithgate, along Bocardo Lane, under the silent, dark mass of St Michael's in Northgate and down into Fish Street. At first they thought the streets were empty but, now and again, they would meet a group of students slipping along the alleyways, whispering excitedly and laughing at their exploits in breaking free of their halls' regulations. Near St Aldate's they met the city watch, a huddle of rather frightened men warming their hands over a glowing brazier. Their leader stopped them but, when Sir Godfrey explained who they were, allowed them to pass without further hindrance. Beggars were everywhere, with their thin, skeletal arms, whining cries and beseeching calls for alms or food. Now and again dark shadows would flit across an alley, but Sir Godfrey dismissed these as the usual city night hawks – a footpad looking for easy prey, some student deep in his cups or a citizen hurrying home from a night's roistering in a tavern.

'Nothing,' Sir Godfrey murmured as they turned their horses back in the direction of the convent.

'Nothing, yet something,' Alexander replied.

'What do you mean?'

'Well, the streets aren't as deserted as perhaps we thought. It's possible that one of these groups we met—' Alexander cleared his throat. 'Let me phrase it more correctly. It's possible that the murderers could pose as any of the groups we met. A group of roistering students asking for directions, two burgesses seeking shelter from a pursuing footpad. Think, Sir Godfrey, think again. What sort of person would you open your door to in the dead of night?'

As the knight and the clerk returned to St Anne's, the Cotterills, a family of tinkers, were just finishing their evening meal in their house in an alleyway just off Bocardo Lane. The occasion had hardly been a cordial one. Isolda, Raoul's wife, had sat tight-lipped throughout, hardly touching her earthenware bowl of soup made from onions and mushrooms. She glared at her daughter Caterina with her dark lustrous hair, creamy complexion and brown merry eyes. She noted how her daughter's ample bosom strained against her threadbare woollen smock and attracted surreptitious glances from her second husband Raoul. Isolda had cause for concern. Earlier in the day, just after Raoul had pushed his hand-cart back from the market, Isolda had caught both of them in the small garden plot behind the house, sharing an embrace hardly fitting between a father and step-daughter. After all, Caterina was her one and only child by Alexander who now lay buried under the old, gnarled yew trees in the corner of St Peter's graveyard.

Isolda's six-year-old son by Raoul, red-haired, freckle-faced Robert, sensed the tensions at the table and, seeing his mother's attention was diverted, slipped upstairs to continue his favourite game. Robert had found a small room, no more than a cup-board in the wall, reached through a small trapdoor concealed behind the iron-bound copper chest in the small passageway outside his mother's room. He had found that by squeezing over the chest and raising the trapdoor he could crawl into his secret chamber, where he could play his favourite game of dragons and monsters. As he lifted the trapdoor his father called his name, but it was too late. Robert crawled in and closed the trapdoor behind him. He took the tinder he had filched from his father's store and lit the old tallow candle standing on the floor in the centre of the room. The little boy watched the candle-flame grow. He giggled softly to himself as he used his hands and arms to make shadows dance against the far wall.

'Here be a dragon,' he murmured, clenching his little fist and holding it up. He watched the shadows flicker ominously on the wall. Then he held up his three little fingers. 'And here be the knight on his horse, come to fight the dragon.'

Robert paused; he heard a knock on the door downstairs, his mother laughing, a scraping of stools, and his father going along the hallway.

'Visitors!' the boy whispered. He strained his ears, but could hear only one voice. 'Just one!' he murmured and went back to his shadow playing. He heard his mother call, 'Robert, come down!' But the little boy sat with his back to the wall and continued his game. He must have dozed for a few minutes. He was awakened by what he thought was a scream, slight, muted. Downstairs the door opened again and Robert heard more people coming into the house. Or were his parents leaving? He heard heavy footsteps on the stairs; that must be Father, he thought, going up to the garret to get a tun of his best ale.

Doors opened and shut. Someone was outside in the passageway, breathing heavily. Suddenly the little boy became frightened. Without thinking, he leaned over and doused the candle and sat crouched in the darkness. Terror tingled every fibre of his body. His legs shook. His hands felt heavy and cold, like the great block of ice he'd helped his father bring in from the river last Yuletide. Something terrible was outside the room. A grotesque creature from one of his worse nightmares was standing on the other side of the wall. The boy crouched, frozen like a rabbit. He allowed the terrible sense of evil to waft around him and ruffle the back of his neck with its cold fingers. Robert dare not move. The devil had come into his house and all boyish games were ended.

Chapter 2

Sir Godfrey and Alexander were up early the next morning, their hearts gladdened by the bright blue sky and the flashes of weak sunlight. They joined Dame Edith in the convent church. They knelt on their prie-dieus in front of the rood screen, listening to the nuns sing divine office, followed by a mass celebrated by the convent chaplain. The priest was dressed in vestments of red and gold, a beautiful white dove made of silk embroidered on the back of his chasuble. Sir Godfrey prayed devoutly, watching every movement of the priest, as he followed the rhythm of the mass through the epistle, the gospel and the offering of the bread and wine.

Dame Edith tried to pray. In her mind's eye, she tried to enter the great column of fire, the entrance to God's kingdom. She didn't know why, but every time she prayed or thought of God she imagined a sea of fire, pure love, which warmed, nourished and strengthened but never burnt. She realized why Dame Constance had asked for this mass to be said; it was a petition to God that he would send his Holy Spirit to guard and protect the convent community after the terrible events of the night before. The exorcist knew the Strigoi had been here; even as she had crouched in her cold, dark cell she'd sensed their malevolence and corrupt influence wafting through the place

131

like the sour stench from a midden heap.

She turned her head to watch McBain, kneeling now in prayer, and had to hide her smile. The young clerk was devout enough, she was sure, but he was more intent on staring at the lovely Emily than on praying for God's guidance. She was right. Alexander said his prayers but every so often he would stare at Emily, sitting so demurely in her stall beside Dame Constance. Alexander stared until he caught her attention and, when he did, pulled a face. The girl smiled and lowered her head. Alexander continued to stare, Emily looked coyly from beneath her eyelashes. Alexander grimaced and rolled his eyes. The girl began to giggle but, when Dame Constance looked up sharply, Alexander's face was fashioned into that of some great mystic, head to one side, eyes intent on the altar, his face and posture as devout as any monk.

After mass, Dame Constance joined the knight and clerk as they breakfasted on ale, oatmeal and bread and cheese in the small parlour of the guest house. She came in, with Dame Edith on her arm, as severe in demeanour as before, but both men knew that the events of the previous evening had deeply frightened her. They all exchanged the kiss of peace. Mathilda set fresh places for the two women. Dame Constance said grace, Godfrey and Alexander looking ruefully at each other, for they had forgotten that. Alexander complimented the abbess on the mass, particularly on the singing of the nuns. Dame Constance smiled thinly and came swiftly to the point.

'Are we in danger here?'

'You mean after the events of last night?' Alexander asked.

Sir Godfrey shook his head. 'I don't think so.' He looked at the exorcist. 'What do you think, domina?'

Dame Edith sipped gently from the horn spoon, wafting her fingers across her mouth, for the oatmeal was hot.

'The Strigoi are demons,' she began, 'evil creatures who love to play games and relish the fear they provoke. They came to frighten you last night, Dame Constance, as well as to warn Sir Godfrey and Master McBain to leave Oxford.'

'Why?' Alexander asked. 'Why didn't they just kill Sir Godfrey?'

'They might not have found that easy,' the knight said grimly.

The clerk gently touched the knight on the back of his hand as a sign of apology. The exorcist put her horn spoon back on the table and pushed away the hot bowl of oatmeal.

'The Strigoi are evil but not foolish. They know you carry the king's commission. An attack upon you is an attack upon the crown. They do not want every house guarded by royal soldiers and royal judges probing into every gutter, sewer and midden heap in Oxford, but that is what would happen if the king's commissioners were murdered. However,' she sighed, 'it's best to be safe. Lady abbess, ask the sheriff for some soldiers to be sent here. Organize a curfew just before dark. Issue instructions that when the bell is rung all doors are to be locked, all windows sealed, the gateways and postern doors barred and bolted. No one is to leave or enter without your special permission.'

Sir Godfrey drummed his fingers on the table top.

'What,' he wondered, 'is their business in Oxford?'

'God knows!' Dame Edith replied. 'But what can we do to discover and prevent it?'

'Well,' Sir Godfrey replied, 'we do have two more places to visit. We would, Dame Constance, like to study the chronicle you've read, the one in the university library at St Mary's church.'

'It will be there,' the abbess replied. 'I have carefully marked, with black crosses, the sections that are relevant. And the second place?'

'The Trinitarian friary?'

'That will be hard. They are an enclosed order, reluctant to accept visitors and even more unwilling to talk about the legends of the place.'

Godfrey pulled his commission out of his wallet. 'This is the king's own warrant. Our good brothers at the Trinitarian friary will certainly speak to me.'

Dame Constance wished them well and left. Dame Edith said she was ready to leave, but warned both men to arm themselves with swords and daggers. She asked Sir Godfrey if he had a crossbow.

'We have two,' he replied.

'Then bring them,' the exorcist advised. 'Don't go anywhere unarmed.'

'So these Strigoi *can* be killed?' Alexander asked.

'Yes, Master McBain, I have told you so. But they must not only be killed; their corpses must be burnt.'

'Why don't we use relics?' Alexander asked, pushing his stool back.

Dame Edith laughed softly. 'I wish we could. But, first, most genuine relics are now sealed beneath the stones of many altars. Secondly, how do we know a relic is genuine? I have seen enough pieces of the true cross to build a warship and still have enough wood left for a manor house.'

Sir Godfrey laughed and drained his tankard.

'Dame Edith speaks the truth,' he declared. 'Just think, Alexander, of the rubbish that is sold. A piece of Jesus's vest, a hair from St Joseph's beard, a feather from the wing of the Holy Spirit!'

'Then why not use the sacrament?' Alexander asked testily.

'How?' Dame Edith asked. 'Make everyone in Oxford receive the eucharist?'

'Well, we could carry it around,' Alexander suggested, 'perhaps in a small pyx?'

'Nonsense!' Dame Edith retorted. 'You saw how we interrogated Lascalle. The host, like the relic, must be held very close against the Strigoi.'

Muttering and cursing, Alexander followed Sir Godfrey up to their chamber where they collected their belongings before escorting Dame Edith to the stable. Grooms prepared their horses and soon they were out of the convent, winding their way through the early-morning streets to the centre of Oxford. The day was just beginning. Traders were setting out their stalls. Apprentices ran hither and thither. The morning air was heavy with the odour of horse-dung and the smell from the sewers mingled with more fragrant odours from the cookshops and taverns. A group of roisterers, now doused with water, their hands tied behind their backs, were being escorted towards the town gaol. A forger screamed and beat his hands against the stocks that imprisoned him as the city executioner, a glowing iron in his hand, burned the incriminating 'F' on his cheek. Farther along, two blasphemers who had shouted drunken abuse during mass stood in barrels of horse-piss while raucous-voiced beadles piled manure on their heads. A whore, found touting for business in the wrong place, stood next to them. She was having her hair shaved before being paraded through the town behind a bagpiper to be mocked and jeered at until she reached the city gates, where she would be expelled.

'Business as usual,' Sir Godfrey murmured.

Alexander smiled, but this time he caught the tension the knight had earlier remarked on. Some students, the food still in their hands, were being driven out of a cookshop by a group of burly labourers. A doctor of philosophy had to scamper quickly through the porchway of one of the halls when some apprentices began to hurl abuse at him, followed by the usual fistfuls of mud.

Alexander grumbled about the unrest as they stabled their horses in a tavern and made their way through the crowds towards the university church of St Mary.

'Is it always like this?' he asked.

'No,' Dame Edith murmured, pressing his elbow. 'This is different. I think the news of the dreadful murders is seeping out to excite and stir up old hatreds and animosities. The Strigoi love that. They thrive in an atmosphere of hatred. They commit their crimes beneath the veil of local animosity. Time and again others are executed for the crimes they have committed.'

They entered St Mary's through a small door and went up the nave. A clerk, trimming the candles on the high altar, came down the sanctuary steps and took them through the sacristy into the great chapter house where the library was kept. The archivist, Simon Neopham, a tired-looking, dusty-faced cleric, greeted them cordially enough. He was eager to show them around the shelves and cupboards that lined the walls, all packed high with leather- or calfskin-bound volumes; the coffers where parchment was kept; and the great carved bookstands, with their thick folios chained to the wall, in the small study carrels at the far end of the room. Neopham looked at Dame Edith intently, then glimpsed the swords and daggers beneath Sir Godfrey's and Alexander's cloaks.

'But you are not here to look around, are you?' he said dryly.

'No, sir.' Alexander smiled dazzlingly. 'I believe you have a secret chronicle, the *Annales Oxonienses*?'

'The Oxford Chronicle?' Neopham looked puzzled. 'There's

no secret about that.' He smiled, offering a display of yellow, ragged stumps of teeth. 'Ah! The chronicle Dame Constance studied.' He waved vein-streaked hands. 'It's not really secret,' he said, 'except Dame Constance noticed a change in pattern, certain items that repeated themselves. Come! Come! I'll show you.'

He made them sit at the long, polished table that ran down the centre of the room and lit the eight-branched candelabra. He then scurried off and returned, huffing and puffing, carrying a thick, leather-bound folio. Alexander stared around the room and shivered. The chapter house was long and dark. He looked up at the rafters and noticed how the candlelight created flickering, dancing shapes. Alexander also caught unease from the exorcist, who pushed her hands up the sleeves of her gown as if she was cold. She kept moving, turning around, listening.

'There's evil here,' she murmured. 'Perhaps it's the record of their wrong-doing!'

Neopham, chattering like a squirrel, pushed the leather-bound volume towards Alexander and began to point out the sections in the centuries-old chronicle that were marked by Dame Constance's black crosses. Alexander thanked the archivist and assured him that all was well, but asked if they could be left alone to study the texts. The clerk then sat, turning over the pages, scrutinizing the sections the abbess had marked.

'What's it all about?' Sir Godfrey asked crossly, peering over his companion's shoulder. Dame Edith drummed her fingers on the table, impatient for Alexander to comment.

'Well,' Alexander replied, 'the chronicle is full of the usual rather boring items of information. Who was sheriff; how the weather affected crops; the doings of the city council; the

fortunes of the university. But, occasionally, about once every
twenty or thirty years, each individual chronicler has narrated
some terrible story.'

'Such as?' Sir Godfrey asked impatiently.

'Well, stories about men who died but who later came back
to life.'

Beside him Dame Edith stiffened.

'What stories?' she whispered. She touched the clerk gently
on the hand. 'Tell us, Alexander.'

Alexander sighed, blew his cheeks out and turned a page.

'Well, here's an entry for year 1297. According to the
chronicler, a certain merchant of depraved, dishonest life, either
through fear of the law or to avoid the vengeance of his
enemies, moved from Herefordshire and bought himself a large
house at Parismead in Oxford. He didn't change his ways but
busied himself in lewd traffic.' Alexander looked up and grinned.
'And I will not describe what it was. However, according to the
chronicler, this man persevered in his evil ways, fearing neither
God nor man. He married the daughter of a local official, a
beautiful woman whom he treated most evilly.'

'Does it say how?' Sir Godfrey interrupted him.

'No, but the merchant travelled abroad. Anyway, on his
return, people began to whisper wanton stories about his spouse,
firing the merchant with the hot flames of jealousy.' Alexander
went back to the chronicle. 'Restless and full of anxiety to
know whether the charges were true, the merchant told his wife
he was going on a long journey to London and would not return
for several days. However, he stole back that very evening and
was secretly admitted into his wife's bed chamber by a serving
wench who used to pleasure him in his bachelor days and was
privy to his designs.' Alexander looked up in mock horror.
'Dame Edith, should you be listening to this? It's more like one

of Master Boccaccio's stories about ladies who are hot and whose husbands like to pry.'

Dame Edith tapped him on the hand as if he was some errant little boy.

'The lures of the flesh,' she assured him, 'hold no attraction for me.' Then she grinned. 'More's the pity! Continue, Alexander.'

'Well, once the husband was in the room he hid away and that night saw his wife being well served by a lusty youth. So angry did he become that he fell from his hiding place. The young cuckolder beat a hasty retreat as the husband lay unconscious on the floor.'

'A bawdy story,' Sir Godfrey interrupted. 'I have heard the likes in many a camp, with a bit more spice and certainly more sauce.'

Alexander waved his hand. 'No, no listen to this! The husband had struck his head against an iron bar. He became very ill. A priest came and told him he was near to death's door and that he should be shriven and receive the blessed sacrament. But the husband refused, he died in his sins and was buried.' Alexander moved his fingers farther down the page. 'According to this, the wicked husband used to come out of his tomb at night, wandering through the streets, prowling round the houses, causing the dogs to howl and yelp. His appearance was grotesque and, if he met anyone, he grievously harmed them whilst the air became foul and tainted with his fetid, corrupting body.' Alexander moved his fingers down the page. 'Eventually, the people of North Oxford, losing all patience, went out to the grave and began to dig. They thought they would have to delve deep but, suddenly, came upon the corpse covered only with a thin layer of earth.' Alexander pulled a face. 'The chronicle describes the body as being gorged and swollen with a frightful

139

corpulence, a face florid and tubby with huge puffed cheeks. The clothes and shroud of the corpse were soiled and torn. One of the townspeople immediately dealt the corpse a sharp blow with the keen edge of the spade and a stream of warm, red gore gushed out. So, before nightfall, they dragged the corpse to Parismead, quickly built a large pyre and set the body alight.'

'Nonsense!' grumbled Sir Godfrey. 'Such stories are commonplace. You can find them in chronicles and manuscripts up and down the kingdom.'

The exorcist just shook her head, while Alexander turned more pages over.

'No, no, there are other stories!' he exclaimed. 'Dame Constance has marked them with her black cross and they are all of the same ilk. Here's one from 1322 which occurred during the civil war between the present king's father and his barons.' He turned the pages. 'Another from 1340. All the same. Individuals, notorious for the wickedness of their life, coming back to life and wandering the streets until the authorities intervene and the corpse is burnt.'

'Is there any time pattern?' Dame Edith asked.

Alexander turned the pages back. 'Yes,' he replied, 'every twenty or thirty years the same story occurs.' He studied the manuscript and tapped the table top as he emphasized the points. 'First, the notorious sinner dies; secondly, he comes back; thirdly, he commits terrible crimes, horrible murders; finally he is destroyed.'

'Is that what's happening now?' Sir Godfrey asked, grasping the exorcist's hand. He could tell by the set of her mouth that she was puzzled.

'No,' she replied, 'what's happening now is quite different. These stories are only precursors of a great event. Mere shadows of the horrors now occurring.'

'But what causes them?' Alexander persisted, closing the book.

'God knows. Perhaps the escape of some baleful influence. It's like a woodland pond, clear and bright on the surface but, if you thrust in a pole and stir the murky depths, all the dirt and filth rise to the top.' She rubbed her mouth with the back of her fingers. 'What was recently stirred has caused these terrible murders to begin.' She got slowly to her feet. 'But I have heard enough. Let's leave.'

They thanked the librarian, who had been secretly watching them from the other end of the library. Although he was a lover of books, Alexander was relieved when they left the church and could feel the cold breeziness of the High Street, where the raucous shouts of the hawkers and sellers were a welcome relief from the baleful silence of the library. They were pushing their way through the throng when Sir Godfrey heard his name called and glimpsed Father Andrew, merry-eyed and bright-cheeked, walking through the crowds, a basket slung over his arm.

'Good day, Sir Godfrey, Master McBain, Dame Edith.' The priest's eyes became serious. 'You are making good progress?'

Sir Godfrey walked on, the priest beside him.

'No, Father, we are not,' the knight replied. 'Indeed, very little. But, thanks be to God, no more murders have occurred.'

'Is there anything I can do?' Father Andrew asked.

Sir Godfrey stopped to allow Alexander to help Dame Edith on to her palfrey.

'Such as what?' Sir Godfrey asked.

The priest shrugged and pointed to his basket. 'I am buying bread and vegetables for the poor we feed outside St Peter's church. I listen to the gossip of the city. I could ask questions.'

Sir Godfrey patted the man on the shoulder. 'Anything you

can do, Father, will be appreciated.'

'And I pray for you,' the priest said, 'every morning at mass that this evil ends.'

Again the knight thanked him. The priest sketched a blessing in the air and slipped back into the crowds milling around the stalls.

Sir Godfrey and his companions paused for something to eat at the Saracen's Head then continued along the High Street, into Eastgate and through the postern gate of the Trinitarian friary. The buildings were large and forbidding, with soaring walls, crenellations, turrets and gables. The ugly-faced gargoyles made Alexander shiver; he noticed that Dame Edith, too, had become quite agitated.

'God forgive me!' she whispered. 'This is a house of God, but I feel uneasy.'

A lay brother hurried over to ask their business. Sir Godfrey nearly asked for Abbot Samson but caught himself just in time and demanded, on the king's authority, to see Prior Edmund. The lay brother shrugged and called for ostlers to look after their horses. He then led them through the cloisters, where the brothers were crouched in their study carrels, making use of the good light to copy or illuminate manuscripts. They went up a wide flight of stone stairs and, knocking on an iron-studded door, were ushered in to where a highly nervous Prior Edmund was waiting.

'You have been expecting us, Father?' Sir Godfrey asked.

The prior hopped from foot to foot, his mouth opening and closing.

'Yes, yes,' he muttered. Suddenly he remembered his manners and waved them to seats before the weak fire. He pulled up a small stool for himself, crouching there like a mannikin, his thin worried face betraying deep anxiety, even fear, at their presence.

Alexander studied the prior's pallid face and noticed that his grey robes were stained and unkempt.

What's he frightened of? Alexander thought. And why has Dame Edith become so restless?

Sir Godfrey, however, was more matter-of-fact. He curtly refused the prior's offer of refreshment and came abruptly to the point.

'Father, you have heard of the ghastly murders in the city?'

'Yes.' The prior tried to force a smile of sympathy, but his blinking became more furious as he constantly wetted his thin, dry lips.

'And you've heard of the legends behind them?'

'There are many legends,' the prior replied hoarsely, 'legends about this house, about the city.'

'Father,' Sir Godfrey dryly asked, 'why are you so nervous?'

The prior bowed his head and plucked at a blob of wax on his robe. 'Sir Godfrey, I am only the prior,' he muttered. 'I have heard about the horrifying murders, but tragedy has occurred here. Abbot Samson is dead.' He looked up, brushing away bits of dried wax. 'I find it difficult to cope. The order should appoint someone else.'

'How did Abbot Samson die?' the exorcist interrupted harshly.

The prior swallowed hard. Of all his three visitors he seemed most fearful of this blind woman, small, white-haired but with a commanding presence.

'He was found dead in his chamber!'

'And the cause?'

'God knows, I am no physician. A sudden stop to his heart, a rush of blood to his brain, an imbalance of humours.'

'But he was a healthy man?'

143

'Many young, healthy men die unexpectedly,' Father Edmund protested.

'Father prior,' Alexander tactfully intervened, 'we are not here to accuse or to pry but to ask certain questions. We have heard the legends and read the chronicles. This house is supposedly built over secret tunnels and passageways. In one of these, in some antique chamber, lies the corpse of a very evil man who lived in these parts many hundreds of years ago, a Strigoi.'

The prior looked up, his face ashen. 'I have never heard the like,' he whispered. 'What is a Strigoi?'

'A man who has died spiritually and whose soul is possessed by an evil spirit from Hell.'

Prior Edmund picked up an iron poker and jabbed furiously at the small log fire, causing a splutter of sparks and a sudden surge of warmth.

'Old wives' tales,' he muttered.

'So, no such tunnels exist?'

'They may have done,' Prior Edmund replied, throwing the poker down. 'But I have never heard of any. This is a house of God, a community dedicated to the service of Christ.'

'Did Abbot Samson ever talk of such matters?' Alexander persisted.

'Never.'

'And you know nothing of these at all?'

Prior Edmund stood up, pushing his hands into the voluminous sleeves of his gown. 'I have told you what I know!' he snapped. 'You carry the king's commission. You may go where you wish, speak to whomever you want. I cannot stop you. However, I am a busy man and, unless you have further questions . . .?'

He walked towards the door and opened it. Sir Godfrey

shrugged. Alexander helped Dame Edith to her feet and the lay brother, who had been waiting outside, took them back to the stables. As they went down the galleries and outside across the cloister, Alexander stared around. The friary seemed no different from the other religious houses he had visited. The smell of good food mingled with that of polish and soap. Brothers and their lay staff bustled about. The infirmarian carried a stack of crisp linen sheets for the laundry room; servitors noisily laid out the refectory for the evening meal. The sounds were normal – a hum of conversation from the study carrels as scholars worked, the ringing of bells, the clatter of noise from the outhouses. Nevertheless, Alexander detected something amiss. It was as if everyone was busily acting out a part as they surreptitiously watched these three strangers to their house.

They had to wait for a while in the stable yard. The lay brother apologized.

'I thought you'd stay longer,' he explained cheerfully, 'so I removed the saddles. It won't take long.'

Sir Godfrey nodded and stared back at the friary buildings. 'Everything is in order here,' he declared, 'but . . .'

'I know what you mean,' Alexander said.

'This is a place of prayer and worship,' Dame Edith murmured, 'but there's something else here.' She shook her head. 'It reminds me of a battlefield where the dead have been buried and masses sung for the repose of their souls. However, if you stand long enough, you can smell the blood and slaughter in the air and experience a deep desolation.' She shifted her head like a hunting dog sniffing the air. 'This place should be burnt,' she continued, 'exorcised by fire, cleansed and purged.'

She stopped speaking as a monk, white-haired and bent with age, walked slowly towards them, his ash cane tapping the cobbles. He didn't stop until he was almost touching Sir Godfrey, then he looked up, his blue eyes rheumy with age.

'My name is Lanfranc,' he wheezed, dabbing the white phlegm at the corner of his mouth. 'I am the historian of this—' He waved a brown-spotted, vein-streaked hand back towards the friary. His eyes darted first to McBain then to the exorcist.

'You have come at last,' he continued hoarsely. He waved a finger at Dame Edith. 'My sight is going, but my hearing is good. Yes, this place should be burnt, cleansed by fire, the tunnels opened and the evil within destroyed.'

Sir Godfrey caught the man's bony wrist.

'You know where such tunnels exist?'

'No,' the old man replied, 'and, if I did, I couldn't show you them – I am bound by a vow of obedience to that fool Edmund. But Samson's death was not an accident. Samson was courageous but headstrong.' He lifted his head and dabbed at his dripping nose. 'He went to places he shouldn't have done, God rest his soul, and it's all the fault of the stranger.'

'Which stranger?' Sir Godfrey asked.

'Come back,' Lanfranc replied, 'come back tomorrow with the sheriff's men. Bring dogs. I will show you the secret manuscripts.'

'You mean the legends?'

'Aye.'

'Why wait till tomorrow?' Dame Edith retorted. 'Sir Godfrey, you carry the king's warrant.'

The old man wheezed with laughter and tapped his cane on the cobbles. 'Aye, that's the way,' he chortled.

Sir Godfrey looked at McBain, who stood tight-lipped.

'What shall we do?'

'We can't very well force our way in,' Alexander replied slowly, 'but the prior did lie.'

Sir Godfrey's hand fell to the hilt of his sword and he was

about to shout an order to the ostler when another lay brother came running into the yard, hands flailing.

'Sir! Sir!' he cried. 'You must return to the convent!'

Alexander gripped the lay brother's arm.

'Why?'

'I don't know, sir, but the sheriff's man was most insistent. Sir Oswald Beauchamp demands your presence there.' The man's voice fell to a whisper. 'He did say something about another killing!'

Chapter 3

Sir Oswald and Proctor Ormiston were waiting in Dame Constance's parlour, an anxious Father Andrew with them. Dame Constance had lost some of her hauteur since her nightmarish fright the previous evening; she sat at her desk pretending to study a book of accounts. Sir Oswald could scarcely contain his impatience.

'More deaths,' he brusquely announced, hardly waiting for Sir Godfrey and his companions to sit down. 'A man, his wife and young daughter brutally slain last night.'

'Where was this?'

'In Bocardo Lane,' Father Andrew interrupted.

'And the corpses?'

'They have already been removed, but they died like the rest – throats gashed, blood drained, no sign of any forced entry.'

'Couldn't this have waited?' Sir Godfrey snapped.

'This one's different.' The ashen-faced proctor spoke up.

'How?'

'First, the corpses were discovered by neighbours and the news is pouring oil on a flame of rumour spreading through the city. You have been in the market place and witnessed the tension. Rumour piles upon rumour and gossip fans the flames. The students blame the townspeople, the townspeople whisper about satanic covens amongst the scholars.'

'And what else?'

Father Andrew turned to Dame Constance. 'May I bring him in?'

The abbess nodded and rang the small bell on her desk; a lay sister answered and was ordered to bring 'the child' up. A short while later a boy, his face as white as chalk, eyes large dark pools of fear, entered the room. He clutched the lay sister's hand and sucked noisily on the thumb of his free hand. He stared round-eyed at the people assembled in the room and hid in the lay sister's skirts. Father Andrew crouched down, arms extended.

'Come on, Robert,' he said gently. 'Come to me. Come here, Robert!'

The boy ran forward and the priest stood up, one arm protectively around the boy's shoulders.

'This is Robert Cotterill,' he announced. 'When his father, mother and sister died, he was playing a game by himself. He was hiding in a secret chamber. The neighbours discovered him only when they heard his crying.'

Sir Godfrey strode forward and knelt before the lad. He unhitched his sword and, ignoring the gasps from the others, pushed the leather scabbard into the boy's unresisting hand.

'We have come to help you, Robert,' he said softly. 'Will you stay here and look after this for me?'

The boy nodded solemnly.

'If you do,' the knight continued, 'I will give you some sweetmeats and we'll find another home for you. However, as long as you hold that sword, because it's sacred, no one can hurt you.'

The boy's face creased into a smile, his thumb came out of his mouth and he touched the knight gently on the cheek. Sir

Godfrey looked at Dame Constance.

'The boy is suffering from deep shock,' he murmured. 'I have seen the same before amongst children in towns taken by storm. They can slip into a sleep from which they never wake, or become violently ill. He must be given warm wine and allowed to sleep. He must never be alone. If these Strigoi, these night-walkers, know there is a survivor . . .' His voice trailed off. He tousled the boy's hair and glanced warningly at the abbess.

'He will stay in the infirmary,' Dame Constance declared, nodding at the lay sister, 'in full view of our infirmarian. Ask her to give him a sleeping draught.'

'Has he said anything?' Alexander asked.

'Nothing,' Father Andrew replied. 'I brought him straight here with the neighbours who found him. They left us at the gate.'

The boy trotted off with the lay sister, Sir Godfrey's great sword sheathed in its scabbard clasped in his small hand. The knight grinned sourly at the sheriff.

'If I could borrow yours, Sir Oswald?'

The sheriff unhitched his and handed it over.

'You did right,' the exorcist declared from where she sat on a stool warming her hands by the fire. 'The boy will sleep and then he will talk, though I doubt if he saw or heard much. Sheriff Beauchamp, you must take precautions.'

'I have already done that!' Beauchamp snapped. 'Every available soldier is now walking the streets. The town council has its own bailiffs and beadles, and Proctor Ormiston has guaranteed the full support of the university.'

'And I have finished here,' Father Andrew said. 'Sirs, if you will excuse me, I must go back to my parish.' He sketched a bow in the direction of the abbess and walked out of the room.

The proctor made to follow, but Alexander restrained him gently.

'We still have questions to ask,' he insisted.

'The students who disappeared,' he went on, 'don't you think it's strange that the last one, the Brabanter, asked you, Proctor Ormiston, for permission to study in the library at St Mary's church?'

Ormiston shrugged his shoulders and spread his hands.

'Such licences are common,' he snapped. 'Many students ask for such permission. What are you implying, master clerk?'

Alexander smiled. 'Nothing, sir, I just remark upon a coincidence which may interest you.'

'Many things interest me,' Ormiston retorted. 'But, at the moment, my hands are full with other matters.'

The pilgrims watched expectantly as the knight paused in his tale to refill his wine cup. When it was brimful he picked it up and silently toasted the crop-headed yeoman sitting next to him. For the first time the pilgrims saw the yeoman's stony face break into a slight smile. Their surprise deepened as the yeoman raised his hand and wiped away the tears brimming in his eyes.

'What is going on here?' the franklin whispered to the lawyer.

'Only the sweet Lord knows.'

'Sir knight,' the lawyer called. 'Your tale, you will continue?'

The knight nodded. The yeoman suddenly got up, went round the table and whispered to the knight, then quietly walked out of the taproom. The lawyer turned and looked through the mullioned glass; in the light of a flickering lamp, he saw the yeoman standing in the yard, his face looking up at the starlit sky. The knight whispered something to the squire, who followed the yeoman out. Then the knight took up his tale again.

* * *

Laetitia, the servant girl from the tavern, hurried through the darkening alleys of Oxford to the convent gate of St Anne's.

'I must see the knight,' she whispered to herself. 'Perhaps what I will tell him will be of use. I owe that to Eudo.' She stopped at the corner of a street to catch her breath, coughing to clear her throat. She pulled a shawl closer around her thin shoulders. She had to be careful of that cough, sometimes it hurt, the pain spreading into her throat and, more frightening, she would spit blood as well as phlegm. She recalled Eudo's happy face and laughter-filled eyes. Deep in her heart the girl knew that the scholar was dead. She owed his memory something and, above all, she owed herself. The clerk had kindly eyes, was a just and honest man. He had not frightened her, but promised her a gold coin if she told him what she knew. Laetitia sucked in a deep breath. Well, she would! She would tell him everything and show him the metal disc Eudo had given her which she had secreted under the heel of her cork shoe.

Laetitia hurried on. She turned a corner where the alleyway became as narrow as a needle, but she glimpsed the walls of the convent and her stomach tingled with excitement. She had almost reached the mouth of the alleyway when the dark shapes suddenly appeared out of a doorway to block her path. They were all cowled and masked. Laetitia stopped, heart pounding. She turned to go back but another figure stepped out, blocking her way. Laetitia whirled round, hands clutched to her chest.

'I am only a poor serving girl,' she whispered. 'I have nothing of value.'

The dark, sinister figures just leaned against the wall.

'What do you want?' she wailed.

The figures began to push her gently back up the alleyway.

'Oh, please don't!' Laetitia looked wildly about. In the poor light she caught a glimpse of an eye, the white of skin between lip and mask. She crouched against the urine-stained wall.

'I am no whore,' she pleaded. 'What do you want?'

'We want nothing, Laetitia,' one of the dark figures whispered. He waved his hand. 'You may run on!'

Laetitia moved forward.

'No, Laetitia, hold your head high. You may be a servant girl but you have every right to be proud.'

Laetitia relaxed, forcing a smile. Perhaps these were only scholars, she thought, out to play some prank. She cursed herself. She wished she had followed the order, so recently issued by the sheriff, instructing all householders to keep within doors and to allow access to no one.

'Can I go?' she asked.

'Of course you can, Laetitia,' the voice mocked, 'on one condition. You may walk, you may run, but hold your head high!'

The figure stepped aside. Laetitia made to run, but her shoulder was seized in a vice-like grip.

'Only if you hold your head high, Laetitia!'

The girl heard a snigger from one of the others which made her flesh creep.

'Go on, Laetitia, run!'

Laetitia needed no second bidding but sped down the alleyway. She stopped, looking over her shoulder to see if there was any sign of pursuit. The dark shapes stayed huddled together.

'Run, Laetitia!' the voice mocked. 'Run proudly!'

Laetitia sped on. She reached the end of the alleyway, her head held high, and the razor-sharp wire strung between the buildings cruelly tore at her throat. The girl staggered back, the blood splashing out. She opened her mouth to scream then tipped over gently, crumpling on to the mud-stained cobbles.

154

* * *

Early next morning, Sir Oswald Beauchamp with Proctor Ormiston and a posse of soldiers rode into the convent of St Anne's, the sheriff bellowing that he had to see the king's commissioner immediately. Sir Godfrey, Alexander McBain and Dame Edith were breaking their fast in the guest house. Sir Oswald flung the door open and stormed in, Ormiston following like a shadow.

'By Satan's cock!' the sheriff bellowed, his face purple with rage. 'It's started, Sir Godfrey, and now we are in a worse pickle than before.'

The knight covered Dame Edith's hand.

'Sheriff Beauchamp, there is a lady present and your language hardly becomes you and certainly offends her.'

The sheriff glowered at him and McBain found it difficult to control his laughter at the sheriff's puce face and popping eyes.

'I apologize,' the sheriff said heavily. 'Lady Edith, I meant no offence.'

'None taken,' she returned. 'I have heard worse.'

'Sir Oswald, Proctor Ormiston,' McBain got to his feet and pushed two stools closer to the table. 'For Heaven's sake, sit down.'

The sheriff mumbled his thanks. He sat down with all the grace of a falling sack and put his face into his hands. McBain, raising his eyes at Sir Godfrey, went to the buttery and brought back two cups half-filled with wine and placed them in front of their guests. Beauchamp dropped his hands.

'God forgive me,' he said hoarsely, 'but the devil himself seems to have arrived in Oxford. Tell me, Sir Godfrey, did you know a servant girl called Laetitia? A slattern from the Mitre tavern?'

Sir Godfrey nodded.

'Well, she's a dead slattern,' Sir Oswald told him. 'Late last night the poor girl had her throat slashed in an alleyway not far from here. I think she was coming to see you. You apparently tried to question her?'

'Yes,' McBain replied. 'She was sweet on one of the students who disappeared. Do you think she was killed by the Strigoi?'

'Oh, yes, but not like the others. They put a razor wire across the mouth of an alleyway and probably panicked her into running headlong into it.'

'You are sure she was coming here?' Alexander asked.

'Oh, yes. She told the taverner at the Mitre where she was going – to see the gentlemen and the blind woman who tried to talk to her a few days previously.'

'Did she have anything on her person?'

'Nothing. Not a scrip, not a wallet,' Sir Oswald replied. 'Except, when they removed her body to the death house near Eastgate, they found this in the heel of her shoe.' He tossed a black, metal disc, no bigger than a penny, on to the table. Both Sir Godfrey and McBain examined it carefully. It meant nothing to either of them.

'They must have been watching her,' Alexander declared. 'Somehow, when we met her, they silenced her by fear but the lure of gold brought her out.' He shrugged. 'Now she's dead and we know nothing.'

'But you've come about more than that haven't you?' Dame Edith asked the sheriff.

Beauchamp sighed. 'You probably can't hear them from here?'

'Hear what?' Alexander asked.

'I heard bells ringing earlier,' Dame Constance said. 'Not the tolling for prayer or divine office but a wild, frenetic clanging.'

156

Beauchamp pulled a face. 'The news of the girl's death has spread into the city and that, together with the rumours about the murders, has caused the deep antagonism in the city to overspill. Not just between the students themselves, the usual rivalry between the northerners and the southerners but, more seriously, between the scholars and the townspeople. To put it briefly, a riot has broken out and it looks as if it's spreading.'

'It began this morning,' Proctor Ormiston interrupted, 'when a scholar from Sparrow Hall posted a bill in the Swindlestock tavern seeking a beadsman to pray for the souls of townspeople who were not yet dead but who soon would be, because of their "crimes".' Ormiston rubbed his tired face. 'As usual one thing led to another. A citizen read this bill, tore it down and said that the scholars were nothing but putrid murderers. Knives were drawn and a brawl broke out which then spread. The great bell of St Martin's was tolled, ox horns blown and both sides took to the streets. In one hall Fulke, rector of Piglesthorne, poured a cauldron of boiling water over a group of citizens who, in turn, stormed into the hall, setting fire to its gates.' Ormiston looked at Beauchamp. 'The riot's spreading,' he repeated. 'And there's little we can do about it.'

'The Strigoi are behind this,' Dame Edith declared. 'They provoke violence and blood and exploit it to veil their own murderous activities.'

Beauchamp looked pleadingly at Sir Godfrey. 'We need your help. We have to restore order. God knows what terrible crimes will be committed. Sir Godfrey, you are the king's fighting man. All I have are rustic levies, with a few serjeants to strengthen them.'

'I'll come too.' Alexander spoke up before even Sir Godfrey could reply.

A short while later they left the convent, the sheriff's soldiers encircling them, and rode down the High Street. It was apparent that the riots were getting out of hand. No stalls were open and gangs of students and townspeople fought in the streets. At the entrance to one hall a man had been hanged by his ankles and a fire lit beneath his head. On a dung hill near Carfax a young scholar, his robes all torn, lay bleeding. In the alleys and runnels that ran off the main thoroughfares the crash of broken glass mingled with shrieks of rage and fear. Columns of smoke were beginning to pour up, hanging above the roofs. No one approached the sheriff or his armed men but, on a number of occasions, arrows and stones whistled above their heads.

Sir Oswald led his group through the city and up to the castle, where he collected reinforcements. He divided them into two parties, one under himself, the other under Sir Godfrey and McBain. It was then a matter of moving from street to street. They tore down the black banners of rebellion, released prisoners, knocked rioters on the head and broke up roving gangs whether of scholars or citizens. Water carriers and bailiffs were organized to douse fires and arrest any looters. McBain admired the knight's ruthlessly cold methods; a street would be cleared, order imposed and a guard left.

Sometimes a group of rioters put up a token resistance, but usually they fled in a flurry of catcalls and jeers. Only once were Sir Godfrey and McBain really threatened. Four scholars in ragged hoods, with leather masks over their faces, appeared at the windows of a hall and fired crossbows, injuring two of Beauchamp's soldiers, one mortally. Sir Godfrey dismounted and with a small party stormed the hall, arrested the malefactors, established who had shot the fatal bow and immediately hanged him before the main gates. Alexander McBain did not interfere; he believed such ruthlessness was necessary. He had seen similar riots in Cambridge; if they were not controlled, arson, pillage and the death of innocent women and children would become the norm. As dusk fell, peace was restored and Sir Godfrey and McBain met up with Beauchamp, who had taken his party to the other section of the city, north of the High Street.

Opposite the Saracen's Head, they all took a respite for they were exhausted, their faces black and streaked with sweat, marked by a myriad of minor cuts and bruises. Then they made one final sweep through the city. By the time they reached the castle, congregating outside Trillocks inn, the sheriff's party and Sir Godfrey's had between them arrested over four dozen rioters. Some of these were herded into the castle dungeons, others led off, roped together, to cool their heels in the Bocardo gaol.

'A good day's work,' Beauchamp breathed, mopping his brow. 'Sir Godfrey, you will join us for some wine?'

The knight shook his head, nursing a wrist where a rioter had struck him with a metal bar.

'Sir Oswald, I thank you, but one day's work is enough. If I dismounted and drank, I'd fall asleep on the ground. What do you say, McBain?'

Alexander nodded. He was saddle-sore, cold and hungry. Above all, he was fearful of what might have happened while he, Sir Godfrey and the city authorities were busily quelling the riots.

They made their farewells and rode back through the now quiet streets of Oxford. Soldiers, bailiffs and men hired by the university stood at the corner of each street and at the mouth of every alleyway. Criers, armed with bells, loudly proclaimed the curfew, threatening dire punishment on any found wandering the streets that night. They reached St Anne's and left their horses to the grooms. Sir Godfrey ordered the gates to be locked and barred and they both returned to the guest house to shave, wash and eat. The exorcist came over and quietly listened as Sir Godfrey, between mouthfuls of bread and meat, explained what had happened. She nodded, now and again interrupting with a question. Alexander watched her intently.

'You think the riot was a veil for something else don't you?' he asked.

Dame Edith adjusted the blindfold over her eyes and smiled thinly.

'In any village or town,' she replied, 'there are always latent jealousies, hatred and rivalries. The Strigoi love these. In Wallachia there was the hatred between the inhabitants and the Turks, the clash between cultures, countries and religions. Oxford's really no different. Northerner hates southerner. Welshman hates Scot. Frenchman detests Spaniard. Scholars detest the townspeople. And so on.' She picked up a small loaf of bread from a platter and broke it into small pieces. 'I just wonder who spread those rumours?'

Her question went unanswered because of a loud knocking at the door.

'Come in!' Sir Godfrey shouted.

A dirty, bedraggled soldier from the castle entered.

'Messages from Sir Oswald,' he gabbled.

'Why?' Alexander asked, half rising from his seat. 'What has happened?'

'Oh, nothing, sir,' the soldier replied. He closed his eyes to remember the message. 'But Sir Oswald says this: "the black metal disc he found on the girl's body"—' He opened his eyes. 'Does that make sense?'

'Yes, it does,' Alexander replied.

'Well,' the soldier continued, closing his eyes again. 'Sir Oswald says that when he went through the belongings of the

Hospitaller, the one murdered in the woods, he found a similar one in the pocket of his jerkin.'

'Is that all?' Sir Godfrey asked.

'Oh yes, sir. That's all he said. Except thank you for today.'

Sir Godfrey nodded and tossed a penny to the messenger, who left as hurriedly as he had entered.

'Black metal discs,' Alexander said. 'What do they mean?'

Sir Godfrey blew his cheeks out and drained his wine goblet.

'God knows, master clerk. Dame Edith, you must excuse me. I find it difficult to keep my eyes open, so I bid you good night.'

He tramped up the stairs. McBain sat down opposite the exorcist, who made no move to leave.

'You must be tired,' she murmured.

'Yes and no,' Alexander replied. 'Tired, yes, but the brain still whirls, the blood beats strong.'

'Get the boy,' Dame Edith said abruptly.

'The boy?'

'Yes, young Robert, whose family were murdered. I understand he rarely sleeps. You have some sweet comfits or marchpane?'

Alexander nodded.

'Then bring them here.'

Alexander had his hand on the latch when the exorcist called out.

'McBain!' Dame Edith controlled the shiver she felt. 'Go nowhere without your sword!'

Alexander was about to argue, but the exorcist had turned her face towards him as if willing him to obey her.

'Please!' she pleaded. 'Do what I say!'

Alexander shrugged, went up to his chamber and fastened his sword belt around his waist. He left the guest house and

161

walked across the dark, silent grounds of the convent towards the infirmary. He found the boy in a small, white-washed cubicle off the main dormitory. He was sitting on the bed, half-heartedly playing counters with the aged and rather forbidding-looking infirmarian. He smiled as Alexander entered and, when the clerk told him to come, leapt from the bed, slipping his little hand into McBain's. The clerk, embarrassed by such tenderness, half muttered an explanation to the infirmarian and took the boy downstairs.

'Are we going home?' Robert asked. 'Are Mother and Father coming back?'

'No,' McBain replied gently. 'But I have some sweetmeats for you, and perhaps I can show you how to cheat the infirmarian at counters.'

The boy gave a little skip. McBain stopped and looked down at him. The gesture probably saved his life for, as he turned, he glimpsed the dark, cloaked figure swooping out of the blackness, softly rushing across the grass, sword raised. McBain pushed the boy away, ducking sideways as the sword blade hissed by his head and struck the earth. McBain, light as a cat, pulled out both sword and dagger, but the attacker swerved from him and, sword half-raised, ran towards the little boy who lay sprawled wide-eyed on the ground.

'*Au secours! Au secours!*' Alexander shouted, rushing towards the attacker.

His assailant turned. In the bright moonlight Alexander glimpsed eyes dancing with malice behind the black mask. The assassin sprang back, his sword snaking out to catch McBain's. Then they parted. McBain dropped his dagger and gripped the hilt of his sword with two hands. He moved to the left, then to the right, trying to draw the cowled, masked figure away from the boy. The attacker advanced, sword high, and suddenly dipped low, aiming for McBain's belly. The clerk blocked the stroke and their swords scraped together before breaking loose. They separated. Again the assailant moved in, light as a dancer on the balls of his feet. The silent yet killing speed of his attacker disconcerted McBain, who could only block his blows. His heart hammered with fear and his stomach curdled; he was no match for this assailant. Sensing this, the attacker closed again. This time the sword came in short, sharp jabs towards Alexander's face. McBain stepped back, praying he would not trip over any obstacle.

'Go, boy!' he screamed. 'Run!'

The attacker paused. McBain moved in, but the man blocked his clumsy stroke. Robert needed no second bidding, he rose but, to McBain's dismay, did not run towards the guest house but back to the infirmary. Again the assailant closed, sweeping his sword, a deadly swathe of steel, aiming for the soft part of McBain's neck. The clerk parried, their blades clashing in a shrill scream of steel. Again the clerk retreated, chest heaving. Sooner or later his assailant would recognize his weakness and close in for the kill.

'Take him now!' McBain shouted. 'Now, Sir Godfrey!'

The black garbed figure turned, though only for a few seconds before he sensed the trick. He swung back, but it was too late. McBain rushed in, moving slightly to his assailant's right. The man's sword thrust was hampered. McBain lunged with all his might and felt the throbbing thud as his sword bit into the sinew and muscle of his assailant's neck. The man staggered back. He tried to lift his sword but it slipped from his bloodied hands. He slumped to his knees, then sideways to the ground; the rich red blood spurted from his deep neck wound. McBain felt its hot splashes on the back of his hand before he, too, fell to his knees, digging the point of his sword into the soft,

163

wet grass. He knelt, sobbing for breath, now and again muttering a prayer or a curse at his narrow escape. His body was coated in sweat, which began to chill in the cold night air. He heard voices, the sound of running footsteps, Dame Edith's voice, strident with fear, asking what had happened and Sir Godfrey's gruff replies. Then the knight prised Alexander's fingers loose from the sword hilt and helped him to his feet. McBain could only point, hand quivering, at the fallen man. Sir Godfrey took his misericorde dagger from its sheath and drove it into the fallen man's chest. As he pulled it out with a loud, sucking noise, McBain turned away, vomiting and retching.

'Are you all right?' Sir Godfrey asked.

McBain nodded. He felt the exorcist's thin arm around his shoulders, a damp cloth wiping away the spittle and vomit from his mouth.

'Shush!' Dame Edith rocked him gently. 'You are a good man, McBain, a fierce fighter.'

'Aye, you killed the bastard!' Sir Godfrey murmured. 'His head's almost taken from his shoulders.'

He pulled back the cowl and peeled the mask from the dead man's face. Some of the nuns came out.

'Go back!' Sir Godfrey ordered.

The nuns retreated. Sir Godfrey pulled the mask off and stared down at the ashen face of a young man, his black hair clammy with sweat. The lips were full and red.

'Have you ever seen him before?'

Sir Godfrey looked over his shoulder at Alexander, who blessed himself hastily and shook his head.

'You are to burn the corpse,' Dame Edith interrupted. 'Burn it now!'

'For God's sake, lady!' Sir Godfrey snarled, 'this man could be just some hired assassin.'

Dame Edith crossed her arms and shook her head. 'He's one of them,' she whispered. 'Lift his lip.'

Sir Godfrey stared at Alexander.

'Do as I say!' Dame Edith ordered. 'Lift his upper lip!'

Sir Godfrey did so carefully and flinched as he saw the sharp dogteeth on either side of the man's mouth.

'You see what I mean, Sir Godfrey? Even though I have no sight, I know the Strigoi. His body must be burnt before the spirit leaves the corpse, recognizes itself and wanders the earth.'

'Children's nightmares,' Sir Godfrey murmured. 'Dame Edith, I must summon both the sheriff and the proctor, they may recognize this man. This corpse may provide some evidence about who the Strigoi are and where they hide.'

'Then do it quickly!' Dame Edith hissed. 'Now, within the hour! Before the devil comes to claim his own!'

Chapter 4

Sir Godfrey pulled the corpse by the legs towards the guest house. He asked Dame Edith to tend the clerk and went back through the darkness to assure Dame Constance and the nuns that all was in hand. He also sent a sleepy-eyed ostler to summon both the sheriff and the proctor, then kept his own vigil over the corpse until both officials arrived. They looked dishevelled and unshaven, but their anger at being so rudely disturbed soon disappeared when Sir Godfrey told them what had happened. They both carefully examined the dead man's features and shook their heads.

'I have never seen him before,' Ormiston declared, 'nor has the sheriff. And he carries nothing on his person to identify him. Perhaps if we stripped him and thew him on the steps of a church someone might recognize him?'

'No! No!' Dame Edith vigorously interrupted. 'The corpse is to be burnt now. I insist on it or I will return to London!'

Sir Godfrey looked in surprise at this defiant little woman, noticing the beads of sweat running down her cheeks. He realized that, in her state of agitation, she would not be mollified so he agreed to her demand. The sheriff and Ormiston left. Alexander, after bathing his hands and face and drinking a cup of claret, declared himself fit and well. He went across to ensure that little Robert Cotterill was well and found him fast asleep after being given a mild sleeping potion.

On his return he found Sir Godfrey in the courtyard, fastening the corpse across a sumpter pony which neighed and whinnied, nervous at the strange burden it carried. Dame Edith insisted on going with him and Sir Godfrey was too tired to object, so they left the convent building together. Sir Godfrey led the pony, Dame Edith rode on a palfrey and Alexander walked beside her, carrying a large jar of oil taken from the convent stores. At one of the city's postern gates they woke a guard who, after seeing Sir Godfrey's warrant, allowed them through. They threaded their way along the narrow pathways that snaked out of the city into the night-shrouded countryside. An eerie journey. The stars shimmered like gems and a hunter's moon slipped between the clouds. The fields on either side were quiet. Now and again the mournful hoot of an owl or the bloody hunt of night creatures in the bracken along the ditches broke the silence. No one spoke; Alexander was still revelling in his narrow escape and Sir Godfrey was too aware of the evil menace that seemed to emanate from the corpse, even though it was swung across the pony like a sack of grain. Dame Edith prayed, time and again repeating the paternoster, emphasizing the phrase *Sed libera nos a malo*, 'but deliver us from evil'.

They followed the pathway over the brow of a small hill and down to a small copse of trees near a thin, silvery stream. In a moonlit glade Sir Godfrey stopped and stared around, then moved into the darkness, ordering the clerk to collect dry twigs and branches. They built a small pyre and the knight laid the corpse on top, dousing it with oil, and struck a tinder, lighting the small bundles of kindling beneath the branches. At first the wood seemed impervious to the flames and Alexander shivered.

Was the corpse resisting? But then, as if in answer to a prayer, tongues of fire caught the oil and, within minutes, the pyre was covered in a sheet of flame which roared up towards the starlit sky. Sir Godfrey threw on more branches, the fire grew, lighting up the entire glade. Alexander felt as if he was in Hell, watching a soul being burnt, as the fire greedily devoured the corpse of the Strigoi. Dame Edith kept up her prayers.

They stood for at least an hour and a half. Only when the flames began to die and a light breeze wafted the acrid smoke towards them, did they go back among the trees where they had left their horses. For a while they stood there; only when Sir Godfrey was satisfied that the raging inferno had reduced the corpse to black ash and yellowing bone did he order their return to the convent. For a while the stench of the fire seemed to follow them, like some evil spirit moving through the cold night air, and Alexander was relieved to slip back through the postern gate into the city. A heavy-eyed porter let them into the convent and took their horses. Dame Edith, lost in her own thoughts, was about to make her way towards the Galilee porch of the convent church when Alexander caught her by the arm.

'Dame Edith, why has the corpse to be burnt so quickly?'

She turned and, linking her arm through the clerk's, walked back to where Sir Godfrey stood watching them.

'I don't know the real reason. But, remember, a Strigoi is a Shape-shifter and if the corpse remains, so does the spirit. This in turn will wait, seeking out a fresh house, another body to dwell in.'

'You mean these men are possessed?'

'Oh, of course.'

'And the sharpened dog's teeth?'

She shrugged. 'One of the signs.'

Alexander wiped his mouth on his sleeve.

169

'And do such men actually drink human blood?'

'In a trance they will. Such practices are not uncommon amongst the heathen. I have heard of tribes in the wildest parts of Scythia who will eat a brave man's heart to gain courage.'

'But does it make them stronger?' Sir Godfrey retorted. 'How can the drinking of blood make any man more skilful or stronger?'

Dame Edith tapped the side of her head. 'Sir Godfrey, you are a soldier. You, of all people, should realize that a man is what he thinks he is. What causes one man to be a coward and another be a hero? After all, they may be the same flesh and blood. They may even be brothers from the same womb. It's what they think. Have you not met knights who thought they were invincible?'

Sir Godfrey agreed.

'And did it not make them more powerful?'

Again he murmured his assent.

'And have you not seen soldiers carry out extraordinary feats?'

'True,' he muttered.

'I have seen ordinary people,' Dame Edith continued, 'perform extraordinary feats in the most difficult situations. In London once a cart toppled over, pinning a young boy to the ground. Burly men couldn't shift the cart but his mother came running out of the house, lifted the cart as easily as if it was a basket and so freed her son. So it is with these Strigoi, these Shape-shifters. They practise their dark rituals. They sacrifice their bloody offerings, make their invocations to the Dark Lord and believe nothing on earth can withstand them.' She patted Alexander gently on the arm. 'Our clerk is most fortunate. He used his brain to escape. If he had depended solely on brawn he'd be dead and so would that boy.' She leaned over, gently kissed Alexander on the cheek and walked quietly off into the darkness.

In the dark woods beneath the Trinitarian friary the hooded, masked figures looked up at the pinpricks of light from the friary. They stood like hounds of Hell watching their prey. Their leader crouched and moved forward, sniffing the night air, ears straining into the darkness. Then beneath the mask his face contorted into a rictus of rage as he looked over his shoulder at his followers.

'Our companion will not join us,' he hissed. 'We must go now.'

They caught the note of triumph in his voice.

'Tonight, you will see what I promised. One of the great ones kept prisoner for so long will be released from his bonds. You have your orders – no killing, no violence, unless it is necessary.' He looked back towards the friary and smiled in the darkness. 'Let's give our mumbling prior something to pray about.'

They slipped up the hill, long, dark shadows in the moonlight, moving like bats towards the friary wall. At the appointed place they stopped and took the small scaling ladder they had concealed there earlier. Once on to the parapet wall, they spread out, the last one pulling the ladder up behind him and placing it gently against the wall. They edged quietly along to the steps and down into the grounds. They moved quickly, keeping to the shadows, well away from the pools of light thrown by the cresset torches Prior Edmund had ordered to be lit in case the turbulence in the city should spill into the friary. A few lay brothers were supposed to be on guard but they were sleeping and proved no obstacle as the intruders climbed walls, going deeper into the friary. They reached the steps leading to the prior's chamber and flitted like ghosts to the top. The leader checked to ensure that the gallery was empty, then knocked softly at the prior's door.

Prior Edmund heard the gentle rapping, rubbed his face and got up from the prie-dieu where he had been praying. Heavy with sleep, he turned the key in the lock and without thinking lifted the latch and pulled the door open. He wanted to scream but a black, leather glove squeezed his mouth and pushed him back into the room. Edmund's heart thudded with terror. The four intruders, clothed in black from head to toe, looked like night crows. He half expected that if they spread their cloaks they would be able to drift like bats across the room. For a moment he imagined he had died and was in Hell, then the hand on his mouth tightened and pushed him up against the wall.

'I will release my hand,' the voice grated. 'But if you scream or raise any alarm, believe me, you will die!'

The hand was released.

'Well, mumbler, do you wish to live or die?'

Edmund was not the stuff that martyrs are made of.

'Live!' he whispered through bruised lips.

'The secret tunnels and passages?'

'There are no such.'

He received a stinging blow across his face.

'Please, mumbler. The secret passageways and tunnels beneath this place.' The man drew back his hand, but Edmund nodded. 'We wish to be taken there. You will show us the secret entrances and take us into the chamber where our master lies. We will move behind you. If we meet anyone, you will not stop or talk but use your authority to protect us. You understand?'

Prior Edmund could only agree. The black-garbed figure grasped him by the shoulder and pushed him towards the door. From outside came a faint rumble of thunder. The leader turned towards the lead-paned glass of the window and smiled.

'Fitting,' he whispered. 'Fitting indeed.'

He bundled Edmund out into the deserted gallery and the prior, sweat-soaked, his heart hammering, stomach churning, legs feeling strangely stiff, led them down the stairs and across the grounds. They entered another building, the oldest part of the friary. This housed the library on the upper floor and a long council chamber, rarely used, on the ground floor. The prior, with shaking hands, inserted his key into the lock and entered the musty darkness, his heart jumping as the black-clad figures slipped behind him. The door slammed shut. Candles were produced and lit. Edmund pushed farther forward.

'Show us!' the leader hissed.

Stumbling and shaking with fright, the prior led them across the rush-strewn floor towards the far end of the chamber, stopping just in front of the wooden wainscoting.

'I can't see,' he muttered.

The candle was pushed closer and he felt a vice-like grip on the back of his neck.

'Find it!'

Edmund moaned with fear. He would have prayed had the grip on his neck not tightened.

'No prattling or mumbling!' the voice hissed.

Edmund's sweat-soaked hands feverishly felt the wooden panelling. He tugged at the hold on his neck.

'Please,' he said. 'Let me go. I can't . . .'

The grip was released. Edmund took a deep breath and stared at the pool of light thrown against the carved panelling. Then he saw the knot of wood on the corner of one of the panels. He pressed it and the panel swung loose. Edmund pulled it open, put his hand inside, drew back a bolt, lifted a latch and pushed against the wooden wainscoting. The entire section of the wall moved silently back on its carefully contrived hinges.

'Go down!' the voice ordered.

A candle was thrust into his hand. Edmund gulped and led his captors down the steep stone steps. At the bottom, unbidden, he lit a huge cresset torch and the ancient chamber flared into light. The leader of the group sighed with pleasure as he glimpsed the great steel-bound coffin placed in the centre of the room.

'So, it is here!'

He snapped his fingers and his companions raced forward and began to prise loose the lid. Edmund, thinking he had been forgotten, edged towards the steps. He thought he would escape. He heard the lid crash off, a cry of delighted surprise, then his shoulder was gripped and, even before he knew it, his throat was slit from ear to ear.

The next morning Sir Godfrey and Alexander slept late. They were roused by a red-cheeked Mathilda, who said that Dame Edith was waiting in the parlour below and would they like to break their fast? Alexander slipped out of his bed, recalled the events of the previous evening and put his face in his hands.

'When will this business be finished?' he groaned to himself. 'When can we go home?'

He shook himself alert, stripped, shaved, washed and put on fresh garments. This time he needed no reminder to clasp the sword belt around his waist. Downstairs, Sir Godfrey was already breaking his fast on bread, fish and watered wine and questioning Dame Edith further on the Strigoi. Alexander made his greetings and joined them as the exorcist described the night-wanderers or herlethingi.

'That's the Saxon word for the night-wanderers,' she explained. 'They are mentioned by Walter Mapp in his chronicle, *De nugis curialium.*'

'Do they really exist?' Alexander asked.

'Well, Mapp says that they have been seen in Brittany – people supposed to be long dead who reappear as living beings and wander the face of the earth in caravans of horses, men and carts. The theologian Peter Le Bois, in his fourteenth epistle, says that in the reign of our Henry II armies of these night-wanderers rambled about in their mad vagrancy, making no sound. They were seen tramping along the marches of Hereford and Wales with carts and beasts of burden, pack-saddles, provender, baskets, birds and dogs, a mixed multitude of men and women.'

'Are they Strigoi as well?' Alexander asked, breaking up a small manchet loaf.

'They might be, though the point I was making to Sir Godfrey is that reality is not what it appears to be; the dead make their presence felt.' She smiled as she put a small piece of fish into her mouth and chewed it carefully. 'What we now face, however, is different; I feel these Strigoi are waiting for something.'

'Such as?'

'A leader, one of their Dark Lords who has been undead for many years.'

Alexander shivered. The exorcist's words brought back the terrors of the previous evening, so he excused himself, saying he needed some fresh air. Once outside the guest house he walked directly to the garden where he had last seen Emily and his heart leapt with pleasure as he rounded a small privet hedge and saw her sitting there. She was clothed in a cream-coloured, fur-lined cloak, jabbing a needle in a piece of tapestry and singing softly under her breath. Alexander coughed. Emily looked up and Alexander's heart leapt again at the beauty of those splendid blue eyes.

'My lady, good morning.'

Emily smiled, stuck the needle into the piece of tapestry and indicated that Alexander should sit on the turf seat beside her. Alexander thrilled with the sheer warmth and pleasure of being so close. He caught a faint whiff of her perfume and marvelled at the golden roundness of her face.

'You are well, my lady?'

She moved her hand closer to his. 'I am, sir, though I am afeared.'

'Of what?'

'Dame Constance told me what happened last night.' Her blue eyes swept up to meet his. 'You were brave,' she sighed, 'so very brave in protecting the boy.' A small pink tip of tongue wetted her lips. 'Dame Constance says you are in Oxford to hunt down evil men. You must be frightened.'

'If I have your favour, my lady—' Alexander moved his hand closer to hers, 'then I would go down to meet Satan himself.'

He half turned to face her squarely. 'And the more I see of you, the closer I come to you, the braver I become.'

'Does that please you?' she whispered, slipping her small, hand in his.

'My lady, my world stops at your gentleness.'

Lady Emily half smiled as she began the courteous, graceful dance of chivalrous flirtation.

'You think of me often, sir?'

'No, my lady, I think of you always.'

Emily pressed his hand and moved in a little closer.

'I am a maid,' she murmured, 'unspoken for and not betrothed.'

'My lady, I could change that.'

'Are you noble born?'

'Aye and of noble heart.'

'Do you easily fall in love?'

'My lady, only once.'

She blinked those beautiful eyes. 'And do you miss her?'

Now Alexander pressed her hand. 'My lady, how can I, when I am sitting so close to her?'

Emily moved her face, turning her cheek slightly away.

'You must capture many hearts?'

'Why many, my lady, when, for me, there's only one.'

Emily looked into the clerk's merry eyes. She felt guilty for she thought of Sir Godfrey with his face of stone and burning looks.

'Do you love me, sir?'

'My lady, you have said it.'

'But, when you are gone?' she whispered.

Alexander slipped off the seat and fell on to one knee, holding her hand and gazing adoringly up at her angelic face.

'Can a man forget his right hand? Can a man ignore the beating of his heart?'

Lady Emily was about to reply when she heard a sound and turned. Sir Godfrey stood there and, by the stricken look on his face and the sheer passion in his eyes, she knew the knight truly loved her. If she was honest, she would have preferred him, proud as an eagle, to be the one kneeling before her.

'Sir Godfrey,' she called. 'Good morrow to you!'

Alexander rose hastily to his feet.

'Sir,' he blustered, 'you come unannounced.'

'Sir,' Sir Godfrey replied sardonically, 'if I thought I needed

177

a herald I would have hired one. Sir Oswald and Proctor Ormiston are in the great house, they demand our presence.'

But Sir Godfrey's eyes were for Lady Emily. She stared coolly back. For God's sake, she thought, make a move, declare yourself. Sir Godfrey, however, turned on his heel and walked back behind the hedge. Alexander sighed, took Emily's hand and raised it to her lips.

'My lady, another time.'

Then he hastily followed, leaving Emily to fume at Sir Godfrey's abrupt departure.

'Sir Godfrey!' Alexander called.

The knight turned and Alexander glimpsed the fury in his face.

'Sir,' Alexander declared, 'you lack manners.'

Sir Godfrey stepped closer, his hand falling to the hilt of his sword.

'You bloody clerk!' he snarled. 'With your glib phrases and flattering words!'

Alexander smiled. So, you have a heart, he thought. Blood does beat in your brains and send fiery messages coursing through your veins.

Sir Godfrey moved closer. 'Do you find me amusing?'

Alexander stepped back, his hand going to his sword.

'Sir Godfrey, I respect you.'

'Don't play with me!'

The knight's hands moved quickly and the sword seemed to leap from his scabbard. Alexander followed suit, stepping back, raising his own sword to cross that of the knight.

'Why?' Alexander pleaded.

'Because, sir, you insult me.'

'Before Heaven, I do not!'

178

Sir Godfrey took a deep breath, closed his eyes and lowered his sword.

'No, sir, you do not.'

He sheathed his weapon, Alexander did likewise and the knight stretched out his hand.

'I find it difficult,' he muttered. 'I am not well versed in words.'

Alexander grinned, took the knight's hand and shook it vigorously.

'Words are nothing.'

'Don't quarrel!'

Sir Godfrey whirled around. Dame Edith stood nearby under the overhanging branches of an elm.

'Don't quarrel!' she repeated. She flailed her hands at her side. 'Why do you men always have to fight for love? You see a pretty face and you become like bucks on heat. You, Sir Godfrey, are a knight. And you, Alexander McBain, are his trusted clerk. You have a task to do. So, finish it! And, afterwards I shall judge between you.' She half smiled. 'I will be your Queen of Love!' She beckoned them forward as if they were recalcitrant boys. 'I know how the heart hungers,' she whispered. 'We crave for love, the human heart is an inexhaustible hunter for it. But let it wait, your visitors expect you.'

The two men sheepishly followed the exorcist back to the guest house, where Sir Oswald Beauchamp and Proctor Ormiston impatiently awaited them.

'God's teeth!' the sheriff snarled. 'Sir Godfrey, you must come with us. Last night the Trinitarian friary was attacked. Prior Edmund is dead. They say a secret chamber has been violated.'

'And what else?' Dame Edith spoke.

'A coffin was emptied,' Ormiston blurted out. 'Why did they kill for a corpse?'

'Oh, sweet Lord!' Dame Edith murmured and sat down on one of the stools. 'That fool of a prior!' She shook her head. 'So, it's happened.'

'What has?' Alexander asked.

'They must have released their Dark Lord,' Dame Edith replied. 'The Strigoi Sir Hugh Mortimer imprisoned there so many hundreds of years ago.'

'Folderol!' McBain snapped. 'Oh, Dame Edith, I accept your night-walkers, your drinkers of blood, your Strigoi, your Shape-shifters! But how can a man survive in a coffin for hundreds of years?'

Dame Edith rapped the top of the table.

'Have you not listened?' she snapped. 'The Strigoi never die! If their corpses survive, they merely sleep!'

'In which case,' the knight intervened, 'why doesn't this Dark Lord just rise from his coffin and walk?'

'He has to be summoned,' Dame Edith replied wearily. 'He has to be invited back. He has to have the blood sacrifice poured over him, then he comes to life.' She looked in the direction of the four men and quietly cursed their uncertainty. 'What is so original about that?' she cried. 'McBain, do you pray?'

The clerk nodded.

'Sir Godfrey?'

'Of course!'

'And you, Sheriff Beauchamp, Proctor Ormiston?'

Both men agreed.

'And when you pray,' Dame Edith exclaimed, 'you call upon Christ to come to you or invoke the favour of your patron saint, yes?'

The men nodded their heads in agreement.

'The Strigoi are no different,' she declared. 'They believe that, if they call, the forces of Hell will answer.' She got to her feet, pushing the bench aside. 'Let us go to the friary. You'll see!' she rasped. 'Before the week is out, you will see the powers of their Dark Lord.'

Words between the pilgrims

The knight paused in his story-telling and looked around the taproom. He particularly watched the monk, whose eyes never left him. Then he turned towards his golden-haired son, the squire, who stood in the doorway with the yeoman beside him. 'Are you well, Robert?' the knight asked.

'Aye, sir. But memory can be a sharp prick and the soul never forgets.'

The knight smiled and gestured his son and the yeoman to sit down, pushing the wine jug towards their empty cups.

'Let's finish the tale, sir knight!' the wife of Bath, half-way down the table, leaned forward, her face beaming in a gap-toothed smile. 'Sir knight, you play with us, you tell us about this beautiful Lady Emily and in your tale today, the one about Arcite and Palamon, the lady is also called Emily.'

The knight raised his eyebrows. 'So?'

The wife of Bath wagged a finger at him.

'In your tale about ancient Thebes all your names are Greek – Arcite, Palamon and so forth. Why, in both tales, the one you tell now and the one you told today, are your heroines called Emily?'

The knight smiled faintly but the wife of Bath was not easy to discourage.

'Tell me the name of your wife,' she demanded.

'I've been married twice,' the knight replied. 'Once to a lady called Katerina.'

'And the second time?'

The knight shrugged. 'Let me finish my tale.'

PART IV

Chapter 1

They found the Trinitarian friary in uproar. The sub-prior, a young man called Roger, met them in the small guest house. He was full of panic, constantly muttering, 'What can I do? What can I do?'

'You can keep your courage,' Sir Godfrey grated. 'Now, tell me what happened?'

'The bell sounded for matins this morning,' the sub-prior replied. 'We assembled in the choir to sing divine office. Only then did I notice Prior Edmund was missing. I thought he was ill, but the lay brothers I sent to look for him came back to report that his room was empty and the door half-open. So I ordered a search. You'd best come with me.'

He led them across the grounds and into the musty council chamber. Dame Edith, however, stopped just outside the door. She moved her head from side to side. McBain could see how her hands trembled, so he took her arm.

'Dame Edith, you are well?'

'Such evil,' she murmured. 'It has gone, but the stink remains, the stench of corruption. The perfume of wickedness hangs heavy in the air.'

'What's she chattering about?' the sub-prior asked anxiously.

'She's not chattering!' McBain snarled. 'For God's sake,

haven't you heard the legends about this place?'

The sub-prior mumbled an apology. 'I thought they were stories for children. We have heard of the secret passageways and chambers but, until this morning . . .'

His voice trailed off as he gestured towards the end of the hall where the secret door was still open. Half-way down the hall he stopped to light some candles, then he led them down the steps to the secret chamber. At the bottom Sir Godfrey drew his sword, for even he felt the hostility of that stark, empty chamber. The sub-prior's hesitancy increased and McBain had an overwhelming desire to run back up the steps away from this dreadful room. Dame Edith, however, recovered her poise.

'The evil has gone,' she murmured. 'Sir Godfrey, there is a coffin, yes? Lead me across to it.'

They went across to the lead-lined oaken casket in the middle of the floor. On either side broken chains hung and the samite on which the corpse had lain was lying rumpled on the floor.

'Describe it to me,' Dame Edith commanded.

Sir Godfrey did so, breaking off at intervals to stare into the corners of the room, fearful that some malignant presence lurked there waiting to attack him.

'Nothing's corrupted?' Dame Edith asked.

'Nothing, my lady.'

'It proves what I said,' she cried. 'The person buried here was one of the undead, a Strigoi lord. Now he has been released. We will have to hunt him down.'

The sub-prior, Roger, listened round-eyed.

'Who is she?' he asked, mystified.

'Never you mind,' Sir Godfrey snapped. He produced a small scroll from his wallet. 'Do you recognize the seal?'

The sub-prior examined the warrant in the light of the flickering candle.

'Why, yes, it is the king's seal.'

'And what does the letter say?'

'What the bearer of this letter orders to be done is to be done immediately and without question.'

'Good!' Sir Godfrey continued. 'You have read it. You understand it, you have seen the seal on it. Now, this is my order. I want the library on the top storey cleared of all possessions, moveables, manuscripts, books.'

'And then what?' the sub-prior whimpered.

'This chamber cleansed by fire and the entire building razed to the ground. Once this is done, the bricks and the timber are to be soaked in oil and purged by fire. What rubble is left is to be thrown into a deep pit.'

'That's impossible.'

Sir Godfrey grabbed the monk by the front of his habit.

'I mean,' the sub-prior pleaded, 'I need the permission of my superiors.'

'And I act on the authority of the king,' Sir Godfrey whispered hoarsely. 'And, if you don't do it, I'll come back, arrest you for high treason and burn the whole bloody place to the ground! If your stupid prior had been honest and co-operative in the first place, this tragedy might not have happened! Now, promise me that by tomorrow evening the work will have been done!'

'It must be done,' Dame Edith insisted.

The sub-prior nodded. The knight released his grip.

'Now, let's get out of this hell-hole,' he said.

'Don't you wish to see Prior Edmund's body?'

'He is dead?' McBain asked.

'Of course, his throat has been slit.'

187

'Then he is in God's hands, not ours. So, what can we do?'

Outside in the grounds Brother Lanfranc, the archivist, was waiting for them.

'Sir knight, the evil has gone?'

'Yes and now this place must be razed.'

The old man's rheumy eyes crinkled and he cackled with laughter.

'I always said it should be. But my books and manuscripts will be safe?'

'Of course.'

The rheumy eyes lit with pleasure. He looked contemptuously at the young sub-prior. 'Then I will show you something kept in my possession, a journal.'

Roger made to protest but Sir Godfrey told him to be silent and go about his business. They followed the ancient one up a steep flight of stairs and into the long library, very similar to the one they had visited at St Mary's church. Lanfranc lit the candles under their protective metal caps and, wheezing and muttering, opened a huge, iron-bound coffer secured by five locks. He rummaged among the contents and brought out a thin, calf-bound ledger which he invited McBain to inspect. The clerk studied it curiously – first the title page, then the different entries – turning the pages over quickly.

'What is it?' Dame Edith asked impatiently.

'It's a secret journal,' Alexander explained. 'The secrets of this house were passed from abbot to abbot. They had a duty every so often to inspect the crypt and ensure all was well.' He tapped the title page. 'They were admonished not to tamper with the coffin and, on their oath of obedience to God, enter each visitation in this ledger.' He smiled wryly. 'But I suspect that though some abbots faithfully followed this instruction others were overcome by curiosity. Years ago one of them actually opened the coffin. Nothing happened, so different successors followed suit.'

'But it would have an effect,' Dame Edith insisted.

'And it did,' Alexander replied. 'Do you remember those incidents mentioned in the manuscripts at the university library?'

'Yes,' Sir Godfrey said. 'How certain people in the city who had an evil reputation later came back from the dead.'

'Well,' Alexander continued, turning to one page, 'we now have the reason. Remember, I described an incident in the summer of 1297? In that same year, according to this journal, the abbot visited the secret room. I suspect he broke his oath and peeped into the coffin.'

'So,' Sir Godfrey declared, 'every time that coffin was interfered with, some evil escaped to wreak its effect in the city?'

'Of course,' Dame Edith interrupted. 'If you put this journal next to the chronicle you would see a correlation. Every time an abbot broke his oath and tampered with that coffin, the evil influence of the Strigoi made its presence felt.' Dame Edith sat down on a stool. 'We must not forget,' she continued, 'that evil is no different from anything else. As the Blessed Aquinas says, following Plato, what is natural only mirrors the supernatural. If you open an oven, heat escapes; unstop a jar of perfume or a flask of wine and the fragrance rises in the air. Every time that coffin was opened some of its evil seeped out to make its presence felt. Now the cause of that evil has escaped and may God help us all.'

'What do you mean?' Sir Godfrey asked.

'This Strigoi lord,' Dame Edith explained, 'will use the coven that rescued him to gather others around him, in this kingdom and across the seas.'

'So all must be destroyed?'

Dame Edith licked her dry lips. She sensed that the confrontation with this evil was not far off.

'We must destroy either the Strigoi lord or his followers; he would be powerless without a coven to sustain and nourish him. But it must be done, and done quickly!' She snaked her hand out and caught McBain's wrist. 'Look at the last entries. What do you find?'

Alexander turned the yellowing pages.

'Oh, sweet Lord!' he breathed, 'over the last year the deceased Abbot Samson went at least a dozen times into that crypt.'

'I thought so,' Lanfranc chortled. 'I thought so. I knew he was up to mischief, he kept asking for the journal. On one occasion I objected but he over-ruled me.'

'What was he after?' Alexander asked.

'He was pig-headed,' Lanfranc hissed bitterly. 'This house has never prospered. He thought the crypt contained the key to secret wealth, which he could use to drain the fens and bogs. But I tell you this, sir knight, forget that runny-nosed sub-prior. I leave this friary tomorrow. I am journeying to the mother house in France. I will go down on my knees and beg my superiors in Christ to burn this place to the ground.'

McBain went back to the journal. 'There's one final entry,' he said, 'not written in the abbot's hand.'

'Ah, that would be that fool Prior Edmund.'

'What is it?' Sir Godfrey asked.

'It just says that in the dead of night Abbot Samson and another went into the crypt. Abbot Samson never left alive.'

'Typical!' Lanfranc jeered. 'Samson lacked the wisdom to consult with me or anyone else. Edmund thought he would clear his conscience by making the entry.'

'How did Samson die?' Alexander asked.

'Fear, fright, poison,' Dame Edith answered. 'But the fool is dead, God rest him!'

'But the other isn't,' Sir Godfrey added. 'I wonder who this Strigoi was?'

'May I keep this?' Alexander asked, tapping the journal with his fingers.

Lanfranc nodded. 'Of course, it won't be needed again, will it?'

They collected their horses from the stables and rode back to the convent of St Anne's. Just as they entered the main gate, Dame Edith pulled in her reins and gestured at both men to draw close.

'No more running about,' she whispered. 'There could be other attacks, other murders. But, terrible as they are, they are just moonbeams, mere shadows of the substance we seek. You, master clerk, have all the evidence you need. You know now what we face, so use that brain of yours! Discover who this "other" is, who joined Abbot Samson in that crypt, and we'll find the Strigoi lord.'

Alexander smiled, dismounted and returned to the guest house. Once he had washed and eaten he collected the journal, with all the other notes and memoranda he had written since arriving at Oxford, and went to sit in one of the study carrels of the convent's scriptorium. At first he was restless, finding it difficult to concentrate. He was horrified by what he had seen at the priory yet he was also distracted by Emily's fair face and the hurt he had seen in the knight's eyes. He sighed, drew a piece of parchment over, carefully wrote out what he wanted and, using his charm, asked one of the lay sisters to take it to the lady Emily. Alexander then returned to his labours but found it difficult to make any sense of what they had learnt. He remembered Robert Cotterill and, leaving his quill and manuscripts, went across to the infirmary, where he found the boy playing marbles in the centre of the floor. Alexander crouched and watched him and, when invited, joined in.

'You are good at this aren't you?' the boy said. 'You are good at everything. You can read and write and you can use a sword. You are even better than that knight who never speaks.'

Alexander smiled. 'I used to be very good at skittles,' he said. 'Have you ever played that, Robert?'

The boy stuck his thumb in his mouth and shook his head.

'You have ten polished pins of wood,' Alexander explained. He took hold of the marbles. 'And you set them up like this and then try to knock them down with a ball. If you are really clever, really good, you can do it with one throw.'

'I'd like that game,' the boy said.

'And I'll buy you it,' Alexander promised. 'But, look, Robert, I need your help, though it may cause you pain. Can you tell me what happened? What you heard or saw the night your sister and parents died?'

He saw fear and pain cloud the young boy's eyes. He would have liked to have given Robert a hug and tell him to forget his question. But, surely, Alexander thought, the boy knew something.

'Please, Robert, try,' he pleaded. 'If you do that, I can bring a very evil man to justice.'

The boy crouched down on his heels and closed his eyes.

'I was playing a game,' he intoned. 'I was playing in my secret chamber. Mother was cross with Father so I thought I would stay there. I was happy watching the candle-flame flicker. I heard a knock on the door. Mummy laughed as someone came in.'

'Did you hear anything?'

'Yes, I thought about that. I heard a man saying "ditch".'

'Ditch?'

'Yes.'

'Then what happened?'

'Mother went into the kitchen, there was a clatter of pots, then she came back. I thought the visitor was a neighbour so I dozed for a while. When I woke up—' The boy's lower lip began to quiver. 'When I woke up I knew something terrible had happened. I stayed still. I heard someone move outside, then they were gone.' The boy crept closer and Alexander put his arm around him.

'Shush!' he said, patting him gently. 'Are you sure there is nothing else?'

'No,' the boy mumbled.

Alexander comforted him for a while, slipped a piece of marchpane into his hand and went back to the scriptorium. He took a piece of parchment, smoothing it out, holding the four corners down with metal weights, and began to list all that he knew. The strange deaths, men and women dying with no sign of forced entry, no commotion or alarm, yet the corpses left drained of blood. The opening of the crypt by Abbot Samson and the attack on Prior Edmund. The death of the Hospitaller in the forest. The disappearance of the relic. The phrase 'Le chevalier outre mer' above the dead Hospitaller's bed in the castle. The death of Laetitia, the tavern maid. The metal discs found on her and the dead Hospitaller. The old legend about the devil returning to 'the rock near the new keep'. Little Robert Cotterill's description and the use of that strange word 'ditch'. Finally, who was the person who had accompanied Abbot Samson, the 'other' – Prior Edmund had used the Latin word '*alius*' – of the journal? Alexander half dozed for a while, different thoughts teeming in his mind, then he shook himself awake. Prior Edmund would have had a classical education.

Why did he use the word '*alius*'? Shouldn't he have used '*alter*', meaning 'the other of two'? Why did '*alius*' seem significant? Where had he read it? Alexander suddenly went cold as he remembered. '*Christus alius*', 'another Christ'!

'Oh, my God!' he exclaimed. 'Of course! Oh, my God!'

He ran back towards the infirmary. Robert was still playing marbles with one of the lay sisters, laughing and clapping his hands at her lack of skill.

'Robert! Are you sure that the visitor to your house said "ditch"? Or did he say "benedicite"?'

Robert stuck his thumb in his mouth and nodded. Alexander gripped him by the arms.

'Robert, did he say "benedicite"? You must answer me!'

The thumb popped out.

'Yes, he did. "Benedicite".' The little boy stammered over the syllables.

Alexander glared at the surprised lay sister.

'Go!' he ordered. 'Tell Sir Godfrey, Dame Edith and Dame Constance I must see them! Tell the lady abbess a messenger must be sent immediately to the sheriff and to Proctor Ormiston. I will meet them all in the guest house. Go on!' he urged. He turned back to the boy. 'Robert! You stay here!' He pointed to where the infirmarian was working, further down the dormitory. 'Never leave her side!'

Alexander went back to the scriptorium, where he began to write hurriedly. Sir Godfrey came storming over to ask what was the matter, but McBain waved him away. He stayed for at least an hour and, by the time he reached the guest house, everyone was waiting in the small refectory. Beauchamp and Ormiston looked furious. Dame Constance sat imperiously tapping the top of the table with her long, slender fingers. Sir Godfrey walked up and down like some hunting dog. Only

Dame Edith seemed composed.

'I know who the Strigoi master is,' Alexander declared as they all took their seats, Dame Constance serving her guests goblets of white wine.

'I have no proof, as yet, but logic and commonsense dictate the truth.'

'Who is it?'

'Father Andrew, priest of St Peter's near the castle.'

'Nonsense!' Beauchamp snarled, half rising to his feet. 'How dare you malign such a good priest?'

Sir Godfrey drew his dagger and banged its pommel on the table top.

'You will hear the clerk out!'

Alexander got to his feet, finding it difficult to contain his excitement.

'First,' he declared, 'we have killers who can gain access to a house in the dead of night, murder their victims and escape scot-free without causing any tumult or commotion. Who better than a priest? He could slip along the streets and alleyways of Oxford unchallenged by the watch. He could even pretend to be carrying a host. He knocks on the door and enters saying "benedicite", a blessing on you all.'

'Father Andrew may be a youngish, fairly strong man,' Proctor Ormiston interrupted, 'but could he kill so many people?'

'Ah!' Alexander picked up his wine cup. 'What happens if he brought some wine, a gift? Robert Cotterill heard the "benedicite" but, being a child, he only caught the second syllable, the one anyone emphasizes, "–dicite". He also heard his mother go into the kitchen for cups or goblets. The wine is poured and drunk but it contains some sleeping powder – crushed poppy seeds or valerian. In a few minutes the householders are drugged.' Alexander put his wine cup down.

'And, if there were young people in the house, Father Andrew might allow them to sip from his goblet. He made sure he never drank any.'

'So, he killed them all himself?'

'Oh, no. He opened the door to allow others in.'

'But my guards,' Beauchamp objected. 'The city watch, they never apprehended anyone.'

'Sir Godfrey,' Alexander asked, 'when we rode the streets of Oxford that night, whom did we see?'

'No one.'

'No, think again.'

'A few beggars.' The knight's jaw dropped. 'Of course!' he breathed. 'Who could dream that some beggar pretending to be maimed, covered in dirt and clothed in rags, was the killer?'

'Of course,' Alexander continued. 'The beggars are always with us. We pass them by, treat them with contempt. Now, what happens if four or five of these beggars are really Father Andrew's accomplices? Some of those young men who help him at the church, giving bread and meat to the poor. A fact I'll return to in a minute. These young men, using their beggarly disguise and the cloak of night, take up position outside a house like the Cotterills'. Once the family are drugged, Father Andrew lets his accomplices in. They slit their victims' throats, perpetrate their abominable practices and slip back into the night.' Alexander paused. 'Never once are they disturbed, except when they came across that drunken student you later arrested, Sir Oswald. They knew of our coming here so they daubed the student with blood to mislead us and passed on.'

'What other proof do you have?' Dame Edith asked quietly.

'Well, both the Hospitaller and the dead slattern from the Mitre carried black metal discs. These are probably counters given out by Father Andrew and his helpers so the poor can

196

claim their bowl of pottage and loaf of bread. Don't you remember when we passed him outside his church?'

Sir Godfrey nodded.

'But why kill those two?' Proctor Ormiston asked.

'Well, I think Laetitia was bringing the counter to us as some proof of the link between her dead sweetheart, Eudo, and Father Andrew. And in the Hospitaller's case—' Alexander smiled sourly and sat down. 'Don't forget he was a fugitive from the law. He arrived in Oxford hungry and thirsty and what does he do? Where can he get free food?'

'Of course!' The doubt ebbed from the sheriff's face. 'He would join the other beggars outside St Peter's church. That's why he had a counter.'

'Ah, he did more than that. He was carrying a precious relic with him. I suspect he went into the church and hid that somewhere. Sir Oswald, or you, Dame Constance, you know Oxford well. In St Peter's church is there the tomb of a crusader?'

'A "chevalier outre mer"!' Ormiston breathed.

'Exactly,' Alexander confirmed. 'A knight who had gone across the sea.'

'Yes, there is,' Beauchamp replied. 'A large tomb in one of the transepts. The effigy of a knight lies on top, legs crossed at the ankles as a sign that he had served in the Crusades.'

'If we go there, I'm sure we'll find the reliquary. Now, Father Andrew was a demon priest. He may have pretended to say mass but he never actually consecrated the bread or wine. He may have pretended to keep the blessed sacrament reserved in the tabernacle but, in reality, he didn't. Accordingly, the church posed no threat to him. However, the presence of a powerful reliquary, if Dame Edith is to be believed, would disturb the wickedness of himself and his followers. Therefore the church was closed on the pretence that the roof needed repair. In reality, the Strigoi, Father Andrew, would have an excuse not to be anywhere near the relic. The Hospitaller, of course, had to die for his crime.'

'What other proof is there?' Dame Edith asked.

'Ah well, now we come to the opening of the crypt at the Trinitarian friary by Abbot Samson. You may remember that Abbot Samson was visited by someone who accompanied him there. Prior Edmund described him as *"alius"*, "another". However, Edmund was an educated man, he should have used "alter". I was intrigued. But when I spoke to little Robert and heard about "benedicite", I understood. Dame Edith, what is a name sometimes given to a priest?'

'*Christus alius*,' she replied. 'Another Christ.'

'I think that is what Edmund meant. Samson and another priest went to the crypt. Somehow or other Father Andrew convinced Samson that his presence there was necessary, playing on the abbot's desire for wealth, the means to enrich his monastery.' Alexander shrugged. 'Father Andrew really wanted to ensure that the Strigoi lord, buried alive centuries earlier by Sir Hugo Mortimer, still lay there.' Alexander toyed with the cup in his hand. 'There are other pieces of evidence: the attack on me, when the Strigoi were really trying to kill young Robert. And who knew he was here except Father Andrew and the people in this room?'

'What about the students who disappeared?' Ormiston said.

'Ah, that's one piece in the puzzle that is difficult to fit. But, don't forget, they disappeared before the attacks in the city itself. Somehow or other Father Andrew got to know the Luminosi, he exploited their secrecy and used them to gain access to the library archives so as to study the manuscripts, then he killed them. But there are limits to the victims he could choose; when he and his coven wanted fresh blood, they began their attacks in the city.'

'Why didn't they just kill the poor they served?' Sir Godfrey asked.

'Perhaps they did,' Alexander replied. 'One or two. Such poor creatures would never be missed but Father Andrew wished to protect his public reputation. Moreover, if the poor began to die, someone might suspect.'

Sir Oswald Beauchamp heaved himself to his feet, his podgy, white face a mixture of trust and disbelief.

'What you say, Master McBain, could be the truth.' He pointed at Dame Edith. 'But why didn't she recognize him? Why didn't she sense the evil?'

'Even Satan can appear as an angel of light,' Dame Edith replied. 'You are a law officer, Sir Oswald, you have experience of crime. Can you tell a criminal just because you are in his presence?' She shrugged. 'Then neither could I tell this demon-possessed priest. Unless he made a mistake, let the mask slip, and he was very careful not to do that.'

'Why did they need so much blood?' Ormiston asked, as if talking to himself.

'To refresh themselves,' Dame Edith answered. 'To practise their rites, to drink, to revive the body of their Strigoi lord.'

Beauchamp walked towards the door.

'Sir Oswald, where are you going?' the knight asked.

'*We*,' the sheriff emphasized, 'we, everyone in this room, with the exception of Dame Constance, will go to the church of St Peter. We'll find the proof there.'

'The proof is there.' Alexander smiled faintly. 'You told us about the ancient legends, when "the devil from the old keep comes to the rock near the new keep".'

'What do you mean?' Sir Oswald snapped.

'Peter is "rock" in Latin,' Alexander explained, 'and St Peter's is near the keep of your castle. The old keep is now the site of the Trinitarian friary.'

Sir Oswald just shook his head. 'Perhaps you tell the truth, clerk, but let's see for ourselves.'

They found the church cloaked in darkness, nor was any light showing from the priest's house. Sir Oswald's soldiers forced the door and, as soon as they were inside, Dame Edith said she felt faint.

'Great evil has been here,' she whispered as Alexander helped her on to a stood in the small kitchen, while one of Sir Oswald's soldiers began to light candles. The knight looked around the clean, gaunt, white-washed chamber.

'Nothing remarkable,' he observed, yet he too felt the fear tightening his jaw and curling the hair on the nape of his neck.

'So clean,' Alexander murmured. 'Too clean. And, have you noticed? No crucifix. Nothing to indicate he is a priest.' He sniffed. 'And that smell, stale as rotting food!'

Sir Godfrey drew his sword and climbed the rickety steps up to the small loft that served as a bedroom. He called for a candle and one was passed up.

'Alexander McBain!' he shouted. 'Come!'

The clerk followed. At first he could see nothing wrong – just a simple chest, a bed and two battered coffers. Sir Godfrey lifted the candle higher and Alexander's stomach lurched. On the far wall a crucifix stood upside down. The corpse of a rat had been nailed to it and, on either side, a red eye had been painted. In the flickering candle-light it looked as if some baleful face was watching them. Alexander cursed, walked over and knocked the blasphemy from the wall.

'He's fled!' Sir Godfrey said, 'and he left that as his farewell!'

Chapter 2

They went back downstairs. Sir Oswald, Ormiston and the soldiers clustered near the door like frightened children.

'Don't eat or drink anything!' the knight ordered. 'Anything at all!'

Sir Godfrey was about to lead them out when he noticed, in the far corner near the hearth, a small iron ring. He went over, kicking the rushes aside to reveal a wooden trapdoor. Sir Godfrey hacked the padlock off with an axe lying near the wall, pulled up the trapdoor and went down. Immediately he caught the stench of corruption, of stale blood. It reminded him of battlefields, when the fighting is done and the corpses have to be buried.

'Lord!' he breathed, looking up at Alexander, who handed down a candle. 'What horrors here!'

McBain followed him down, covering his nose and mouth with his cloak. At first they thought it was just an ordinary cellar, though it stank like a slaughterhouse. Above them they could hear the cries and exclamations of the rest as the stench seeped out into the kitchen.

Sir Godfrey edged his way forward. As the flame of the candle grew stronger, he saw that a pit, about three feet deep and ten feet square, had been dug in the middle of the cellar. Sir

Godfrey fought back the inclination to gag, went to the edge of the pit and looked down. It seemed to be covered in some sort of drape and he tested this with his dagger. He held the candle closer to discover it was ox-hide, large pieces sewn together and laid across each other to cover the entire pit. He leant down and scraped his dagger along the leather. He then examined his dagger point in the full glow of the candle-light.

'Blood!' he exclaimed. 'Like some rotten wine vat. Oh, my God!'

He looked over his shoulder at the clerk, but McBain was now leaning against the wall retching violently.

'They brought the blood here!' Sir Godfrey whispered to himself. 'They drained their victims and brought the blood here, probably using wineskins, turning this into some sort of horrible vat!'

The knight could stand no more so he helped McBain up into the kitchen. The sheriff and proctor had already left. Only Dame Edith sat slumped on a stool, her head forward, mouth gaping.

'Take me from here!' she whispered. 'Get me out of this damned hell-hole!'

McBain wiped his eyes and face on the edge of his cloak and gently led her out. Sir Godfrey dropped the burning candle on to the dry rushes and slammed the door behind him. McBain stood, sucking in the clean, night air, with Dame Edith resting on his arm. The knight walked over to inform Sir Oswald and Ormiston of what they had found. Proctor Ormiston could stand no more. He glared speechlessly at the sheriff, gathered up his robe and fled into the darkness. The sheriff himself had lost all his usual bombast and bonhomie. He was a mere shadow of his former self, while his soldiers muttered among themselves that they had no business here. Sir Oswald dismissed them as the knight shouted, 'Send them back to the castle!'

The sheriff walked over to the men. 'You are to tell no one!' he declared.

'Don't worry about that, sir!' one of them replied, mounting his horse. He tugged the tabard over his head and flung it on the ground. His companions did likewise.

'God damn you, Sir Oswald, for bringing us here! And I say a fig for your orders!'

The soldier glanced at the fire now burning the priest's house and pushed his grizzled face down towards the knight.

'We are country lads, sir, not your hardened mercenaries. Our homes lie in the villages miles from here. We intend to go back there. This city is cursed. Let the likes of Sir Oswald tend to this business!'

He turned and he and his three companions cantered off into the darkness.

Sir Oswald was about to shout after them, but the knight stopped him.

'Let them go,' he muttered. 'No need to swear them to silence. We will not see them in Oxford again.'

'What about Ormiston?' the sheriff asked.

'I suppose he'll go back to his hall and drink himself stupid. God knows, I don't blame him. Such sights would break a lesser man.'

'I have had my fill, too,' Beauchamp said wearily. 'Oh, don't worry, Sir Godfrey, I'll see this matter through but, when it's done and you have gone, so will I. I'll go back to my manor, marry some sweet-faced wench, settle down and till my soil. Never again will I work in royal service.' He turned, hawked and spat into the darkness. 'I became a sheriff to maintain the king's peace, to hunt down, arrest and punish felons, not to cross swords with the powers of darkness. Are we finished here?'

'One more thing,' the knight replied. 'McBain, you stay with Dame Edith. Sir Oswald, come with me!'

They walked round to the front of the church. They removed the bars, hacking off the padlocks, and entered the musty darkness. Sir Oswald handed the knight a spluttering pitch torch and they walked cautiously up the deserted nave. Both men fought to control their panic, prompted by their own shadows flickering and dancing in the torch-light.

'The tomb's over there,' the sheriff indicated.

They walked into the transept. Sir Godfrey held the torch up as they carefully made their way forward. At last they reached a huge marble tomb with the life-sized effigy of a knight on top. The figure was clothed in chain mail, legs crossed at the ankles and resting on a small dog, both hands clasped on the hilt of a sword. Sir Godfrey took the torch, ignoring the strange sounds and creaking noises from the church. At last he found a small aperture just beneath the neck of the effigy. He put his hand in and drew out a small case about three inches wide. Its sides and back were made of gold and small precious jewels encrusted the rim around the glass front. In the centre, resting on white samite, was a small piece of wood.

'The relic!' Sir Oswald breathed. 'The Hospitaller must have hidden it there. Come on, man!' he pleaded, peering over his shoulder into the darkness of the church. 'We have the relic, the devil priest has gone. We can do no more tonight.'

Sir Godfrey agreed and they went to join McBain, who was talking quietly to Dame Edith beneath an outspread yew tree. The knight gave her the reliquary and Dame Edith clasped it reverently and pressed it against her cheek.

'Now we have something,' she whispered. She raised her

head as if staring up into the starlit sky.

She gripped McBain's wrist with one hand and Sir Godfrey's with the other.

'They have brought their Dark Lord back to life,' she whispered, 'and we must hunt them down. Kill them for what they are. Send them, body and soul, back to Hell!'

Sir Oswald, exhausted, agreed but said such matters would have to wait until morning.

'Then tonight,' Sir Godfrey ordered, 'when you go back to the castle, tell no one of what has happened here. Send your swiftest courier to the chancellor in London, asking for all ports on the south coast to be sealed.'

The sheriff nodded.

'Use only your mercenaries,' Sir Godfrey continued. 'Have this place cordoned off. Tomorrow morning, at first light, search the cemetery!'

The knight, the clerk and Dame Edith rode back through the darkness to St Anne's. A porter let them in and took their horses. Dame Edith joined her two companions in the guest house for some bread and wine. Sir Godfrey could hardly keep awake. McBain found he was trembling and gulped greedily at the wine. Only Dame Edith seemed composed. She shook Sir Godfrey gently.

'We must,' she insisted, 'make plans for the morrow.'

The knight rubbed his eyes wearily. 'I am tired, my lady. My orders were to root this evil out of Oxford and I have done that.'

'Nonsense!' the exorcist retorted. 'We must pursue them now. They are devil-worshippers, felons, traitors and plan more murderous mischief!'

'What more can we do?' Alexander murmured. 'Sir Godfrey has asked for all the southern ports to be sealed.'

'Of course he won't use those!' Dame Edith replied. 'The

priest is no fool.' She nibbled on a morsel of bread and took a small sip of wine. 'When we met the priest at the church, he said he hailed from a town in the north.'

'Whitby,' Sir Godfrey said wearily. 'A small fishing port between the Tees and the Humber.'

'I know it well,' Dame Edith continued smilingly. 'You forget I hail from those parts. A small harbour overlooked by a steep hill with an abbey on top. Ah, yes, the abbey of St Hilda's.'

'Why should he go there?' Alexander asked.

'Oh, master clerk, apply your logic. He knows the southern ports have been sealed, yet he has to escape from England. So, where can he go? To France where English armies roam at will? To Holland and Zeeland full of English merchants? No, he will try to get back to Moldavia or Wallachia, those wild countries where I spent years as a prisoner. And what better route than through the northern lands, vast open spaces where he will not be recognized, free of any official or inquisitive church clerk.'

Sir Godfrey rubbed his eyes. 'I agree,' he said, 'and Whitby is the best port for such destinations. Moreover, the priest knows the routes well and will have a good two days' start on us. The rains are stopping. The roads will be hard and he will carry little baggage.'

McBain got to his feet and bowed to Dame Edith. 'Sir Godfrey, my lady, I must sleep.' He smiled. 'Or at least think. I bid you good night.'

'Wait! Wait!' Sir Godfrey went over to stand at the window and stared into the darkness. McBain paused, one hand on the door latch, Dame Edith glanced in the direction of the knight.

'What is it?' she murmured.

'All my life,' the knight began slowly, 'I have fought against flesh and blood: in the lists, on the tourney ground, in battles such at Poitiers where I helped to break the French advance. I have fought with dagger and sword either in blood-filled drenches before the towns of Normandy or against French scouts in some desolate, rain-soaked glade. But this,' Sir Godfrey shook his head. 'Corpses being revived after hundreds of years, blood sacrifices, demon-priests.' He breathed out noisily.

'And yet,' McBain interrupted, 'you go to mass, Sir Godfrey? You take the sacrament. You believe a wafer of bread and a cup of wine are, substantially, the body and blood of Christ?'

'Yes.' The knight turned around, rubbing the side of his face. 'But that's religion, a matter of faith. Different from . . .' his voice trailed away.

'From reality?' Dame Edith asked.

'Yes, yes, from reality!'

Dame Edith pushed the sleeves of her gown back. 'But what happens, Sir Godfrey, if there's no difference? If everything is only part of the one reality. And, as the great Aristotle says, we only draw dividing lines to make things appear more reasonable?'

'What do you mean?' the knight snapped.

'What she means,' McBain declared curtly, 'is often debated in the schools of Oxford and Cambridge.'

The knight made a rude sound with his lips.

'No, listen,' McBain explained patiently. He walked over to the window and pointed to the shutter where a small insect was crawling. 'Do you think this flea, or whatever it may be, is aware that we are in this room? Even better, Sir Godfrey, do you think that insect understands the concept of this room or our existence?'

The knight shook his head.

'But,' McBain pressed the point, 'just because that insect

isn't aware of our existence, surely it does not mean that we don't exist?'

The knight shrugged.

'The clerk is right,' Dame Edith chuckled softly. 'Like the insect, we define our reality, Sir Godfrey, by what we see, touch, feel and understand.'

'But the Strigoi?' Sir Godfrey exclaimed. 'With their sharpened teeth and blood sacrifices? Your story, Domina, about the spirit of one Strigoi being able to leave a corpse and take up residence in another body?'

'Have you seen the effects of the plague?' Dame Edith asked.

'Yes.' The knight answered softly. 'My first wife died of it.'

'I am sorry, sir knight. Yet can you explain how the plague moved from one person to her? Or from her to someone else?'

The knight shook his head.

'The same is true of the Strigoi moving from one body to another,' Dame Edith continued. 'To put it bluntly, Sir Godfrey, just because I can't explain it, doesn't mean it can't happen.' She sighed and spread her hands. 'The sharpened teeth, well that is a small matter, teeth can be filed down. Some may have it, some do not.'

'But the spirit of the Strigoi?' Sir Godfrey persisted.

'Sir Godfrey, you fought at Poitiers, you helped break the French advance?'

The knight nodded.

'You became tired? Weary?'

'Aye, Domina, to the point of death.'

'But brother knights, comrades in arms, were cut down?'

'Aye they were, God assoil them!'

'And what effect did their deaths have on you?'

Sir Godfrey raised his eyebrows. 'I fought all the harder as if given a new lease of life.'

Dame Edith leaned forward. 'But how do you know that the spirits of your dead comrades did not strengthen you?'

The knight smiled thinly and walked back to the table.

'Everything,' Dame Edith explained, 'everything under the sun has an explanation. As I've said, just because we can't find one doesn't mean it doesn't exist.'

'But the Strigoi Lord?' McBain asked, sitting down next to Sir Godfrey. 'A corpse which can survive uncorrupted for hundreds of years and then be revived.'

Dame Edith shrugged. 'All I can say, Alexander, is that there must be an explanation.' The exorcist rubbed her face in her hands. 'When I was a prisoner in Wallachia, I heard stories from the east, strange tales about men who could sleep for years, appear as dead. In Wallachia there were similar stories about the Strigoi. Now, the peasants there have a name for the Devil. They call him the "Great Dragon" or "Dracul" and claim these Strigoi lords are his sons.' Dame Edith tapped the side of her head. 'God knows the power of the human mind. Its goodness is eternal and so is its malice. The good Lord said that if we have enough faith or power we can ask a tree to uproot and plant itself into the sea. Why can't the Lords of Darkness have similar powers, if their malice is thick or deep enough? We live in a world of signs and symbols. I shake your hands, that means we are comrades. I put my hand on the book of the gospels to make a promise and I am bound by oath.' She shrugged. 'The demons of the air and their retainers on earth also have their sinister, dark ceremonies.'

Alexander stretched forward, grasped the exorcist's thin hand and gently squeezed.

'A scholar as well as a fighter,' he teased gently. 'Sir

Godfrey, Dame Edith is right. If you read the history of Eusebius you'll find a story, well documented, about seven young brothers who, in the reign of one of the Roman emperors, hid and slept for centuries in a cave outside Ephesius.'

'Yes, yes,' Sir Godfrey interrupted. 'I have heard of that tale.'

'And go to churches,' Alexander persisted. 'Why is it the bodies of certain holy men and women never corrupt, such as those of Saint Philomena or Saint Lucy?'

Sir Godfrey stretched. 'Perhaps you're right but,' he added abruptly, 'this Strigoi Lord. Now we must hunt this son of the devil down and kill him!'

'Exterminate him!' Dame Edith declared harshly. 'Extinguish all sign of him and his followers from the face of the earth. We must give him no resting place under the sun. Believe me, there is a tie between the Strigoi Lord and this kingdom. One day he will return, coming back along the same route by which he left. He'll either come alone or with his followers but he will return to wreak great evil!'

Both men sat quietly for a few moments, chilled by the passion in Dame Edith's words. Then the exorcist quietly excused herself and walked out of the guest house, politely refusing both Sir Godfrey's and McBain's offer to accompany her. She walked unerringly through the darkness, moving her face gently, remembering the different paths and obstacles. She paused for a while, feeling the breeze on her cheeks. She choked back a sob as she recalled her youth in Northumberland, walking along the parapets of her father's castle, letting her hair be tossed and whipped by the wind. The dead thronged about her but she felt comforted not frightened by their presence. They were only friends standing on the other side of a river, patiently waiting for her to cross.

'Soon,' she murmured. 'Soon I'll be with you. No more pain. No more terror. No more darkness.'

Dame Edith walked along the gravelled path. She hoped McBain and Sir Godfrey would stay with her. 'Good men and true. Christ strengthen their arms and sharpen their wits.' Then she stopped. She remembered McBain's hand in the upper room at the tavern, ice cold! Was that a warning of things to come? She hurried along to the church. A lay sister, just inside the postern gate, led her back to the cell. Dame Edith closed the door behind her and lay down on the simple cot bed, chanting her prayers, asking for God's mercy, not for herself, but for her companions. Dame Edith thought of tomorrow's journey and raised her head.

'Oh, God have mercy!' she whispered. In her mind's eye, Dame Edith glimpsed the Strigoi Lord and his party galloping along the deserted roads, cloaks flapping, like ravens speeding to their nests.

'They'll need strength,' she murmured. 'Oh, God have mercy, they'll need strength! Oh, sweet Lord, bless all travellers on this terrible night!'

Words between the pilgrims

'By pig's bones!' Harry the taverner exclaimed, stretching his hands out towards the candle-light. 'An eerie tale, sirrah.'

The knight sipped from his wine goblet and stared down the table at the monk who had now pulled his cowl well over his head.

'Is this possible?' the nun's priest asked in his rich, mellow voice. 'Do such things happen?'

'I have seen them!' the wife of Bath explained.

'Seen what?' the cook shrilled.

'I have seen the uncorrupted bodies of holy men.' The wife crossed her arms. 'And if the good Lord looks after his own, so does Satan.'

'Where are the corpses?' the Manciple interrupted harshly.

'What bodies?' Harry the taverner asked.

'The bodies?' the Manciple persisted. 'Those of the students killed by the Strigoi?'

The knight dabbed his lips with a napkin. 'My tale is not yet finished,' he declared quietly. 'Listen to the truth . . .'

'Truth?' the summoner sneered. 'Nightmares to frighten children!'

The knight shrugged eloquently. 'Sir, I was asked to tell a tale and that's what I am doing.'

'It is true!'

The shipman sprang to his feet, knocking his stool over. He pointed down the table. 'St Anne and all God's holy angels be my witness. You mentioned Whitby, Sir?'

The knight nodded.

The shipman now seized the wine jug and filled his own cup. 'Sir,' the shipman lifted his cup, 'I salute . . .'

'Sit down!' the knight ordered. 'And, as I have said, I'll finish my tale!'

PART V

Chapter 1

The carts and caravans of the Moon people trundled along the moorland path under forbidding, iron-grey skies. The rain had stopped falling but the gorse and brambles on either side were still heavy with water and the cobbled trackway had turned to a soggy morass. The painted sheets of the wagons had begun to run, the dye streaming down the sides of the four-wheeled carts. Even the horses seemed dispirited, raising their hooves lack-lustrely, heads down against the cold, biting wind. The drivers and carters, huddled in their shabby cloaks, cursed the elements and the driving rain which had forced them to shelter in caves for most of the day. They'd never reach the next village by nightfall and would have to camp out on the open heathland.

Imelda, the dancing girl, trailed behind one of the carts, her jet-black hair hidden by a shabby cowl; her voluptuous, sinuous body was covered in an old blanket with a hole cut in the middle, her only protection against the icy rain. Every so often, cheap bracelets jangling on her wrists, Imelda would wipe the rain from her face and trudge on, mindful to stay at least a yard behind the cart, away from the mud and dirt flung up by the iron-rimmed wheels. She heard her mother, lying on a bed in the cart, moan and groan. Imelda closed her eyes. Her mother groaned again.

215

'Oh, shut up!' Imelda whispered to herself. 'There's nothing wrong with you!'

There never was but, whenever any journey became arduous or difficult, Imelda's mother immediately became ill.

'I am too tired!' she would wail. 'Too sick to walk!' And she would climb into the gaudily painted wagon to take her ease as if she was the queen or some great lady.

A curlew, braving the driving wind, swooped and shrieked eerily across the lowering sky. Imelda looked up. She saw the flash of its wing and wished she could fly. She'd flee from here! Far from the cold, the poverty, the pennies flung at her in some tavern or ale-house, the hot-eyed glances of the men, their greedy pawing and the jealous glares of the womenfolk. Her father had similar dreams which, she knew, he would repeat tonight as they gathered round the camp fire.

'This is not our land,' he'd begin. 'We are of an ancient and noble people, driven from their lands after the Romans came.'

Raquerel, her father, would then begin to describe strange lands, dark forests, lush river valleys and rich meadows, a land on which the sun always smiled. Imelda wondered if such a country did exist and, if it did, whether her father was telling the truth. Her grandmother, who now sat beside the driver of the cart in front, wrapped in her dark-blue cloak with strange symbols painted on it, told a different story. How the forests of that country sheltered demons and strange beings called Draculs lurked in fortresses built by devils on top of lonely crags. Imelda smiled. What did it matter? She was cold, soaked to the skin, and her feet, protected only by loose-thonged sandals, were beginning to turn to blocks of ice.

'Will you dance tonight, Imelda?'

The girl turned and glared at the thickset man who suddenly appeared beside her and, as usual, drew close until their shoulders brushed. Imelda wrinkled her nose in distaste at the man's sour breath. She didn't like Osbert. He wasn't one of her people. A juggler, a mountebank, Osbert had joined their caravan two or three months earlier. Father had taken him in; Osbert was strong, he earned some pennies and provided good protection on the lonely roads. Nevertheless, Imelda disliked him, not just his wart-covered face and hairy nostrils, but his thick fingers always ready to touch her.

'Will you dance tonight?' Osbert repeated, drawing even closer.

'No,' Imelda replied through clenched teeth. 'All I want is to be warm.'

'I'll keep you warm,' Osbert whispered.

'Have you ever seen my trick?' Imelda demanded.

Osbert drew back. 'What trick?'

'I can make a knife appear between any man's ribs?'

The mountebank opened his mouth to reply when they both heard a shout behind them.

'Riders on the road! Coming fast!'

Imelda heard the drum of hooves. The carters began to pull aside. Her father was always subservient, every ready to concede the road to haughty noblemen and their well-armed bully-boy retainers or to merchants, so self important, for whom every second counted. As the cart in front lurched to one side, Imelda climbed into it.

'What is it, girl?' her mother whined.

'Shush!' Imelda replied. 'It's only riders!'

She looked out through the mist. The horsemen had slowed to a canter.

'How many are there?'

'Four, no five!'

Imelda peered. 'They are dressed in black, cloaked and

cowled but their horses are fine. Perhaps they are a group of black monks, Benedictines.'

The riders drew close. Imelda shivered. The strangers now clustered together. She could glimpse no weapons or glint of steel but they had a quiet, sinister purpose. They looked neither to the left nor the right. Imelda heard her grandmother gasp and begin to chant something in that strange tongue Imelda could only barely understand.

'Silence, Grandmother!' she hissed.

But the old one continued her chant, an ancient verse against the evil one. The riders approached, the leader pulled back his cowl and smiled. Imelda relaxed. The man had a serene, smiling face, soft and gentle and, as he bowed his head in greeting, she glimpsed the tonsure.

'Good morrow, Father!'

'And greetings to you, my girl.' The priest pushed his horse closer to the back of the cart. 'How far to the next village?'

'A few miles.' Imelda smiled back. 'You'll reach it before us, sir, though you're welcome to stay with us tonight.'

The priest smiled and shook his head. 'We are expected,' he said. 'And time is short but I thank you for your offer.'

Osbert came round the side of the cart and glimpsed the priest.

'Father Andrew!' he cried.

The smile on the priest's face faded. His eyes became hard and Imelda shivered with fear as the other horsemen, their faces concealed by the cowls, urged their horses forward as if Osbert's greeting posed some threat. The mountebank, however, impervious to this, grasped the priest's bridle.

'Father Andrew, don't you remember me, Osbert? I stopped at your church in Oxford some months ago. You were most kind to me.'

The priest shook the bridle loose and pulled the cowl back over his head.

'I think you are mistaken!' he snapped and, giving his reins an abrupt tug, led his party off at a gallop, the sharp hooves of their horses scattering mud and pebbles in every direction.

Osbert watched them disappear into the darkness.

'Strange,' he mused. 'I am sure it was Father Andrew. And yet he was so kind. He and his helpers.'

'I didn't know you were ever in Oxford?' Imelda scoffed. 'Are you a scholar, Osbert?'

The man scowled up at her. 'I have been to places,' he muttered, 'and seen sights you'll never see, Imelda!' And he stomped off.

Imelda poked her tongue out at his retreating back and made her mother comfortable. She climbed off the cart and they continued their dreary journey. Grandmother was still chanting her ancient prayers. Every so often Imelda heard her break off and ask the carter: 'Have those riders gone? Have those riders gone?'

'Of course they have!' the man growled back. 'Why, what do you expect, more custom for tonight, eh?' He cackled with laughter but Grandmother went back to her prayers.

Now the carts and wagons were back on the road, Imelda wondered what Osbert was doing in Oxford. She would like to go there and see the sights. Perhaps even glimpse a book, like the one she had seen at that monastery two summers ago. She could have cried at the brilliance of the pictures and the fine strokes of the pen. She'd called it beautiful and tried to stroke the pages but the novice master had just gently closed it. Imelda bit her lip; her father would never go to Oxford. She'd noticed that, how, in their peregrinations up and down the kingdom, he stayed well away from the valley of the Thames and the area around Oxford. Others claimed it was a good source of income. Raquerel just shook his head and murmured about great evil and ancient legends. Imelda smiled to herself, father was full of such tales. She looked up. Darkness was beginning to fall. She watched an eagle owl soar above the gorse, talons outstretched only to be mobbed by a group of raucous crows.

At last her father gave the order to leave the track. They would not reach the village that night: instead they would camp in a small copse where the trees would afford them some shelter against the rain and driving wind. The carts and wagons were pulled in a circle, kindling collected and dried and soon a huge fire roared in the centre. Imelda sat between her father and mother, the latter still moaning at the knocks and jars of the journey. The dozing girl stretched out her hands and revelled in the warmth. She closed her eyes and slept for a short while. When she woke, her father and brothers had set up a huge spit on either side of the fire ready to roast the pheasant and quail they had brought down by slingshot. They had slashed the birds' throats then hidden them beneath the cart lest they were stopped by some sharp-eyed bailiff or manor steward.

'Get some more kindling, Imelda!' her father ordered.

'I'll help,' Osbert cried.

Imelda tossed her head, her long black hair flowing around her. 'There's no need.' Imelda's lower lip came forward. 'There's no need, Osbert.'

The man just laughed. Father was still shouting so Imelda had no choice but to walk into the dark ring of trees and sift beneath the wet fern and brambles for the dry bracken and kindling which lay there. Osbert, too, was busy, chattering away. Imelda heard him gasp but she refused to look up.

'Don't play your games, Osbert.' She moved deeper into the trees and straightened up. 'It's so silent,' she murmured and looked back towards the encampment, the welcoming glow of the fire, the dancing flames, the chatter of her kinsfolk. Here it was so dark and cold.

'Osbert?' She stared around but the man had disappeared. She heard the branches above her swish. Imelda looked up and her throat constricted in terror at the dark cowled, pallid face grinning maliciously down at her.

The next morning McBain was aroused by a now alert and vigorous Sir Godfrey.

'Come on, clerk!' the knight shouted. 'The sun's up, I have packed my saddle bags. I suggest you do the same. Dame Edith insists on joining us. We will leave for London within the hour.'

'Why London?' McBain sleepily asked, swinging his legs off the bed and softly cursing the knight's boisterous cheerfulness.

'I have already sent one of Dame Constance's couriers to the Admiral of the East Coast based at Queenshithe. I have asked for a war cog, the fastest ship in the Thames, to take us north to Whitby. We can either blockade the port or, if necessary, go in pursuit.'

Alexander agreed and stripped and shaved, teeth chattering at the coldness of his chamber. He dressed carefully in vest, shirt, woollen jerkin, hose and his special fur-lined travelling boots. He threw his belongings into the saddle bag, including the journal he had taken from the Trinitarian friary, and went downstairs to break his fast. Dame Edith had already been across and then left with Sir Godfrey to prepare their horses at the stables. Alexander ate hungrily and stared around the small, white-washed guest house. He knew he was finished here. He had a feeling he would never return and this made him uncomfortable as he remembered Emily's golden ringlets, blue sparkling eyes and the warm silken sheen of her hand. He leaned against the table and thought of the last tumultuous days – his arrival in Oxford during the rain, the dreadful scenes he had witnessed, the apparent holiness of Father Andrew, the growing silence of Dame Constance and the utter collapse of Proctor Ormiston. He sighed, finished his tankard of warm ale, blessed himself and went out to join the rest.

The horses were being saddled. Dame Constance had agreed to lend her own palfrey, a gentle but sturdy cob, to Dame Edith, and two of her stable boys would ride with them until they entered London. Saddle bags were thrown on to the backs of the sumpter ponies, girths, stirrups and reins checked. All three took their leave. The abbess seemed relieved that her convent would now be free from the strange guests and the wicked business they had been investigating. Although neither admitted it, both Sir Godfrey and McBain hoped that the lady Emily would appear and the knight was about to ask Dame Constance for her permission to say farewell to her when an exhausted-looking Beauchamp rode into the convent. The sheriff almost fell out of the saddle. His once rubicund face was now white and drawn and great black shadows ringed his eyes. He looked a man who could do no more. He walked slowly towards them, rubbing his thighs and quietly groaning at the pain of spending so much time in the saddle.

'You are leaving?' he asked abruptly.

'For London,' Sir Godfrey replied. 'We intend to pursue Father Andrew, his coven and the nightmare creature they took from the crypt.'

'Then I wish you well.'

Beauchamp put both hands in the small of his back and stretched, then rubbed his unshaven face.

'I sealed off the church,' he said, 'claiming that the whole edifice is now unsafe. My soldiers, the few mercenaries I lead, have already dug up corpses from the cemetery. I believe they are the missing students.'

The sheriff turned and, not bothering about Dame Constance's presence, hawked and spat.

'They are not a pretty sight,' he added hoarsely. 'They are like the rest, throats slit from ear to ear, bodies drained of blood. Some are already rotten. They were slaughtered like pigs and buried in shallow graves.'

'And Proctor Ormiston?' Alexander asked.

The sheriff tapped the side of his head. 'Proctor Ormiston is witless, with a sickness of the mind. He sits in his chamber mumbling to himself, moving the papers on his desk. He is terrified of leaving, even to relieve himself. His days of scholarship are over. God send him good fortune!' Sir Oswald's red-rimmed eyes stared at the knight.

'Wickedness!' the sheriff breathed. 'Sheer wickedness! I tell you this, sir knight—' His eyes moved to McBain and Dame Edith. '—and you others, I have been in the Valley of Death.' He licked his lips. 'Another courier is already on his way to London. If God wills, and the king agrees, I will be out of Oxford within the week.' He clasped the knight's hand and that of McBain, then gently kissed Dame Edith's fingers. 'God speed and farewell!'

He went back to his horse, mounted, grabbed the reins in his hand and looked once more at them. 'Farewell, I hope we do not meet again.' And, turning his horse's head, he galloped out of the convent gates.

Sir Godfrey and his party finished their farewells. They were almost level with the gate when Dame Constance reappeared, her arms linked through that of Lady Emily, who looked as fresh as a summer-filled May morning. Alexander made the usual courtesies, stretching down to kiss her hand, which he held a little longer than he should have done. Lady Emily then went to stand beside Sir Godfrey. She put her hands gently on his muscle-hard thigh and stared at the knight's face, made all the more forbidding by his chain-mail coif.

'Sir Godfrey,' she whispered, 'you will return?'

The knight grasped her hand awkwardly. 'Aye, perhaps.'

'Thank you.' She smiled. 'Thank you for the lovely poem.'

Sir Godfrey drew his eyebrows together.

'The poem,' she insisted. 'The one you composed and asked Master McBain to write out.' She shook her head slightly. 'It was beautiful.'

Sir Godfrey looked up across her head at Alexander, who smiled, winked and shrugged. Sir Godfrey stared back at the young woman, grasped her hand, stooped down and kissed her passionately on the cheek.

'God willing,' he whispered hoarsely, 'I shall return.'

The girl stood back and Sir Godfrey led his small party out into the winding lanes of Oxford. Within the hour they were free of the city and deep in the countryside, following the ancient Roman routes back to the capital. The sky was cloud-free, the air cold but the roads were good and hard. Dame Edith proved to be a skilled horsewoman and posed no hindrance to their progress. By nightfall they had reached Bishopsgate, where they thanked and dismissed Dame Constance's porters. Sir Godfrey then insisted that they must ride on through the city, to the admiral's quarters in the Vintry, just north of Queenshithe docks.

Admiral Sir Clement Chaucer had already received their message. A small, portly man with a weather-beaten face and light blue eyes, he was an old acquaintance of Sir Godfrey's.

He greeted him cordially and his two companions without question.

'I have already received orders from the chancellor,' he boomed, leading them into a small dining hall on the ground floor of his three-storeyed house.

'I have a ship ready for you. The *Star of the Sea*, a three-masted war cog, under a good captain, Humphrey Grandison. You will sail at first light. But now you must break your journey. Some good food, eh? Beef roasted in pepper and mustard, wine and the softest bread? And feather-filled mattresses?'

Sir Godfrey and Alexander could not object and Sir Clement proved to be an excellent host. He chattered about the sea, hardly asking them any questions, while paying Dame Edith the courtesies due to any lady. All three ate their fill. Sir Godfrey fell asleep at the table and had to be aroused by servants. Alexander saw Dame Edith to her own quarters at the back of the house and, within minutes of his head touching the bolster in the chamber he shared with Sir Godfrey, he was fast asleep, snoring as loudly as Sir Godfrey beside him.

Servants woke them just before dawn and they broke their fast. Sir Clement promised to look after their horses before leading them through the still dark streets and down to the quayside of Queenshithe. The river was full of shipping – small skiffs, barges, cogs and the huge, heavy-bottomed sterns of Hanseatic merchantmen. Already the quayside was busy as ships prepared to catch the early-morning tide. Small cranes were depositing barrels, chests and huge leather bags in ships' holds. There was a confusion of sound, strange oaths, cries and orders. Sir Clement paid no heed, leading his small party along the quayside, ordering people aside and ignoring the catcalls and oaths that followed him.

Eventually they found the *Star of the Sea*, a large ship with a bluff hull and darting bowsprit, its sides rising high above the quayside, its stern crowned by crenellated fighting platforms to protect archers and soldiers during battle. Sir Clement hailed the ship and a broad, greasy gangplank was lowered. Sir Clement went first. Alexander helped Dame Edith, who stoutly refused Sir Godfrey's half-hearted invitation to remain behind, and the knight brought up the rear. On board, bare-foot sailors moved about, jostling each other; some stopped and watched Dame Edith curiously. Sir Godfrey heard their muttered curses and dire warnings about a woman being on board ship.

'Just ignore them,' Sir Clement whispered out of the corner of his mouth. 'Sailors love any excuse for dark prophecies. It's another matter when it comes to bringing their whores on board!'

The ship moved slightly and Alexander's stomach heaved as he looked up at the soaring rigging and towering masts. He stared around the deck, full of coils of rope and leather buckets. Under canvas sheeting stood two large catapults. Beside one of them, Alexander glimpsed a patch of dried blood. He guessed the ship must have been in one of the many skirmishes that took place at sea; beyond the mouth of the Thames, the ships of various nations, Norway, Denmark, England, Scotland and France fought a long and bloody war.

A young, red-haired man dressed simply in a leather jerkin, dark hose and boots came up and introduced himself as Humphrey Grandison, captain of the ship. Sir Clement made the introductions and handed the captain a small leather packet. 'These are your orders, sir,' he said tersely. 'You are in command of the ship but under the direct orders of Sir Godfrey. You are to sail north to Whitby and act on Sir Godfrey's instructions.'

The captain nodded, then, rolling his tongue round his mouth, he pointed at Alexander.

'I can see Sir Godfrey's been at sea,' he declared in a broad, flat accent. 'But the clerk'll be sick before we clear the Thames. And who is she?'

'My name is Dame Edith Mohun,' the exorcist tartly replied. 'And I have been on more ships than I care to count. In northern waters and the Middle seas. I was bobbing on the waves when you were dangling on your mother's knee, young man!'

The captain stared speechlessly at her, stroked his sparse beard then burst into laughter which drowned all the clamour from the ship. The captain glared round and, in a stream of filthy oaths, told the sailors to continue with their work. He then took Dame Edith's hand and raised it gallantly to his lips.

'Madam, no offence.'

'Sir, none taken.'

Sir Clement took his leave and Grandison began to issue orders. Quayside ropes were released, the decks were cleared of all impedimenta. Sailors climbed like monkeys up the rigging, unfurling the great sails. The ship turned and lurched. Alexander was sent sprawling, much to the amusement of the sailors. Grandison helped him to his feet, grinning from ear to ear.

'You'd best get out of here.'

He took the three of them down to a small cabin under the forecastle, a small, dingy room smelling of tar and salt containing a simple cot bed, a table and a number of stools.

Alexander, unused to the gentle rocking of the ship, banged his head as he straightened up. The pain was intense and, though the captain laughed at his discomfort, he offered McBain and his companions cups of surprisingly good wine to ease the pain and 'strengthen their stomachs' for the coming voyage.

'Dame Edith can stay here,' Grandison explained. 'But,

gentlemen, I'm afraid you've got to share below decks with the rest.'

And, whistling merrily under his breath, Grandison left them to their own devices.

Within the hour the *Star of the Sea* had cleared the river and was sailing north by north-east through a cold, choppy sea. The pain in Alexander's head subsided, only to be replaced by a growing sense of nausea as the ship rolled in the water.

Sir Godfrey sat, amused by the poor clerk's discomfort, until McBain's face took on a greenish tinge.

'Come on, Alexander,' he said jovially. 'Dame Edith, stay here. If our clerk is going to be sick, it's best if he did it elsewhere.'

Alexander, muttering curses, followed Sir Godfrey up the ladder and on to the deck. The sails billowed and snapped in a strong southerly wind. Grandison came up, hanging on to the halyards.

'Do you feel sick, clerk?'

Alexander nodded.

'Then let me give you some advice. Try not to think about the motion of the ship but busy yourself.'

Alexander grimaced, then promptly fled to the side to vomit his breakfast into the choppy, grey sea. He felt better afterwards and leaned against the rail, drawing in deep breaths and staring out at the receding land, listening to the smack of the sails and the creak of timbers.

Grandison glimpsed the pleasure in the clerk's face.

'Aye, she's a bonny ship!' he shouted. 'Goes straight and true as an arrow.'

He dug inside his jerkin and brought out a brown roll of parchment. He unrolled this, spreading his legs to steady himself against the roll of the ship. The captain pointed with a stubby finger at the crudely drawn map.

'We should reach Whitby by tomorrow evening,' he said. 'And then what?'

'We are hunting for four fugitives, possibly five,' Sir Godfrey explained. 'They will take ship from Whitby.'

'And what then?'

'If they haven't left we will blockade the port.'

'And if they have?'

'Pursue them with all speed.'

'And?'

'Destroy them utterly.'

Sir Godfrey pointed to the large catapults farther down the deck under their canvas covering.

'At my orders, Master Grandison, they are to be loaded and fired. No prisoners are to be taken.'

Grandison pointed to a group of men dressed in brown leather jackets lounging on the starboard side of the ship, just near the forecastle.

'They'll be useful too,' he said. 'They are Cheshire archers, master bowmen.'

Sir Godfrey smiled and said that was enough and, leaving Alexander to regain his sea legs, went below decks to converse with Dame Edith.

The *Star of the Sea* proved to be a fine craft and Grandison a most skilful sailor. By dusk the following evening, they had sighted Whitby's soaring cliffs and the large abbey on its summit. At Sir Godfrey's request, three officers and two of the archers took a dinghy and rowed into the harbour. Returning two hours later they whispered to their captain, who took Sir Godfrey and Mcbain down to Dame Edith's cabin.

'Bad news, I'm afraid,' Grandison began, leaning against the door and watching the simple leather lantern swing on its hook. 'Your fugitives have been seen. In fact one of them is well known in these parts – Andrew Melbray, a priest. He was with five others, one a dark hooded stranger who never showed his face. They did business in the taverns along Whitby's quayside and hired a fishing smack with a crew of four to take them across the northern sea. They left early this afternoon.'

'You'll pursue them?' Dame Edith asked.

'I'll pursue them,' Grandison replied, 'but the weather's changing.'

'You mean storms?'

'No, not storms, fog. It's already thickening. We have to go carefully. There are hidden sandbanks in these waters and we are pursuing a craft manned by people who know this sea and its cruel tricks.' Grandison paused. 'These aren't common criminals, are they? I mean, for you to commandeer a king's warship?'

'No, they are not,' Sir Godfrey declared. 'And, Master Grandison, you may see things that chill your blood. But do your best, not only on your loyalty to the king, but for the good of your eternal soul!'

Grandison looked surprised, but merely shrugged and went back on deck. They heard him shout orders. The anchor was raised and the ship moved slowly out to sea.

Alexander went up on deck, drawing his cloak tightly about him. Tendrils of mist were seeping across the ship, giving it a ghostly, eerie aspect. Alexander shivered. He was confident that they would catch up with the Strigoi and he felt, deep in his heart, that all his life had been a preparation for that dreadful meeting. He went below decks, gagging and retching at the fetid, sour smell but lay down, closed his eyes and said his prayers until he fell asleep. Sir Godfrey shook him awake with a bowl of hot oats and a cup of strong wine. After that he joined the knight on deck and felt a thrill of apprehension as he saw the ship prepared for battle: the catapults were being uncovered and archers stood ready on the sterncastle, in the rigging and on the forecastle. Look-outs were high on all three masts.

Daylight came as full as it could in the mist, which boiled thick as steam from a cauldron. Alexander was about to go back down to Dame Edith's cabin when he heard one of the look-outs shout.

'Sail! To the north-east! Not far!'

'How can you tell?' Grandison shouted back through his speaking trumpet.

'The mist cleared, captain, just for a while, but there's a fishing smack! It's not moving!'

'What do you mean?' Grandison shouted back.

'I can't see!' the look-out roared. 'Yes, yes, I can! The fog's cleared again! It's gone aground on one of the sandbanks!'

Grandison turned and grinned at the clerk.

'I've found your quarry!'

Chapter 2

The captain rapped out orders; somewhere a drum began to sound, beating to quarters. Sailors rushed around, their bare feet slapping the wet decks, jostling and shoving Sir Godfrey and McBain aside. Dame Edith heard the excitement and came to the top of the steps leading from her cabin. Surprisingly, the mist began to break. Sir Godfrey went below and brought up his and the clerk's weapons.

'Come on, Alexander!' he said. 'We have to fight the good fight. These sailors cannot go on board that ship. We must!'

The *Star of the Sea* edged forward. Now and again the mist would break and they would catch a glimpse of the sea, even of faint sunlight, then it would close in again like a curtain, leaving Grandison and his officers to curse. Dame Edith leaned against the rail, hands clasped, staring into the fog banks. Alexander could see she was fervently praying. Then, as if in answer to her prayer, the mist cleared. They were in open sea and, half a mile away, a low-slung fishing smack, its one sail furled, bobbed and turned as if trapped by some giant underwater hand.

Sir Godfrey and McBain joined Dame Edith at the rail. Grandison came up behind them.

'Can't you get any closer?' Sir Godfrey asked.

Grandison shrugged. 'I dare not, sir. The fishing smack could easily break free but a ship of this size might be trapped and then pounded to pieces by the sea.' Grandison turned and hailed the look-out. 'What can you see?'

'Nothing, sir. It looks deserted.'

'Oh, Lord, no!' Dame Edith breathed. 'Don't say they have abandoned it. Perhaps they met another ship out at sea?'

'The boat's gone!' the look-out shouted down.

'What do you want me to do?' Grandison asked.

'Burn the fishing boat!' Dame Edith snapped.

'No!' Sir Godfrey breathed. 'We can't do that. God knows, there may be innocents on board and we have to make sure. Captain, I want your boat launched!'

'I'll come with you!' Grandison declared.

'No, sir, you won't. The boat can only take six people. I want one of your best archers and two seamen to row us across.'

'Are you all going?' Grandison asked quietly.

'Yes,' Dame Edith replied before the knight could open his mouth. 'All three of us began this, all three of us must be in at the end.'

Grandison shrugged, clapped his hands and shouted his orders. The boat was lowered and a rope ladder dropped down the ship's side. Two sailors clambered down into the boat. Sir Godfrey went next then Dame Edith, carrying a flask of oil, assisted by Alexander. They were followed down by a wiry little man, his monkey face sun-tanned, his toothless mouth gaping in a grin. He reminded Alexander of a court jester; nevertheless, the longbow the fellow carried, the quiver of goose-feather-tipped arrows and the leather wrist brace proclaimed him to be a bowman. The small boat bobbed on the waves. Alexander's stomach heaved. He wanted to retch; the sea rose on either side and the *Star of the Sea* now seemed like a haven of comfort.

'God be with you!' Grandison shouted, his words snatched away by the wind.

Sir Godfrey, sitting in the prow, nodded acknowledgement. 'Pull!' he ordered.

The two oarsmen began to row, the muscles of their shoulders and necks rippling as they leaned over the oars, chanting some doggerel verse to maintain the rhythm of their dipping oars. Alexander sat in the stern and put his arm around the exorcist. She felt so thin and frail, yet the tension thrilled in her body. The monkey-faced archer watched both of them curiously. He must have caught their fear for, by the time they reached the trapped fishing smack, his seemingly perpetual smile was beginning to fade.

The fishing boat, a narrow, swift-looking craft with a jutting prow and small stern, was low in the water. Sir Godfrey noticed that the sail was neatly furled but there seemed to be no sign of life on deck, empty except for mounds of canvas. The oarsmen brought their boat alongside, bobbing and crashing against the fishing smack. Alexander looked down and, through the swirling waters, saw faint traces of the sandbank.

'We can't stay here!' one of the oarsmen shouted over the grinding of wood against wood and the noise of the wind-whipped waves. 'The sandbank will trap us and the waves batter us against the smack.'

'Don't worry,' Sir Godfrey shouted back, his eyes now bright with the light of battle. 'Put me on deck, then stand off!'

'No, you won't!' Alexander roared. 'I'm coming with you!'

'And so am I!' Dame Edith stood up, swaying perilously in the boat. 'Either I go on board or into the sea!'

The sailors were now shouting at them to hurry. Sir Godfrey

shrugged and clambered over the side of the fishing smack, making sure his sword did not obstruct his movements. He leaned over and helped Dame Edith, then the monkey-faced archer gave a hand to Alexander and all three were aboard. They were soaked, their faces whipped by the wind, gasping for breath as the boat pulled away leaving them to stare around the silent deck of the fishing boat. They saw heaps of canvas, pieces of rope, lobster pots made out of wicker and leather buckets full of brine, but nothing seemed out of place.

'Nothing,' Sir Godfrey growled, drawing his sword. 'Let's go below!'

They edged their way forward. The fishing boat moved slightly, creaking as the waves lapped against its timbers. Now and again it gave a judder as if trying to break free from the ensnaring sandbank. Sir Godfrey started down the ladder that led to the tiny cabin. He wrinkled his nose at the sour, fetid smell that came up to him. But there was something else – a foulness that caught at his throat. He felt his way down the slippery steps. The light was poor but he glimpsed a fat, tallow candle on an iron spigot in the centre of a table bolted to the deck. He took a tinder and struck it a number of times until the flame caught and the candle flared into life. By this time Alexander and Dame Edith had followed him down.

'God have mercy!' Alexander breathed.

He stared at the corpses of the four fishermen, their throats slashed from ear to ear, eyes half-open, mouths gaping. They had been thrown like refuse, sprawling in grotesque positions, their blood giving the swilling sea water a scarlet froth.

'Murder again!' Dame Edith whispered. 'I can feel the horror in the air. More innocent lives!'

Sir Godfrey held up his hand. The ship suddenly creaked and they heard the faint shouts of the oarsmen who had brought them over. Dame Edith cocked her head slightly and shivered.

'Someone's on deck!' she said hoarsely. She wrapped her arms around the flask of oil she had taken from the cog. 'We are not alone.'

Sir Godfrey uttered an oath and sprang up the ladder. Alexander, behind him, stared in horror. The canvas sheets had been cast aside and, in the prow of the ship, swords and daggers drawn, black cloaks swirling about them, stood the priest and his followers. Sir Godfrey had faced the charge of armoured knights but had known nothing as fearsome as these sinister individuals standing, legs apart, at the far end of that gently heaving deck. They were clad from head to toe in black, which emphasized the stark whiteness of their faces. With their haunted eyes they looked like demons from Hell, ghouls spat out from the heart of darkness. The priest stood silently forward of his companions, the fury in his eyes and the drawn whiteness of his face belying the cunning smirk that twisted his lips.

'Is he here?' Dame Edith asked huskily. 'The Strigoi lord?'

'He's gone!' the priest shouted, pointing into the mist. 'Gone, but we have stayed to protect his departure and wreak vengeance on those who should have left matters well alone!'

Alexander drew his sword and dagger and stood shoulder to shoulder with Sir Godfrey. He glanced quickly over the side and saw the small boat bobbing on the waves. The archer, his bow unslung, was shouting at them, uncertain what to do. The *Star of the Sea*, under Grandison's skilful direction, was attempting to draw close.

Dame Edith began to pray. 'Jesu Misere!' She was half-way through when the priest and his companions closed with Sir Godfrey and McBain. Alexander fought with all his skill. He was conscious of the deck heaving beneath him, white ghostly faces, black swirling cloaks and the jar and shatter of steel. His attackers retreated. Sir Godfrey and Alexander stepped back, Dame Edith behind them. The sides of the ladder leading down to the small cabin jutted up and afforded them some protection. The priest and one of his companions returned to the attack in a whirling arc of steel. McBain and Sir Godfrey parried their thrusts. Father Andrew stood away. Another took his place and the fight continued. What McBain lacked in skill he made up in fury. Sir Godfrey suddenly lurched forward. He knocked his assailant aside and, with a quick swooping movement, drove his dagger straight into the man's belly. His writhing body blocked the path of another dark-clad figure who moved forward to take his place. Sir Godfrey then turned and with two hands drove his sword straight into the side of McBain's opponent. The blood gushed out, carried by the sea water lapping around their feet down the steps towards Dame Edith.

'God save us!' the exorcist shouted. 'They must be burnt!'

But the priest's remaining companions were edging, like two great black spiders, towards them. Alexander heard an arrow whirl across the deck and plunge into the sea on the other side; the archer had begun to fire. But now the two Strigoi closed in, and they were more skilled and more cautious than the two who now lay dead. McBain began to tire and he realized that both he and Sir Godfrey were being forced back to the ladder behind them. Sir Godfrey lunged forward, pushing his assailant back and, as he did so, the archer shot again; this time his arrow flew true and took one Strigoi full in the neck. His companion fell back, not one whit less determined. He even smiled at the Strigoi priest, his black-garbed master.

'They are ready to die,' Sir Godfrey whispered, wiping the sweat from his face with the back of his hand. 'They are here to die! To kill us and protect their master's going.'

Alexander opened his mouth to reply and, as he did so,

caught the priest's throwing knife full in the belly. He turned, face drawn in surprise; the pain was so intense he dropped his sword, falling back on the exorcist. Both of them tumbled to the bottom of the ladder. Dame Edith sprawled in the darkness.

'McBain!'

The clerk could only groan, conscious of the searing, hot fire in his belly, the sudden weakness in his arms and legs. He flailed around and caught the exorcist's thin wrist.

'The oil?' he muttered. 'You have the oil?'

He felt further. The exorcist was now scrabbling in the darkness around him.

'I have it!' she whispered.

Alexander made one last effort.

'I have it!' she repeated. 'But the steps. Where are they?'

Alexander pulled her across him until one of her hands, stretching out, caught the bottom rung.

'Climb!' he whispered. 'For the love of God, climb!'

Dame Edith did so, trying to ignore the bruising to her chest and legs caused by her sudden fall. She made her way slowly up. Above her Sir Godfrey was fighting for his life against two assailants, aware of the clamour and destruction behind him. He tried to pray but couldn't. Dame Edith pulled the relic which she wore on a cord around her neck and flung it in the direction of the deck above her. The small gold casket hit the priest in the face. He screamed as if burnt and staggered back, dropping his sword. Sir Godfrey turned and, taking the second attacker by surprise, drove his sword straight through the man's neck.

The priest staggered, his face now drained of its arrogant smirk. Sir Godfrey leapt towards him.

'You bastard whoreson!' he snarled. Then he slipped. He knew he was falling but couldn't stop. He dropped his sword, the fishing smack rolled and the sword slipped farther away. Sir Godfrey looked anxiously over the rail. The *Star of the Sea* was closer but of little help. The archer was still firing, but the arrows whirled futilely through the air. He glimpsed a dark shape. He tried to roll, but the movement of the ship sent him sprawling. Then the priest staggered back as Dame Edith blindly flung herself at him. He shrugged her aside, sword raised, but Sir Godfrey was back on his feet. The priest turned, mouth snarling. Again they clashed, a scrape of steel, the stamp of boots. The knight knew something was wrong. The priest had not wearied but seemed stronger and more alert and the knight remembered the exorcist's warning about how the spirits of the dead Strigoi can enter the bodies of others. He began to pray.

'De profundis . . . Out of the depths I have cried unto you, O Lord, Lord hear my voice.'

The priest grinned, his lips curling like those of a dog. He wielded his sword in scything cuts that Sir Godfrey could barely fend off. The knight was soaked in sweat, his arms felt like lead, his legs weak from the strain and shock of combat.

'Die!' the priest hissed. 'Die! In the name of darkness, die!'

Sir Godfrey could only retreat further, even as he was aware of faint shouts from the *Star of the Sea*. He took one step back and went sprawling over one of the corpses. He looked up, the priest nicked his chest with the point of his sword, about to push the killing blow. Sir Godfrey closed his eyes.

'Jesu Misere!' he whispered.

Then he heard a scream and looked up. Dame Edith had launched herself at the Strigoi, her pathetic, slight body wrapped around his, dragging him away from Sir Godfrey. The priest roared with rage as Dame Edith blindly struck at his face with her nails. He pulled a dagger from the top of his boot and struck her once, twice, but she hung like a leech. Again and again he plunged the dagger. Dame Edith, screaming prayers, dragged him over, turning his body so that his back was turned to the prostrate knight. As if in answer to a prayer, the deck heaved and both fell, the Strigoi still stabbing relentlessly. At last the exorcist groaned and lay still. The Strigoi rose, just as Sir Godfrey, at a half-crouch, swung his sword back for the killing blow. The Strigoi opened his mouth but the knight's blade sheered through his neck and sent his head bouncing across the deck. The blood shot up, a crimson fountain of gore. Sir Godfrey cursed, gave the decapitated torso a kick with his boot and fell to his knees, gasping for breath. He looked around. The decks were awash with blood, flowing backwards and forwards as the fishing smack rocked on the sandy bank. Sir Godfrey crawled to where Dame Edith lay, a huddle of bloody rags beneath the rail of the ship. He picked her bleeding body up in his arms and staggered across to lay her against the mast. The bandage slipped from her eyes and Sir Godfrey thought how peaceful she looked. He saw her lips move and pressed his ear close to her mouth.

'Dying!' she whispered. 'Thank God, dying at last! In Paradise I'll see again!'

Then she slid sideways. Sir Godfrey felt for the pulse in her neck but there was none. He stopped, waved with both hands towards the *Star of the Sea*, then staggered across, down the ladder to where McBain lay. He saw the red bubble on the clerk's lips and could have wept at the sheer waste of it all. McBain opened his eyes.

'Dying?' he asked faintly.

Sir Godfrey nodded.

'And Dame Edith?'

'She's gone.'

241

The clerk forced a smile. 'Then she'll wait for me!'

His eyes fluttered. 'And the Strigoi lord?'

'Fled!' Sir Godfrey replied.

'You must hunt him down. Promise me!'

'I promise.'

The clerk smiled. 'You are a hard man, knight.'

'And you are a good one, McBain.'

Alexander tried to laugh, the blood dribbling between his lips.

'I thought you'd never say that,' he whispered. Then he shuddered. The knight thought he said 'Edith!' McBain's head fell to one side, eyes open in death. Sir Godfrey laid him gently on the floor, checking his blood-soaked neck for any sign of life, but there was none. The knight whispered a prayer that Christ would welcome these two brave souls and glared fiercely into the darkness.

'And damn those hell-hounds into the pit of blackness!'

The knight struggled up the steps. He collected his sword and dagger from the deck. He picked up the relic from where it had fallen, kissed it and put it carefully around his neck. He stared once more around the fishing smack, which looked and smelled like a butcher's yard. Dame Edith lay by the mast, small and pathetic, and from under the far rail the priest's decapitated head glared back at him through half-closed, heavy-lidded eyes. Sir Godfrey felt a spurt of rage. He walked across, picked the head up by the hair and tied it to a loose rope so that it swung in the wind like some rotten fruit. He then clambered over the rails into the waiting boat and, sitting in the stern, kept his eyes fixed on that grotesque head as the oarsmen rowed him back.

Grandison helped him up the rope ladder and back on to the deck of the *Star of the Sea*. All the ship's company were assembled – soldiers, archers, even the cooks. They stared in open-mouthed astonishment at the corpses littering the little fishing smack, the deck awash with blood. The bodies appeared to have an eerie life of their own as they moved on the sea-washed decks, black cloaks flapping, at the motion of the waves.

'God save us, sir knight!' Grandison exclaimed. 'What terrible tale is all that?'

'Woven in hell and told by demons,' the knight replied.

'What happens now?'

'We burn it!'

Grandison rapped out orders. Charcoal blaziers were lit on deck. The catapults were loaded with balls of fiery pitch. The archers strung their bows and waited to catch a flame from the braziers.

'Wait!' Sir Godfrey shouted.

He grasped the rigging and climbed on to the ship's rail. He held his drawn sword in his free hand, blade down, like a cross.

'Alexander McBain!' he shouted above the noisy wind. 'I salute you! Dame Edith, a woman with a crusader's heart, I salute you! By the cross, I swear my sword will not rest until the Strigoi lord is dead!'

The wind caught the words. The knight crossed himself and climbed down. He nodded at the captain, who raised his gauntleted hand.

'Prepare!'

Sir Godfrey heard the crack of the catapults and the shouted orders of the master of archers. Grandison's hand dropped.

'Loose!'

Fiery arcs sped towards the fishing smack, some dropped, hissing, into the sea, others landed on deck.

'Again!'

The archers loosed a shower of fiery arrows. The catapults twanged and, again, a thin wall of fire fell upon the fishing boat.

'Again!'

Once more the fire, like God's vengeance, dropped from the skies. Sir Godfrey glimpsed a ball of burning pitch go through the small cabin door. Tongues of flame began to appear. There was a large tearing sound as the fire reached the oil and the fishing smack and all on it were enveloped in a sheet of flames. Grandison would have stopped but Sir Godfrey insisted that the shooting continue. He stood for an hour until every shred of the fishing smack was reduced to blackened timbers which the sea lapped gently before pushing away.

Amen.

The Epilogue

The knight finished his tale and stared into the flames of the taproom fire.

'What happened?' the wife of Bath breathlessly asked.

Now the knight smiled. He shrugged.

'My tale is ended.'

'And the Strigoi lord?'

'He lives still.'

'Is it a tale?' the man of law shouted. 'Fable or fact, sir knight?'

'It's the truth, isn't it?' The shipman was now standing on his feet, eyes staring as he pointed at the knight. 'It's true isn't it?' he whispered. 'I was there. I was on the *Star of the Sea*.'

The knight just stared back.

'But, if it's the truth,' the man of law continued remorselessly, 'there is some explaining to be done. You, sir,' he looked at the poor priest, 'said Father Andrew was much respected. And you, the Oxford clerk, said St Peter's church housed his remains. And you, sir monk, said that the Trinitarian friary has no knowledge of such legends?'

'No, I know what happened,' the quiet manciple intervened. 'Sir Oswald Beauchamp retired. Proctor Ormiston is witless.

Sir Godfrey achieved his task and the Church and crown drew a veil over this. The friars were laid under a solemn vow of silence and Father Andrew will be remembered as a much-loved priest. I am correct am I not, sir knight?'

The knight shrugged, rose to his feet and stretched. He glanced at the host.

'My tale is done, sir.'

'And a good one, too,' Harry asserted vigorously. 'Hell's teeth! I'll not sleep easy in my bed tonight!'

The knight yawned, looked quickly at the monk and walked to the door.

'Sir knight?'

He looked round where the prioress sat, coyly fingering her brooch with *Amor Vincit Omnia* inscribed on it.

'Monsieur,' she pleaded. 'Excusez moi. La belle dame Emily?'

'Oh, she married the love of her life.'

The knight smiled and went out into the night air. He walked across the yard, sat on the edge of a stone wall and stared up at the starlit sky.

'Father!'

The knight turned and looked at his son.

'Yes, Alexander?'

'You were the knight?'

'Of course!' The knight smiled through the darkness. 'Emily was your mother. I returned to Oxford and wooed her with all my strength and power. She loved me and bore you, the noblest son any man could ask for. But,' the knight looked sadly at his son, 'until the day she died, there was a small corner of her heart, an enclosed shrine, a memorial to Alexander McBain.'

'And that makes you sad?'

'No, it does not. I am a lucky man, Alexander. Throughout

my life, I have served Christ and his holy mother. I have loved and been loved. My first wife, the Lady Emily, Alexander McBain and Dame Edith Mohun.' The knight looked over his son's shoulder and saw a movement in the darkness. 'And you, Robert Cotterill, who, ever since I took you from Oxford, have served me loyally.'

The yeoman emerged from out of the darkness and drew close.

'But the hunt will go on?' Robert asked.

'Oh, yes,' said the knight. 'I have dedicated my life to hunting the Strigoi lord down. I pursued him to Alexandria, to Algeria, Wallachia, Prussia, Spain, Asia Minor. One day I will catch him, take his head and send his soul back to Hell!'

'But I thought you had?' the squire declared softly.

The knight clasped his son's hand. 'No, but I give him no rest. I do not allow him to stay and build up his strength or gather a new coven around him. Now and again, I do catch one of his followers when he sends one of his ilk against me. It always ends in their deaths.'

'And you always burn their corpses?'

'Yes, and now you know why.'

'But not in Canterbury?'

The knight smiled and rose to his feet. He spread his arms, put one round his squire, the other round the yeoman and hugged them close.

'No, not in Canterbury. I go there to give thanks and beg for the help of the Blessed Martyr Thomas. Now, come, one cup of claret and a good night's sleep.' He dropped his arms and fingered the relic still hanging from his neck. 'I've told my tale and tomorrow let's give our buxom wife of Bath a fair hearing.'

Laughing and talking they walked back into the taproom.

* * *

In the darkness a shadow, deeper than the rest, moved. The eyes, half-hidden in a hooded cowl, glittered maliciously through the darkness and the lips curled in a grin like that of a hunting dog.